THE
TALKING
PICTURES
MURDER
CASE

THE TALKING PICTURES MURDER CASE

BY
GEORGE BAXT

ST. MARTIN'S PRESS
NEW YORK

Design by Claire Counihan

Library of Congress Cataloging-in-Publication Data

Baxt, George.
 The talking picture murder case / George Baxt.
  p. cm.
 ISBN 0-312-05043-7
 I. Title.
PS3552.A8478T34 1990
813'.54—dc20

90-36897
CIP

First Edition: November 1990

10 9 8 7 6 5 4 3 2 1

This book is for
MARTIN WITTMIER
``Bleepin' A, Babe!''

◆

THE
TALKING
PICTURES
MURDER
CASE

ONE

It sounded like one gigantic supernatural howl coming from the mob storming the church in Forest Lawn cemetery in the Hollywood Hills.

"This ain't no funeral!" shouted one policeman to another as they tried to hold back the clamoring mob. "It's a bloody uprising!"

"Have you no respect for the dead?" a woman asked a man who had just knocked her hat off her head. "Honest to Christ a body can't get themselves decently buried in this rotten town! Poor little Dolly Lovelace!" she shouted, but went largely unheard. "Let her rest in peace! The poor thing!"

"Aw, banana oil!" yelled a pickpocket as he lifted the billfold from her purse.

Fifty policemen had been assigned to Dolly Lovelace's funeral, but an hour before the service was scheduled to begin, it was obvious to the lieutenant of police in charge of the funeral force that at least another fifty would be needed to keep order. A half hour later he requested an additional fifty, and his superior officer had to borrow some policemen from neighboring Beverly Hills. The start of the services was postponed twice because the celebrities' limousines were moving at a snail's pace through the unruly mob.

"My God," said Norma Shearer to her husband, Irving Thalberg, "this is Nineteen twenty-nine. You'd think we'd be civilized by now."

Thalberg said, "Your voice is recording better. It's not so nasal."

"My voice is *not* nasal."

He patted her knee. "Like you don't have a cast in your eye." He yelled at the chauffeur. "What's holding us up? Why can't we move any faster?"

"It's those crazies out there! They're running riot! This funeral is worse then Valentino's!"

"Oh, I loved Rudy's funeral," said Miss Shearer. "Pola Negri was so funny sobbing her heart out draped over his coffin, and Gloria Swanson made such great wisecracks about Pola . . ."

In the back of his limousine, Hollywood's most powerful independent producer, Samuel Goldwyn, conferred with his henchwoman, Sophie Gang. "You mock my words, the talkers will save Hollywood a lot of money. We can get rid of all the stars who are commending a million dollars a year. Did you tell Vilma Banky's agent we're canceling her contract?"

"Yes. He's suing you."

"What's to sue? That Hungarian can hotly talk English as good as me."

Sophie suppressed a guffaw at the infamous Goldwynisms. "Do you want to discuss some of these New York actors available at very little money?"

"My three favorite words, very little and money. So who's available that all the other bastards haven't already signed up?"

"There's Arthur Lytell. Not bad-looking, very popular on Broadway, and he's toured a lot."

"Is he tall or short?"

"Five foot ten."

"Not bad. How's his health?"

"Well, he suffers from diabetes."

"You mean sick, he suffers from diabetes. Does he inject himself with insolence?"

"You can always cancel him if insurance rejects him. Jascha Heifetz is interested in doing a talker."

"Heifetz the fiddler? The one who's marrying Florence Vidor? Say, he's not such a bad-looking guy." He thought for a moment. "Take a memo. Think of a story for Heifetz in which maybe he's the conductor of a sympathy orchestra."

The crowd was frighteningly out of hand. A limousine was almost overturned and actress ZaSu Pitts, emerging from her chauffeured car, had a string of pearls torn from her neck. Other hands snatched at her fox fur and a policeman on horseback struck a man over the head with his truncheon as he tried to grab the actress's handbag.

In the back of their limousine, Douglas Fairbanks said to his diminutive wife, Mary Pickford, "I don't like the look of this. This crowd's dangerous."

Little Mary leaned forward and spoke sharply to the chauffeur. "Get the pistol out of the glove compartment."

"For Pete's sake, Mary, we can't go around shooting people!"

"Why not, dear, we're Doug and Mary, America's sweethearts. We can do anything we like."

Annamary Darling's limousine was the longest, most sparkling, most overpopulated vehicle in the line snailing its way to the entrance of the church. Pretty Annamary sat sandwiched between her athletic husband, Willis Loring, the swashbuckling hero of numerous moneymaking adventure epics, and her mother, Marie Darling, the infamous battle-ax. Spread across the two jump seats was Annamary's younger brother, Jack Darling, whose fame in country bumpkin roles was as legendary as his doping and drinking.

In a cross between a growl and a snarl, Marie Darling said, "Alexander Roland ain't dumping any of you." She was referring to the powerful head of Diamond Films, to whom the three actors were contracted. ("If it sparkles, it's a Diamond!") "I know what all them studio bastards are up to. I've been outsmarting them for years, and I'll outsmart them into their graves."

"My money's on you, Mama Marie," rasped her son-in-law, with an unsubtle mockery in his voice.

"It better be, smart aleck." She folded her arms and restrained an urge to stick her massive tongue out at a youngster whose face was pressed against the car window. "Beat it, sonny, before I crush your skull!" The youngster favored her with an obscene gesture. Marie directed her tongue at her daughter. "You've got

3

an ironclad contract, sweetie pie, and it's good for another three years, three million per, and we ain't moving off easy street."

Annamary's wispy voice was now surprisingly husky. "What good is it if my voice doesn't register?"

"Your voice'll register or it'll answer to me!"

"Mama, this is February. They've been making talkers at Diamond for the past four months with just about everybody under contract except us three. Alex Roland is destroying us!"

"No he won't." The voice sounded distant and disembodied. It was fully half a minute before the others realized it was Jack Darling who had spoken. He sat up, yawned and stretched, scratched himself under the right arm, looked out the window, winked at an ugly girl who was displaying a naked breast, and asked, "Where are we?"

"Dolly's funeral," Mama Marie told him.

"My Dolly's funeral?"

"Your Dolly's funeral."

"My pretty witty shitty Dolly's funeral? She's really dead?"

"As dead as a glassful of acid can make you."

"I don't have to pay her no more alimony?"

"Account closed."

"Stop it, you two!" raged Willis Loring.

"What's wrong with you?" Mama Marie was genuinely startled. Her son-in-law was usually too preoccupied with the development of a new muscle to have such outbursts.

"This is so ghoulish! The poor girl's dead." He stared at Jack. "You loved her once."

"I love her still."

Loring was perplexed. "Then why'd you divorce her?"

"Because Mama told me to. Dolly was taking too much dope and Mama said there'll be a scandal Jack and it'll ruin your career but I should have stayed married to her because I don't have any career. I haven't made a movie in over a year because Alexander Roland hates my insides and now there are talkers and he says I can't talk but I can talk as good as all of them, Alexander just hates my guts. I stole Dolly away from under him and he's never forgiven me. And that's when he said he'd ruin Dolly too be-

4

cause he knows something about her if it was ever made pub-lic—"

"Stop it, Jack," begged Annamary.

But there was no stopping Jack. "—it would truly ruin her. And that's what started her drinking and then she graduated to cocaine and that's when I joined her because I loved her—"

"You could have stopped her," admonished Annamary sharply.

"There was no stopping Dolly, you know that. She was a wild thing . . . dancing naked on top of grand pianos at the Co-coanut Grove . . . shooting out windshields driving along Sun-set Boulevard . . . gang-banging the UCLA football team. . . . God, she was an original—and Alex Roland destroyed her." He reached into his jacket for the ever-present flask of gin. "Dolly's secret. My poor Dolly's secret. Oh God, the look on her face when I told her I was leaving her . . ."

It had been a year earlier in the solarium of their home in the Pacific Palisades, with its magnificent view of the ocean a mile away. It was late one Sunday after returning from a luncheon at film star Mae Murray's mansion. Jack was at the bar of the play-room mixing sidecars. Dolly sat on a bar stool aggravating a fingernail with an emery board.

"What's wrong, hon?" she'd said. "You ain't been yourself all week. Still mad at me for stripping down to my teddy at Carmel Myers's Passover dinner?"

"I'm getting a divorce." She'd stared at him. He might have been telling her he was buying a new automobile or thinking of a game of tennis while there was still daylight.

"You want to leave me?"

"You know why."

"My God, we only been married a couple of months! Don't you love me no more?"

He was fighting tears as he poured the drinks. "I'll never love anybody else."

She was at his side, clutching at his arm, causing him to spill the drinks. "Then why are you doing this? Why? Why, baby, why?"

"You know why! Mama says I have to because Alex Roland's

5

going to ruin your career with a scandal and if I stay married to you it could ruin me too."

"That old fucker."

"Yeah, Alex is an old fucker."

"I mean your mother."

"Don't you say nothing bad about my mama."

"Of course not. Nothing bad about your mama. But anything bad about me. Sure, sure. Roland can't ruin me! I'm in the top ten at the box office along with you and Annamary and Willis and Mary and Doug and goddamn it I ain't giving you no divorce. I mean that. I'll fight you into the grave."

In the limousine, Jack's voice was ghostly. "I'll fight you into the grave. Little did I know how prophetic she was. Well, a fat lot of good divorcing her did me. I haven't worked since, damn Alex Roland!" He ran a hand through his handsome mop of hair. "I should never have divorced her. I should have stuck by her."

"It's no use crying over spilled milk," said Mama Marie.

"I wish I could hold her in my arms just once more. Beg her to forgive me. I should have taken us both to Europe. There they wouldn't give a damn. We could be making pictures together in Europe. I shouldn't have listened to you, Mama. Who gives a shit her grandfather was a nigger!"

The chauffeur's eyes flew open, a small trace of a smile played on his lips. This little tidbit ought to be worth a nice chunk of cash from a newspaper. He was too involved with greed to feel the intense power of Marie Darling's eyes boring into the back of his head.

Still more police reinforcements converged at the funeral. The cops were ferociously fighting back the mob, forming flying wedges to assist the celebrities into the church.

"Wheeee! Ain't this fun!" yelled redheaded "It" girl Clara Bow as she and Gary Cooper hurried up the steps to the church. "I hope the show ain't started yet. I don't like to miss the beginning of a pitcher."

Cooper punched a man who had broken through the cordon and attempted to kiss the actress. "Son of a bitch," muttered Cooper as the man fell back and flashbulbs popped like a Fourth of July celebration.

6

"Gee whillikers, Gary. Papa Zukor ain't gonna like them pitchers of you bopping one of our fans."

Cooper grabbed her arm and hurried her inside. "Didn't you care the way he was going for you?"

"I only care when they stop going for me, you big lug."

He-man movie star Milton Sills sat with his actress wife, the blond and strikingly beautiful Doris Kenyon, at the far end of a pew. Above them was a stained-glass window donated by Adolph Zukor, the head of Paramount Pictures, in whose hands lay the futures of Bow and Cooper. "Look at this turnout," Sills said, in the voice that had registered magnificently when tested for sound. "I didn't think Hollywood cared."

"This isn't caring, darling," said Miss Kenyon, who didn't give a damn if she succeeded in talkers as long as her husband's career would continue to thrive, "this is publicity at the expense of poor Dolly. I hope she's happy where she is. If there's an afterlife, I hope she's truly happy."

"If there's an afterlife, I hope she's got herself a good agent."

Doug and Mary were followed down the center aisle by the Thalbergs, their usher displaying his best profile in hopes of an offer of a screen test. At the head of the aisle, Mama Marie stopped her group until the others in front of them were seated. As if by mass instinct, everyone in the church turned to stare at them. And then the whispering began. Mama Marie sensed the whispering was too intense; someone else must have joined them. She turned and saw Alexander Roland, czar of the most powerful studio of all, Diamond Films.

Roland was a little man, just an inch or two above five feet, but by the imposing way he carried himself, he seemed taller. Actually, he *thought* taller. He was dressed in his usual Bond Street uniform of navy blue suit, gray vest, Asser and Turnbull shirt, and Countess Mara tie. His diamond stickpin was the only thing about him that sparkled. The flunky behind him carried his fedora and walking stick and cache of Cuban cigars with his initials printed on the bands.

The others were also staring at Alexander Roland. Willis Loring spoke first. "Why, Alex, how nice to see you, but how sad under this tragic circumstance."

Annamary was next. "Why, Alex, it's been so long since I've heard from you, I was wondering if you'd returned to the smoked salmon business." Roland's face betrayed nothing.

Mama Marie was next up at bat. "We need to have a long talk, you *gonif*, and when I say long talk you goddamn well know I mean a *long* talk."

Mr. Roland anticipated Jack Darling and had him in focus.

"Hypocrite," said Jack with a very old-fashioned sneer, "you helped put her in her coffin."

The czar finally spoke. "And I shall help carry it to her grave. I'm a pallbearer. Shall we proceed down the aisle? Sam Goldwyn's behind us and he's famous for his lack of patience."

Willis Loring signaled their usher to lead them down the aisle. Behind them they heard Goldwyn insisting to Sophie Gang, "We have to change the scene. They would never fire the housekeeper; after all, she's an old family container."

They could hear screaming and the yelling outside. The police had linked arms to form a human chain to prevent the mob from storming through the entrance. Dolly Lovelace's priestly confessor, Father Justin, was in the pulpit and speaking in his soft, mellifluous voice, which was slightly marinated with sacramental wine.

"What really killed our darling Dolly Lovelace?" He stared down at the sea of celebrities before him, his eyes sweeping the interior like a klieg light, stopping for a few seconds to focus on a couple in the last pew on the right who were practically fornicating while chewing gum; and then, as his face reddened with envy, he stared at the ceiling. "What really killed you, Dolly? Was it the drugs? The alcohol? The rumor of advanced syphilis? Or was it bad scripts?"

The screaming mob broke through the human chain and went tearing into the church at full cry. The ushers were the first to flee for their lives. Marie shrieked at Annamary, "Hide your jewels! Willis, lift Annamary above the crowd, I'll take care of Jack!" The police came racing in after the mob, using their truncheons and cracking skulls and breaking limbs and poking out eyes as the crush reached the coffin, which began to teeter precariously.

Jack's agonized cry sounded as if it had been wrenched from the bowels of hell. People scratched and clawed at each other. Actors punched actors and actresses had an excuse to settle old debts with hair-pulling matches.

"Jack! Jack! Come back!" yelled Mama Marie.

Jack rushed to the coffin in an attempt to steady it, but a hoodlum tripped Father Justin, who fell against the coffin and sent it crashing to the floor with an ugly thud. The lid flew open. Jack reached the coffin as Dolly Lovelace's corpse came flying out and landed in his arms.

"Oh my Dolly," wept the gin-soaked actor, "oh my lovely Dolly. You forgive me. You've come back to me!" He peppered the face with kisses while Father Justin upchucked and Mama Marie screamed, "Let go of the cadaver, Jack—the photographers!"

But she was too late. Flashbulbs popped, eyes popped, and another bizarre event found its permanent niche in Hollywood history.

TWO

It took four members of the Los Angeles riot squad to subdue Jack Darling after separating him from Dolly Lovelace's corpse. Another four were needed to help get the family out of the church, into their limousine, and safely out of Forest Lawn. In the wake of the lawlessness they saw tombstones overturned and private chapels vandalized. They heard a woman scream at no one in particular, "Where's the Tomb of the Unknown Extra?" People attempted unsuccessfully to jump on the limousine's running boards.

Sitting in her magnificent Beverly Hills estate, "Annawill"—a double entendre that escaped no one except gossip columnist Louella Parsons, who was proudly illiterate—Annamary knew she would never forget the looks of hatred and horror and thirst for blood; the desecration of Dolly Lovelace's corpse would surely give her nightmares into her years of senility. She could still see those women who kicked the body as Jack held it while sobbing bitterly, in fulfillment of his wish "to hold her in his arms just once more." Now Jack was upstairs in his bed, sedated by their doctor, who'd clucked his tongue at the sight of Jack's bruised face and predicted there would most likely be no scars. From her seat in the living room Annamary could see her husband blithely working out on the parallel bars he'd set up on the lawn. Marie sat at a small table devouring a turkey sandwich washed down with a large chocolate milk. Annamary warmed a snifter of brandy between the palms of her hands, but it couldn't stop her from trembling. Mama Marie polished off the last of her snack and lit a cigarette.

"I didn't see Louis B. Mayer, did you?" Annamary shook her head no and Mama Marie continued. "Probably out at the track doping his string of horses. And what about Louise Fazenda?"

Annamary asked, "How what about her?"

Louise Fazenda was a popular comedienne. "That cow! Did you see what she was wearing? Purple! At a funeral, purple! What the hell did Hal Wallis see in her? Why do you suppose he married her? It can't be her looks, her face is like the rear end of a dying rhinoceros. He's got a cushy spot with the Warners, he could snap his finger and land any pretty kid on the lot he wants. Well there's no accounting for tastes. If it suits him to be the prisoner of Fazenda—"

"Mama . . ."

"Yeah?"

Annamary leaned forward, the expression on her face making Marie think of poor little Oliver Twist asking for seconds. "Promise me, I want you to promise me." Marie said nothing. Annamary licked her lips and continued. "If I die before you do—"

"Booshwah!"

"If I do, Mama, promise me a private burial. A secret burial; no one will know where to find me and do to me what they did to poor Dolly today. Promise me, Mama. Promise me."

Warmth didn't come easy to Marie Darling, but she had recognized her daughter's tender sensibilities as far back as the first time she pushed her out on a stage at the age of three. "I promise you, baby. Now gulp your brandy and I'll pour you another stiff one."

Annamary continued staring at her mother. "Did you really force Jack to leave Dolly?"

Marie was picking at her teeth with a fingernail. "He could have stood up to me."

"He's afraid of you. Why is that?"

"I don't know." She retired the fingernail and sucked at the tooth instead. "I think it started when I turned your father in to the cops the week you signed your first deal with Alex Roland. Don't look at me like that. You were six then, old enough to know what I was doing. He was a professional criminal, and if it got out it could have ruined us." Marie clenched her fists. "By

God I was determined to see you kids make it to the top and I didn't give a damn who I had to destroy to get you there. I ran my steamroller over anybody who got in my way. And I'm damn proud of what I accomplished."

"But Poppa hung himself."

"Well, he didn't have to. Nobody forced him. He didn't have to take my suggestion." She sighed. "Just look back on it as a nice fatherly gesture." She smiled, baring a set of stained dentures. "God, but was he a brilliant pickpocket. They called him 'the dip's dip.' Do you know—did I ever tell you this before?—anyway, it's worth repeating. At the intermission of Charles Dillingham's Famous Revue back in Nineteen hundred I think it was, dressed in his soup and fish and looking more elegant than Adolphe Menjou, he swept through that crowd and you know what he came out with?" Annamary wasn't listening. She was thinking about Dolly's parents and sisters and why there was no sign of them at the funeral. "I'll tell you what he came out with. Seven diamond bracelets . . . six pearl necklaces . . . four rings, one of them studded with emeralds the size of your teeth . . . three cigarette cases, and"—she slapped her knee and roared the remainder of the inventory—"two diaphragms!"

"I wonder where they were?"

"Are you kidding me? Where do you think they were?"

"Dolly's family."

"Oh, them. Ask Alex Roland, he did the arrangements."

Annamary sipped the brandy. "Irene Rich and Estelle Taylor have accepted mother roles. They're not even thirty, and they're still as beautiful as ever."

"So what?"

"I'm tremendously wealthy . . ."

"So?"

"I need never worry again for the rest of my life."

Marie said sternly, "The rest of your life is gonna be a long time in coming. What are you getting at?"

"She's thinking about retiring." They hadn't heard Willis Loring enter.

Marie jumped to her feet, eyes afire and cheeks ablaze. "Not

12

in my lifetime you won't! You got plenty of good years ahead of you. Retire? Retire to what?" She waved a hand like a semaphore. "Live here in this big mausoleum of a dump?"

"Hey! It cost half a million!" remonstrated Willis.

"Not your money, kiddo!" Willis shrugged and mixed a scotch and soda for himself. Hands on hips, Marie advanced slowly on her daughter, who seemed mesmerized by the brandy in her snifter. "Irene Rich and Estelle Taylor and most of the rest of them, they ain't never been the real big star you are and they ain't never going to, so they can take mother roles. You want to go into vaudeville like so many of the others are doing? Evelyn Brent, Ben Lyon, Jimmy Hall . . . even May McAvoy with her hilarious lisp—you want to do that? You can't sing, you can't dance, you don't do card tricks; what'll you do?"

Annamary said vehemently, startling both her mother and her husband, "I'm rich! *Rich!* Very *rich!* I don't have to denigrate myself. I've seen pictures of these pretty young things and the elegant Broadway and West End stars they're bringing in by the trainload. I can't compete with them!"

"Yes you can!" stormed Marie. "They don't know nothing about making pictures! It took you years to get to where you are, right up on top of the heap. Millions of fans around the world adore and worship you! You're more famous than the Prince of Wales or the President of the United States or Queen Marie of Romania, and none of them knows diddlyshit about acting!" She mimicked her daughter cruelly: "'Pretty young things and the elegant Broadway and West End stars' indeed. You know where most of those pretty young things will wind up if they aren't smart enough to go back home and marry a ribbon clerk—they'll end up whoring for Madam Blanche." Willis winced, remembering his account at Madam Blanche's was long overdue. "And them Broadway and West End stars? Well what about them? I seen some of them around town. Ruth Chatterton? She's forty, for chrissakes! Them limeys Fay Compton and Beatrice Lillie? Compton's a bore and Lillie's nuts. She already hates it out here and wants out. So what makes you think they're better than you are?"

13

Annamary slammed the snifter down on an end table and cried, "They can *talk*!"

"What the hell do you think you've been doing all your life, communicating by tom-tom?"

"Goddamn it, Mama, get your head out of the sand. Look what's happened to Jack Gilbert. He sounds perfectly fine when you talk to him, but look what he sounds like on the screen. It's embarrassing."

"Don't believe everything you hear, baby. Louis B. Mayer hates his guts. He told the sound engineer to ruin Jack."

"But Jack just signed a three-million-dollar contract!"

"Louis B. doesn't care what it costs when he's out to destroy someone. Look what he did to gorgeous Francis X. Bushman after he did *Ben-Hur* for Louis. Francis can't get a job anyplace. And look how Louis has ruined Mae Murray, just because he fancies she crossed him when she married that phony Prince Mdvani who's taken her for every nickel she had. Poor bitch is so broke she's doing a quickie on Poverty Row, *Peacock Alley* or something like that."

Willis reminded her, "Mae's no chicken, Mama. She's at least ten years older than Annamary."

"On her good side," snorted Marie. "And look at what Louis's done to Lillian Gish. Deliberately put her in two flops in a row and neither one of them got any fair distribution. Well, Lily's made of sterner stuff. She's headed back to New York and Broadway. Anyway, her mama was as smart as me. She invested for Lillian and her sister, Dorothy, and they can retire if they want to."

"Why can't I?"

"Because I ain't ready!"

Willis freshened his drink. Annamary sank back in her seat. *Because I ain't ready*. She should have burst into laughter, but didn't. She was reminded of the perennial silent film intertitle: *Came the dawn*. Dawn had come to Annamary and settled over her like an invisible cloak. Her mother saw herself as an extension of her daughter. Annamary's fame was Marie's fame. And Annamary's fame was all that kept Marie from drying up, shriveling and crumbling and drifting away into a dusty oblivion.

Willis cleared his throat but neither of them acknowledged him. "You know girls, I'm a bit of a big box-office star myself." Now they loooked at him. Annamary with patience, Marie like a cannibal about to devour a missionary. "I've been having talks with Joe Schenck over at United Artists." Schenck was chairman of the board of the independent distribution organization, United Artists, which was owned by Charles Chaplin and Mary and Doug. To keep the distribution arm operating at top speed, Schenck lured the biggest stars into the fold with lucrative promises of untold fortunes and, especially, the right to choose their own properties. Gloria Swanson had left Paramount to join UA, and it was rumored that her first talker, *The Trespasser*, in which she also would unveil a surprisingly beautiful soprano singing voice, was going to be a smash hit, if the enthusiasm of preview audiences was a true barometer.

Willis discoursed briefly on Swanson and then returned to his favorite subject, himself. "Schenck has offered me a three-picture deal, a quarter of a million apiece."

Marie folded her arms and tapped a foot. "And what about your contract with Alexander Roland?"

"Mama, we both know when I ask Alex to release me, he'll dance around the room with unrestrained joy and lift me in his arms and carry me out to the parking lot and gleefully dump me into my Rolls-Royce or my Hispano-Suiza or my open touring car or whichever pleases my fancy to drive the day I decide to leave."

"You damn fool. You're getting a million a picture from Diamond Films and you'd throw that over for a quarter of a million from UA? You damn fool! Diamond can't dump you! I negotiated your contract myself! There's no way they can get you out without paying you off!"

"There's one way they can get me out." Willis spoke calmly and reasonably. Few people credited him with any intelligence to speak of, as he seemed so firmly under the thumb of his formidable mother-in-law. But his lawyer often said, and not

15

disparagingly, "Willis has brains he hasn't had to use yet." Willis looked at Annamary, who guessed what he was going to say. "They can get me on the morals clause."

"Booshwah! Everybody knows if it moves you screw it!"

"Not if the moving object was sixteen years old."

"Willis, you fool." Annamary crossed her legs and stared out the window. The beautiful college student who cleaned the pool was out there stripped to the waist, his slender bronzed body giving her an appetite she knew would not soon be fulfilled.

Mama Marie was pacing the room. "That's nothing for you to worry about."

"I could go to jail."

"Horsefeathers! I could send Alex Roland to jail." They stared at her quizzically. "I've got plenty on him. I've got plenty on a lot of them. I know a lot of things I've come close to forgetting. You want to leave Diamond, then leave. But you don't have to." She went to her daughter. "And you're going to make your first talking picture very, very soon."

"What about me, Mama?" Jack Darling was standing somewhat shakily at the head of the stairs that led into the room, wearing a terry cloth bathrobe and clutching a bottle of gin by the neck. "Are you going to throw me to the wolves?"

"What are you doing out of bed?" she asked sternly.

"Asking you questions." He was descending slowly, stopping on every fourth step for a swig of gin.

"The doctor sedated you!"

"That was hours ago. It wore off and I been lying there and thinking about my future. Or do you plan for me also to swallow acid?"

"Shut up! You're gonna get back into pictures and you're gonna be bigger then you ever were!"

"Rah rah rah!" He stumbled on the last step but caught himself and grinned foolishly at his mother.

Marie stomped across the room and grabbed his arm. "No more of that hayseed crap for you. It ruined Charlie Ray and now he's playing bits. We'll be smart like Richard Barthelmess.

16

He's playing gangsters and smart reporters and he's gonna make good in talkers. The Warner brothers are solidly behind him. I've got a great idea for your first talker." Nobody cheered, so she continued. "You're gonna play a real chick dip!"

"A chic pickpocket?" Jack asked. Marie had deposited him on a couch and grabbed the gin bottle out of his hand, leaving him briefly forlorn with a feeling of abandonment.

"Yeah, like your father, rest his criminal soul. I got it all here"—she poked her head with an index finger—"and I just might write the scenario myself."

Annamary was in another chair now, busying herself half-heartedly with her needlepoint. Willis patiently waited for Marie to resume the subject of Willis. He heard Jack ask, "And who's going to produce this maybe picture?"

"Who the hell do you think? Alex Roland. He can't break your contract and he knows it."

"He could offer a settlement, which I think I would gladly grab."

"You'll gladly grab nothing while I'm still on this earth. Now the three of you, you listen to me—I'm the captain of this ship and if it ever sinks, it's because I chose to scuttle it. But while I've still got my sea legs, we go sailing together into a prosperous and successful future in the talkers!" She paused, possibly awaiting a fanfare, and then addressed Annamary. "I don't want you worrying about the invasion from Broadway and London. And forget about all them drippy ingenues they're importing from New York—"

"Yeah, yeah!" shouted Jack. "You forget about them, sis! They can't topple you! You're too big! You're really big!" His eyes misted. "You're the best sister I ever had and I don't ever want no other. You're going to be bigger in talkers then you ever were in the silents. You better believe me. You mark my words." The last two sentences were slurred as his head dropped and he fell asleep, more purring than snoring.

Willis spoke. "I promised Joe Schenck an answer by the end of the week."

"You won't have to bother. I'm going to take care of everything."

Willis didn't doubt her.

The talkers, as the early talking pictures were called, had turned the movie industry topsy-turvy. Silent pictures would no longer speak an international language. The major studios had assigned their European offices to sign up actors in France, Germany, and Mexico to be featured in foreign-language versions of their talkers. Metro-Goldwyn-Mayer had contracted the fine French director Jacques Feyder and his actress wife, Françoise Rosay, to come to Hollywood to do both French and German versions of Greta Garbo's first projected talker, an adaptation of Eugene O'Neill's *Anna Christie*. Garbo was studying English with Broadway actress Laura Hope Crews. When it was learned that fading suave leading man Adolphe Menjou spoke fluent French (though it was later learned he came not from Paris but from Pittsburgh), he found a new career in foreign versions, which led to new stardom in talkers. Mexican-born Lupe Velez and Dolores Del Rio worked overtime both in English and Spanish.

The new horizon beckoned Broadway playwrights, novelists, phony speech teachers, singing teachers. The studio hummed with activity strictly pertaining to the talkers and the telephone wires sang high C, communicating all over the world in search of talent.

"Hello Russia?" asked a secretary at Fox studios. "Moscow in Russia? Do you speak English? Oh, thank God. Yes, I'll speak very slowly." She enunciated clearly. "Do you have a number for a songwriter named Peter Tchaikovsky?"

At Paramount, a secretary was talking to London. "I'm trying to locate a writer named Charles Dickens? He wrote something called *Great Expectorations* I think? He's where? In public domain? Can you tell me where that's located?"

Jack Warner was talking to his office in Berlin, and it was a poor connection. "For crying out loud, Harry, we're dumping the foreigners here and you're trying to sell me a whole other batch! You crazy? Sure, we can use replacements for those we're unloading. We're getting rid of Monte Blue and Jack Mulhall, and Dolores Costello sounds like a sodomized canary. The only two at the studio that passed their talk tests are Jack Barrymore and Rin-Tin-Tin . . . and believe me, Barrymore may have been a great Hamlet, but Rin doesn't slur his barks!"

At Universal Pictures, little Carl Laemmle, who headed the studio and whose name was synonymous with nepotism, was explaining to a cousin abroad, "I can't hire any more nephews! No nieces either! And cousins are strictly out! I got a nephew here now who wants to direct, he calls himself William Wyler so help me God, but Junior says he ain't got no talent!" His son, Carl Junior, was in his own office at the moment auditioning a potential starlet, the two of them stretched out on the couch moaning and groaning between nibbles. Junior was a very precocious twenty-one-year-old and the starlet's talent was confined strictly to horizontal activities.

Earlier that day Sam Goldwyn had auditioned the British singing star Evelyn Laye, although he had already signed a one-picture deal with her. Smiling beatifically, he asked Miss Laye if she could sing one of his favorite songs, "Lo Hear the Gentile Lox." She bit her lip and then offered to do a number from Noël Coward's *Bitter Sweet*, a show in which she had triumphed in New York.

An hour later Goldwyn was behind closed doors in a story conference. Under discussion was the first talker planned for his major male star, Ronald Colman. "Now then, boys"—he pronounced it "boyess"—"and ladies, it is agreed we begin Ronnie in *Bulldog Drummond*. Let's be together on this. I want it should be an anonymous decision." It was a unanimous decision. Goldwyn beamed with satisfaction. "Wasn't that simple? It's like water falling off a duke's back." His secretary said Sophie Gang, his henchwoman, needed to speak to him on his private line. The story conference was declared ended and the three men and two women who had participated made hasty departures.

"What is it, Sophie?"

"Everybody's meeting at six o'clock in Louis B. Mayer's office."

"Who's everybody?"

She named every powerful studio head. Laemmle, Warner, Adolph Zukor, William Fox, Alexander Roland. Goldwyn nodded and then said, "That's quite an aggravation." He listened to something Sophie was advising. "Do you take me for a fool? How long have you been working for me? Of course I want to establish a rappaport with them!"

It had taken over five years for Bertha Graze to win the confidence and the trust of the great, the near-great, the not-so-great, and the never-will-amount-to-anythings of Hollywood. But now she reigned supreme as the official astrologer to the stars. Articles about her appeared in newspapers around the world, and she photographed superbly, although she was built like the stereotype of an operatic soprano. A bosom so huge that Jack Darling had insisted she could accommodate four for dinner on it; hips powerful enough to send steel pillars crashing; hands that one suspected could crush coconuts without spilling a drop of the milk they contained; but that face, that dear, sweet, angelic face, it was the same enchanting face that had won her a contract with Alexander Roland's Diamond Films ten years earlier. Then she was the winner of a beauty contest held by a popular movie magazine. She arrived in Hollywood at the age of seventeen, slim, blond, and tragically naïve. At Diamond Studios she was passed around from executive to executive, from star to star like a tray of after-dinner mints, and they all found her equally refreshing. Two years later, at nineteen years of age, she was a stag party joke.

But Bertha had evolved from solid Junker German stock and had always taken an interest in astrology. Recognizing that show people were highly superstitious, she had subscribed to a mail-order course in astrology offered in a science magazine. She was a brilliant student. She wisely began operations by recruiting a network of spies who could supply her with information about the denizens of the studios. She blackmailed a series of lovers and had enough of a cash reserve to pay premium prices to butlers, maids, housekeepers, secretaries, and chauffeurs. The tidbit Annamary Darling's chauffeur sold her about Dolly Lovelace's black grandfather was especially valuable. Marie Darling was one of her most faithful clients.

Oddly enough, it was Bertha who had predicted the coming of the talkers. When the prediction became a reality, she was as surprised as everyone else and further predicted the talkers would give her a whole new lucrative army of clients.

After convincing her son, her daughter, and her son-in-law that they would soon be making their debuts in talkers at Alexander Roland's Diamond Studios, Marie, feeling in need of some moral support, phoned Bertha for an appointment. Bertha told her to come right away; Bertha was getting weird vibrations, brought on, she was positive, by the disgraceful behavior of the mobs at Dolly Lovelace's funeral, and somehow these vibrations put her in mind of Marie and her brood.

Over a pot of tea and assorted biscuits, Bertha explained her vibrations to Marie, who kept nodding her head in understanding. "So you see, my dear, I've since consulted the tarot cards, my Hebrew Kabala, and the crystal ball for confirmation and they tell me I'm right. There is an ominous darkness settling over the film industry, an ominous darkness like a shroud knitted by the children of Satan."

Marie felt her blood turning to ice water. She interlaced her fingers and held them tightly.

"I'm not foreseeing the awful horrors that are being inflicted on those unfortunates who were once the greats of the silent screen, though among them there will be an epidemic of degradation and disaster and it won't be fun . . . but I see something worse. I see death creating mayhem with his bloodied scythe, cutting a swath through the flesh of the young and eager new breed of aspirants descending on Hollywood like the biblical locust plague . . ."

Marie blinked her eyes rapidly as Bertha paused to demolish a crisp ladyfinger biscuit. Bertha held her crystal ball in the palm of her left hand, her right hand necessary for the stoking of biscuits into her hot furnace of a mouth.

Bertha's eyes moved from the crystal ball to Marie's face. "You ask me if Alex Roland will agree to your demands." She paused dramatically. Though she never could act, her sense of timing was native born and sensational. "You've got him by the short hairs." Marie smiled at last. "He will agree, reluctantly and swearing revenge . . ."

"That's all he ever swears," growled Marie.

"He's capable of murder."

"So am I, sweetie, so am I."

THREE

In Louis B. Mayer's imposing conference room at the MGM studios in Culver City, the Hollywood potentates who had gathered to sow the seeds of destruction sat around a table constructed of hewn oak, a gift from William Randolph Hearst. The conspirators smoked expensive cigars, which seemed to be asphyxiating Mayer's comely secretary, who sat behind Mayer taking notes. Seven rugged individualists who had been in motion pictures since their infancy; seven robber barons who listened to the sounds of their own distant drummers; seven men who for once were of one mind: it was time to destroy their overpriced silent screen stars. Those stars were no longer needed. Expendable. Redundant. An unnecessary overhead to be consigned underground. Some would soon be sweeping the rooms they once swept into. Many were in financial thrall to their studios, who were eagerly ready to call in their markers.

A hardy few would survive the holocaust, but only for another two or three years, by which time the new faces would have replaced them in the hearts of the fickle audiences. Fairbanks and Pickford would fight valiantly to retain their hold on the public. Gloria Swanson, Richard Barthelmess, Betty Compson, Bebe Daniels, and Dorothy Mackaill would enjoy a brief renaissance in the talkers; others would continue in the industry starring or featuring in Poverty Row quickies; some would continue appearing in major productions in small parts or as extras. A lucky handful would make a successful transition as character actors, no longer billed above the title of the film but enjoying steady employment because they were smart enough to accept and adjust to the new career of being a subordinate player. To new generations of filmgoers, many of these players were new faces and enjoyed a new prosperity.

Tragedy stalked too many others. Comedian Karl Dane would commit suicide. John Bowers, husband of actress Marguerite de la Motte, walked into the Pacific Ocean and his body was never recovered, inspiring the many versions of *A Star Is Born*. John Gilbert would continue at MGM until 1933 because of his unbreakable contract, and then drink himself into death by a heart attack. Marie Prevost was found dead in her furnished room, part of her eaten away by her hungry dog. James Murray also chose drink as a solution and ended up floating in the drink, off a New York pier in the Hudson River.

Several actresses and actors chose prostitution and found that lying on their back was just as profitable as, and less exhausting than, keeping on their toes.

There were the lucky silent stars who were even bigger in the talkers: Ronald Colman, Janet Gaynor, Wallace Beery, Norma Shearer, Joan Crawford, Greta Garbo, Lewis Stone, Jean Hersholt, Gary Cooper, William Powell, Del Rio, and Velez. Talkers proved a blessing to some silent screen actors whose careers seemed destined to go nowhere. Talking pictures refreshed the static careers of Myrna Loy, Fay Wray, Nancy Carroll, Edna Mae Oliver, Conrad Nagel, Bessie Love, and Reginald Denny, if only briefly for some of them. William Haines and Ramon Novarro made successful transitions into talkers until Louis B. Mayer put them on the skids because he found their flagrant homosexuality intolerable.

Louis B. Mayer was summing up the decisions of the meeting. "So it's agreed, boys, once we start dropping our stars, none of the others go after them to buy them up cheaply, all right?"

Sam Goldwyn pointed an accusing finger at Mayer. "You should talk! I drop Vilma Banky and right away you sign her to do a picture."

"I had to!" insisted Mayer impatiently. "I needed Rod La Rocque to play opposite Shearer in *Let Us Be Gay*. You can imagine what Norma is like when she wants something, especially now she's married to Thalberg. So when Rod says you can have me Louis if you give my wife a job, what am I supposed to do? Anyway, it's a nothing picture with a homely nobody from New York, Edward G. Robinson. Vilma will disappear and so will Robinson."

"So will La Rocque," predicted Adolph Zukor. "I heard his talker test. Silent he has sex, talking he has nothing."

Mayer shrugged. "Norma likes him. She brings in the customers. He doesn't. Anyway, let's get down to the *kishkas*. I'm unloading Aileen Pringle and Lew Cody and Karl Dane to start with. When their contracts are up, we're not renewing Eleanor Boardman, Roy D'Arcy, or Nils Asther."

William Fox said, "You shouldn't have dropped Lillian Gish. She talks real good."

"The stubborn bitch! Who could deal with her? She's such an *artiste*." He spat the word at them. "*Pfeh!* You tell her to do something and she says, 'Mr. Griffith wouldn't dream of asking me to do a thing like that,' or 'I never worked this way with Mr. Griffith.'"

Adolph Zukor chimed in. "We're letting go of Raymond Hatton and, while Evelyn Brent's still good, she's beginning to photograph old. As for Clara Bow, well, we'll see. So far her first couple of talkers are profitable, but you know how disgracefully she carries on in private."

Jack Warner spoke up. "What do we do about Harry Cohn?"

"What about him?" asked Alexander Roland. "His Columbia Pictures is another quickie operation; he's no threat to us."

"He's buying up a lot of has-beens and giving them good parts."

"He has to," said Roland. "He can't afford to hire any real names. On the other hand, you have to hand it to him. He casts half a dozen old-timers in a movie and then advertises it as an all-star cast and, you know, it brings in enough customers for him to either break even or show a small profit. But he's a drop in a pail of water. He's no more a threat then Pathé or Tiffany or this new Radio Pictures bunch that's beginning to operate.

Listen, boys, I'm the one with the big problem. Mama Marie and her three marionettes."

Carl Laemmle finally spoke. "I can understand wanting to lose Jack Darling. He's a wreck. But Annamary and Willis Loring? They're still big names."

"They're costing me millions and I don't need them anymore," said Roland coldly. "Actors aren't the box-office draw. It's the movies that talk and sing! I'm planning a dozen musicals to go into production right away."

"So am I," said Jack Warner with a sigh. "Where are the women singers who are lookers? God, the dogs that are blessed with glorious voices."

Alexander Roland said to Adolph Zukor, "I hear Emil Jannings has gone back to Germany. He refused to do a voice test."

Adolph Zukor ho-ho-ho'd like a dwarf Santa Claus. "Oh yes, he did a test. So did Pola Negri and Paul Lukas. Talk about a melting pot! Emil you couldn't understand a word; Pola was hopeless and knew it and so she quit. But Lukas, you gotta hand it to him. He hired a good teacher so his Hungarian accent is a little less Hungarian every day. Actually, instead of leading men, I'm lining him up some good gangster parts. For some reason audiences find villains more menacing if they have a foreign accent."

"Oh yes?" Mayer's eyebrows were arched. "Maybe I should hold on to Nils Asther?"

Laemmle asked, "Is his Swedish accent so thick? Is it as bad as Garbo's?"

Mayer replied, "Garbo, Carl, is Garbo. Believe me, she's going to be bigger than ever and even more impossible. Anyway, now we all understand each other, right?" He chuckled. "How's for some schnapps to seal the agreement?" There was a smattering of applause. Mayer signaled his secretary to bring in the whiskey and she fought her way through a sea of cigar smoke into the next office.

Her girl friend asked her as she entered, "How many heads are dropping?"

"Don't ask. But listen, Belle, this is a riot. They're talking

26

about finishing off all the actors who have thick accents. Well, can you believe it? Ain't it hot? All seven of them inside come over in steerage and there isn't one of them who hasn't got an accent you could hack with an ax! Listen, be a doll and get the hooch out of the cabinet and set it up on a tray with some seltzer and ice water. I gotta make an important call." She hurried to her own office. She closed the door behind her, sat at her desk, and gave the switchboard operator a number.

Bertha Graze was cuddling her calico cat, Mephistopheles, when the phone rang. She draped the cat around her neck, popped a cookie in her mouth, and, while chewing, spoke into the phone. "Oh hello, honey. Hmmm? Why sure it's worth ten to me if it's any good." She listened and chewed, then smiled her very special wicked witch's smile. "He *thinks* he'll get rid of Annamary and Willis. He'll have to get rid of Mama Marie first. And let me tell you honey, it'll be easier to transfer the Rocky Mountains to Florida!"

The great influx of acting hopefuls from Broadway and abroad intensified over the following weeks, causing film director David Wark Griffith to comment to his former star, Mae Marsh, now among the deposed, "It recalls the invasion of my beloved southland by the carpetbaggers at the close of the Civil War." He always talked like a silent film intertitle. "Ah, my poor lovely Mae, the barbarian hordes are swarming over the territory and a great art is being smothered to death. Are you terribly unhappy, my poor little Mae?"

"Not really," replied the actress. They were having afternoon tea on the porch of the Hollywood Hotel. "I had ten good years. I have a happy marriage. I have my children. I'm still young. It's some of the others I feel sorry for. Poor Henry B. Walthall is taking it badly, and accepting small parts. But then, D. W., he was having a hard time of it long before the talkers became a threat. Blanche Sweet is heartbroken, but she's behaving well."

"She's a good actress."

"She's doing something at Metro and she says she has offers

from First National and the new Radio Pictures. But I advised her to marry young Raymond Hackett and go back to New York with him and try her luck in the theater."

"Isn't he tied to a Metro contract?"

"It's only for a year, He doesn't like the competition. They've brought out lots of young boys who'll be competing for the same parts. I met some of them at Blanche's party last Sunday. There was a Robert Montgomery and an Elliot Nugent and a Kent Douglas and"—she laughed—"so help me, I couldn't tell one from another."

Griffith said, "Blanche had a party last week and didn't ask me?"

"Oh dear," said a chagrined Mae Marsh.

Griffith's face was a gray study. "I wonder if she knows something I don't know."

A few tables away from Griffith and his guest and well out of earshot sat former silent stars Marie Prevost and Betty Bronson, sipping bourbon out of teacups. Bronson, who had been a major sensation four years earlier as the screen's first Peter Pan, was looking at her friend with astonishment. "You're not going to do it, are you?"

"Listen, kid," said Prevost, who had once starred for Ernest Lubitsch, "I gotta believe what my agent tells me. Marie Prevost in Lubitsch pictures looked chic and sexy and had a certain *je ne sais quoi*. Prevost in talkers has a voice that goes with nightclub floozies, waitresses, and manicurists. Why kid myself? If Louis B. is offering me a stock deal at three hundred a week, I'd be a dummy to turn him down."

"But you used to make three thousand a week!"

Prevost drew herself up with indignation. "Six thousand a week, you mean! Ah, the hell with it. Even my ex"—actor Kenneth Harlan, who was high on the list of the doomed—"is pleading poverty so he says he can't pay me my alimony no more. Listen, Betty, don't try to kid me. I know you're getting the shaft, too, and we can't fight them." Bronson dabbed at her eyes with her napkin. "Look at the sunny side, kid. You're still in your twenties and you got a knockout bozo in love with you.

Get married and get pregnant, in no particular order. Hell, I'm so up to my neck in hock, my lawyer tells me even if I get a decent price on my house and the furnishings, I'll still have to pawn some of my jewels. Anyway, kiddo, three hundred smackers will pay for a lot of groceries and it'll feed my precious little poochie and I'm guaranteed good featured billing."

"But what will your friends say?"

"*What* friends? That strong breeze you feel is the backlash of a small tornado created by the departure of my nearest and dearest. Anyway, we're better off than poor Dolly Lovelace. Wasn't that funeral a scandal? I'm sure glad I didn't go. I thought about it and then I figured, oh what the hell, we never did a picture together. I really only knew her to sneer at. Crikey, it took over three hundred cops to bring that mob under control and they took over two hundred people to the hospital. I hope the hell that ain't the way I go. I hope I die nice and peaceful in my own bed with my poochie-woochie howling over my body which will then be discovered and given a peaceful burial. Did you see that awful picture in the *Herald* of Jack Darling kissing the corpse? Oh my God, she must have tasted awful of embalming fluid."

"Stop that, Marie. That picture gave me nightmares. I once . . . well . . . you know . . ."

"With Jack Darling?" Prevost winked an eye. "So we have something else in common."

In the lobby of the Hollywood Hotel, New York actresses Ruth Chatterton and Nance O'Neil were sharing an afternoon tea and enjoying the music provided by a trio consisting of violin, piano, and triangle. There was a sly tone in Chatterton's voice as she asked Miss O'Neil, "Come on, Nance. 'Fess up. Is it true you and Lizzie Borden were companions those last years before her death?"

O'Neil lifted her chin and said with pride, "She was a magnificent woman and a wonderful friend. We traveled everywhere together and I'm pleased I was able to bring some light into her somber life. And my dear, she used to make the most *superb* chopped liver." O'Neil paused for a sip of tea. "Tell me, Ruth, are you happy with your contract with Paramount Pictures?"

"Well actually, darling, they see me as some sort of *grande dame*. Little Mr. Zukor, a quaint old thing with the tongue of an adder, assures me that mine will be prestige pictures. Well, Clive Brook, who's an old hand out here and proving to be more valuable talking than miming, tells me prestige picture means one that loses money but can be pointed to with pride when the censors accuse them of trying to pull the wool over their eyes with something salacious from Clara Bow. Anyway, that's not important. What matters is they're paying me a lot of money, which I sorely need, and at my age it's a godsend."

O'Neil smiled. "You never were one to fool yourself."

"Hell no. I was prepared to do mothers, aunts, or high school principals for that kind of dough. I haven't had anything decent on Broadway in years and touring was beginning to wear me down. What really hurts is coming on the set as I did yesterday and among the small part players and extras were some familiar faces who used to command the best dressing rooms and my kind of salary. Oh hell, Nance, what does one do? Should I talk to them? Should I try to be friendly?"

"Chatterton, keep your distance. If they hate your guts, you don't want to know about it. You didn't bring about their unfortunate circumstances. Sooner or later they'll realize that and adjust to their lot and make the best of it. Don't forget, girl, a couple of decades ago I was big stuff on the Great White Way. But . . . ." She shrugged and they both laughed.

In the club car of the Twentieth Century Limited, out of Chicago and bound for Los Angeles, Rita Gerber, a pert young actress in her early twenties, was advising her traveling companion, another young actress named Alicia Leddy, "Listen, baby, there's only one way never to grow old."

"What's that?" asked Alicia eagerly.

"Die young."

"You mean like Dolly Lovelace? Brrr. I wouldn't want to die a suicide like she did. God in heaven, how could she have swallowed acid? What agony she must have suffered!"

30

Rita looked around to make sure she wouldn't be overheard and then signaled Alicia to move forward on her chair. "Listen, baby, I got this from the schmuck who directed my screen test. He says she didn't commit suicide, she was murdered."

"No kidding?"

"Would I kid you?"

A traveling salesman interrupted them, favoring the girls with a toothy grin. "Excuse me," he asked Rita Gerber, "haven't we met before?"

"No," snapped Rita, "I've never been in a train wreck." He went away quietly. "Anyway, this director has a pipeline to this Alexander Roland's secretary and he says that she says that he says—"

"That's who signed me!"

"Who?"

"Alexander Roland." When she smiled, Alicia Leddy looked like an amusement park Kewpie doll. "He saw me a couple of months ago in *Cutie Pie* and liked me and he never forgot me."

"*Cutie Pie?* I saw that. I don't remember you. What part did you play?"

"I didn't have a real part. I was in the chorus."

"I see." Her voice had gone flat. "You must have done a pretty damned good test."

"I didn't do any test."

"Say, listen, baby, are you sure you're being brought out there to *act?*"

Jack Darling watched with a mixture of fascination and distaste as Mephistopheles, Bertha Graze's calico cat, worried a baby mouse in a corner of the room. Oblivious to the unimportant drama, Bertha popped a Fig Newton into her mouth and swiftly ground it to pulp and then said to the surprisingly sober young actor, "Why'd you come to me? You usually ridicule my predictions. But then, you don't take anything seriously except your boozing."

"Because you know the source of just about every rumor that springs up in this town. Where did it start? Who began spreading it? Do you think Dolly was murdered?"

Bertha washed down the remains of the Fig Newton with a swig of the nauseating California soft drink, Orange Julius. "It's possible. There was no autopsy."

"How come?"

"Her father wouldn't permit it. You haven't forgotten your former father-in-law, have you?"

"He's not easily forgotten. He didn't want Dolly to marry me. He did everything possible to talk her out of it."

"Maybe if you hadn't let your mother bulldoze you into divorcing the poor kid, she might still be alive today."

"Who told you that? Who told you Mama made me divorce her?"

"You said it yourself, handsome, I'm the source of just about every rumor that springs up in this town. Have a a bite of my Baby Ruth?" She was holding out a candy bar.

"No thanks." He averted his eyes as she demolished the candy. The cat was demolishing the mouse. Jack covered his mouth with his hand. Bertha was staring into her crystal ball.

"My my, lookee what I've got here." His eyes traveled back to her face. "Why, here's your mama and you know where she is, she is in Alex Roland's office and giving him what for."

"She's in Pasadena visiting some old friends."

"So what? What I see in the ball is the future, that's what crystal balls are for." She resumed studying her prop. "He's standing his ground like he always does. He's giving as good as he's getting. But your mama's gonna beat him down. You and Annamary and Willis are soon gonna be making a talker, each of you. The crystal ball never lies."

"How can it lie when Mama tells you everything? You don't need that thing to feed me a plate of applesauce. Say, did you start the rumor Dolly was murdered?"

"Next thing you know you'll be accusing me of starting the Chicago fire."

"Who would want to murder Dolly?"

"Who would want to murder anybody in this town? Everybody's got a reason to kill somebody else out here. Aren't there some old scores you'd like to settle?"

"If anybody murdered Dolly, I'm going to find him and kill him."

"What makes you so sure it's a 'him'?"

Chief Inspector Herbert Villon of the Los Angeles Police Department sat behind the desk in his claustrophobic office with his feet propped atop the desk. He was reading in the latest *Photoplay* magazine an interview with the up-and-coming young Paramount Pictures actress, Jean Arthur. Seated in the room's only other chair was an almost homely young woman named Hazel Dickson. Hazel was a reporter for the United Press and was considered a brilliant scavenger of hot Hollywood items.

"Come on, Herb, put down the magazine and talk to me."

"Get a look at this Jean Arthur. What a cute hunk of flesh."

"I'm built better." And she wasn't lying, but her face was something else. Not exactly ugly, not exactly homely, not completely undistinguished, it was the kind of face that drew admiration only when her mouth was open and talking. Her tongue was a dangerous weapon and she wielded it indiscriminately.

Herbert Villon set the magazine aside and folded his arms across his impressive chest. He was in his mid-thirties and insisted he was a direct descendant of the French poet, François Villon. Despite this, there was nothing poetic about Herbert Villon. He was probably one of the youngest chief inspectors in the United States and could still not understand why he had landed the job over several others who held greater seniority. Still, Villon reserved his detecting for more important problems.

"Why don't you interview Jacob Udell? He's in one of the cells upstairs and very lonely. Nobody comes to visit him."

"What's he in for?"

"He raped a seventeen-year-old virgin."

"I'm not interested in breaking and entering. I want to know why there was no autopsy performed on Dolly Lovelace."

"The coronor said her mouth, her throat, and a lot of her guts were burned by acid, so why bother?"

"I heard different. I heard her father wouldn't permit it. That's

33

never stopped you guys before. I think somebody high up in the studios pulled some strings and schmeared some palms to call the autopsy off."

"Nobody bribes me, Hazel, you know that."

"Sure, sure. But that's a hell of a hot rumor going around that her suicide was no suicide. Why don't you exhume her body and order an autopsy anyway?"

"Because that would take a lot of red tape and a lot of explaining and you don't exhume a body to help kill a rumor."

"You might also substantiate the rumor."

"I wish you hadn't gone to college. I wonder if Jean Arthur went to college."

"Aw, screw Jean Arthur!"

"I'd love to."

She left the chair while opening her handbag and surveying her face in a pocket mirror. After a moment she sighed and said, "God might have done worse."

"I think you're cute."

She leaned across the desk. "You know something, Herbert, meeting you must be the lowlight of my life."

"Why don't you take me to dinner on your expense account?"

"Because I've got me a previous engagement."

"Oh yeah? Who with?"

"I don't mind telling you. Ezekiel Lovelace, Dolly's poppa." She wiggled her hips as she walked out of the office. "Don't take no wooden nickels!"

It was Villon's face that was wooden.

FOUR

Hazel Dickson's Model T Ford clattered at the breakneck speed of forty miles an hour toward her rendezvous with Ezekiel Lovelace in Inglewood. Like Annamary Darling, Hazel had been curious as to why none of Dolly Lovelace's immediate family had attended her funeral. Following the outrageous ceremony, Hazel had beelined to the morgue at *Picture Play* magazine and read up on the departed Dolly. A few of the purported interviews sounded genuine; the rest were easily detected as sham press agent puffery. There were the early photos of Dolly when she was just beginning: Dolly dressed as a Pilgrim and menacing a turkey with an ax; Dolly as Santa Claus on the roof of a house, a pack of toys on her back, one foot already in the chimney; Dolly at the seashore frolicking in the waves with some other curvaceous bathing beauties. Dolly seemed to have graduated quickly to portrait shots by the studio's ace photographers. She had been proving herself in supporting roles, the final step into stardom unless she tripped herself up. But Dolly had matriculated into stardom with top honors and flying colors and was being wooed by the Prince Charming of Hollywood, Jack Darling. Was it really possible that her whirlwind ascent had occurred in less than two years?

Hazel pulled up in front of a mailbox on which was printed LOVELACE. The mailbox was sagging to the right, possibly exhausted by its years of service. There was a fence of wooden palings badly in need of Tom Sawyer and his pail of whitewash. Hazel went up the path leading to a gate that had hinges thirsting for oil. The front lawn needed mowing. A cinder path led to some sagging wooden steps that in turn led up to a porch of a bungalow shingled with poverty.

It was a warm and humid day, contradicting Hazel's ice-cold fingertips. There was a knocker on the door and Hazel used it. After a short wait, Hazel used the knocker again. She crossed to a window and looked in. She saw a shabby interior with threadbare furniture and wondered if she was the victim of a hoax. Dolly Lovelace had made good money; surely she could have provided her father with better surroundings than these.

She tapped on the window. "Mr. Lovelace? Hello? Hello, Mr. Lovelace?" Her voice rose an octave. "It's Hazel Dickson!" She went to the door and rattled the knob. The door opened. Hazel stuck her head inside and shouted his name. She waited. No response. She thought, in for a penny, in for a pound. A newshen must get her story any which way. She crossed the shabby living room. There were some framed photographs of Dolly on a table, so she knew she was in the right place. On a sideboard there were other frames but no photographs. Odd, she thought. There was a hallway off which there were two bedrooms, one on the left and one on the right. This led to the kitchen in the back of the bungalow. It was obvious whoever furnished and decorated the bungalow was not a candidate for any awards. From the hall Hazel could see dirty dishes stacked in the sink. There was a foul odor of garbage and Hazel was of a mind to make tracks out of there. But no, she was the stalwart scavenger of juicy tidbits and she was determined to have her interview with Ezekiel Lovelace. Ezekiel. How biblical, how quaint, how dead.

Or at least as first seen, she assumed he was dead. He was sitting in a kitchen chair, his head hanging back, his mouth gaping open, and if Hazel wasn't mistaken, those were acid stains burning his lips. Hazel hurried back to the living room where she had spotted a telephone and gave central Herbert Villon's private number.

*   *   *

Stage 6 at the Diamond Films Studios was still waiting to be converted to sound. But it was being used anyway because the Diamond chain of theaters across the United States was clamoring for talkers and more talkers and even more talkers, and Alexander Roland was committed to grinding out at least fifty-two talkers a year, a staggering one a week. He was not alone. At Metro and Paramount they were shooting around the clock. Stars whose contracts still had some months to go were doing as many as three pictures at a time. The greedy studios wanted more than their pound of flesh, so actors shot sequences for one film in the morning, bicycled in the afternoon to another stage for service in the second film, and then after bolting a hasty supper of a sandwich and a cup of coffee, continued into the night filming on the third film. Some lucky ones even managed to get some sleep.

"Is it no wonder," moaned Diamond second-string actress Laura Gates, "I look like a hag of forty, I haven't had any sleep in twenty hours!" She was sitting in the makeup room with several other Diamond contract players who were suffering a similar circumstance. She said to the woman doing her face, "Listen, Gert, make me look the way I think I look."

Gert cracked the gum she was chewing and said, "In this next scene you're a corpse, honey. You gotta look as lousy as you look."

"What do you mean corpse? I'm supposed to be a bridesmaid at this society wedding!"

"That's tonight. This afternoon you're a corpse."

"I'm going mad! I know I'm going mad! I was a corpse yesterday morning! Ain't I been buried yet?"

"You're the same corpse today. The sound was ruined by that plane what flew over and today's a retake."

"Nobody tells me nothing."

"That's what you get for not sleeping with the right people," said Tessa Main, who was sitting in the next chair patiently waiting for her makeup girl to finish penciling in her eyebrows.

37

"The trouble with sleeping with the right people is that there are too many of them," replied Laura Gates wearily. "If the men I slept with in this town were laid end to end, they still wouldn't be satisfied. Like when I slept with Sam Goldwyn he kept making cracks about my eyeglasses."

Tessa Main squinted at Laura Gates. "You wear eyeglasses when you're getting laid?"

"Well, for crying out loud, I've got to see what I'm doing, don't I? Well, anyway, finally I'm fed up with the cracks and I say, 'Okay, Mr. Goldwyn, when you sign me to a contract you can tell me what kind of glasses I should be wearing.' And he says, 'Girlie, I can tell you now. You'd look better in bisexuals.' Which explains why I'm at Diamond Films and not with Goldwyn." She looked at her reflection in the mirror and howled. "Oh my God, I look like Buster Keaton!"

Jack Darling had wandered onto stage 6. One of the grips greeted him. "Hey, kiddo, where you been keeping yourself? Long time no see!"

"I've been resting, Bugsy. What's shooting here?"

"Some piece of turd called *The Bride Wore Sneakers.*"

"They'll have to change the title."

"They'll have to change the cast. Boy, are they stinko. All from New York. Watch 'em rehearse. Look at 'em. They're frightened stiff. Look at the blond bitch."

"I'm looking. She's cute."

"Watch her walk, she moves like a robot with a spear up its ass."

Jack watched her walk. She moved like a windup doll. She was terrified of the camera, an affliction not easily cured. But she was so pretty and so young and so anxious to make good. Perhaps she would. He remembered the first film he'd ever appeared in some fourteen years ago, when he was a callow sixteen. It was the first of his long and tiresome series of films with a rural background. He was walking barefoot along a path through the woods with his fishing pole over his left shoulder, a battered straw hat on his head, wearing dirty overalls and chewing on a strand of straw. He remembered Henry Turk, the director, patiently explaining, "No no, Jack, you mustn't look at the camera. Just amble along lazily and casually, look up at the sky, and be glad it's a beautiful day. Off camera you can hear a lark trilling and you smile because you love the trill of the lark. Now let's take it again, Jack, nice and easy."

Jack remembered Henry Turk's hysteria four hours later. "Don't look at the fucking camera, you stupid sonofabitch! I don't give a mother's fuck if your sister's the biggest star on the lot! You're the stupidest fuck-up I've ever worked with! Oh God, have mercy and strike him with a bolt of lightning!" He was glaring into Jack's face, frothing at the mouth, shaking him savagely by the shoulders. "Don't you know how to amble? You're still walking like you're stalking a fucking deer. When you see the sky don't you know how to look glad? You look like you just took a dump in your pants! Did you never hear a bird singing? Oh my God, oh my God!" He was tearing at his hair. "Doesn't anybody around here know how to make a silk purse out of a sow's behind?"

"No no no no no, Miss Leddy! You are crossing the room to greet your lover who has just returned from the war! His left eye's been shot out! His right arm's in a sling and he's lost his left leg!" It was the same Henry Turk who had directed Jack's film debut, now looking about eighty years old though he couldn't have been more than fifty. "You have to look brave and compassionate and there must be no trace of pity in your eyes. He's a hero and you're proving to him you're just as brave. That you're also a good little soldier." He paused as though shot from behind with an arrow. He shouted at the continuity girl. "Cecelia! Take a note to Alexander Roland. Maybe instead of *The Bride Wore Sneakers*, which is to vomit, we should maybe retitle it *The Good Little Soldier*."

As the continuity girl scribbled in her pad she said under her breath, "Which is also to vomit."

Henry Turk was down on one knee, his hands clasped together, imploring the impossible of Alicia Leddy. "Please,

please, Miss Leddy, when I go to my grave, let me go to my grave with a smile on my lips and a song in my heart."

"If you're dead," said the amiable Miss Leddy, "how can you have a song in your heart?"

"I'm going to kill her! I'm going to kill her!" He was jumping up and down while Miss Leddy shook her head from side to side and contemplated returning to New York and settling into the pleasant oblivion of a rich and loveless marriage.

Jack Darling strolled over to Alicia Leddy, who recognized him immediately. "Oh, it's Jack Darling!" she gushed. "Oh, it's really you! Oh, you've been my favorite ever since my mother held me in her arms when we saw *The Barefoot Boy*."

Jack ignored the "held me in her arms" bit and smiled his famous smile, the one reserved only for young ladies he intended to take to bed: a clever combination of warmth, helpfulness, and seduction. It was an asset that paid handsome dividends. "I think I can help. May I, Henry?" From a prone position on the soundstage floor, Henry Turk nodded approval, while Jack wondered why all directors named Henry seemed to be so untalented. Jack took Alicia by the hand and led her to her first position, which was marked in blue chalk on the floor.

The second assistant whispered to the continuity girl, "You are now witnessing at first hand some fancy footwork by the notorious Jack the Zipper."

Jack was asking the first assistant, "Where are the microphones placed?"

The first assistant told him, "There's one in the vase on the table next to Miss Leddy. There's one in the piano, and there's a third in the bowl of fruit on the table just to the left of Mr. Holt." Holt, of course, was the wreckage of a hero.

"Ready, Miss Leddy?"

"That rhymes," said the heady Miss Leddy.

Jack stifled a groan and favored her with a heart-melting smile. "You speak your first line here by the vase with the microphone . . . go ahead."

"Ummm . . ." She asked the continuity girl, "Line, please."

The continuity girl gave it to her. "'Irving, you've come home.'"

"Oh yes," said Miss Leddy, as she smoothed her dress with her hands. "Irving!" The soundstage trembled with the force that came out of her mouth.

Mercifully, Jack stopped her. "Softer, dear. This is film, not the theater. Talk conversationally. You don't have to reach the rear of the balcony when you make a talker." The vocal coach Mama Marie had assigned him had done his job well.

Miss Leddy blinked her eyes, possibly to prove she was still alive, and spoke the line again. "Irving . . . you've come home."

"Speak to Irving, not into the vase," Jack cautioned her.

"But that's where the microphone is."

"Irving is more important. They're paying him a lot of money."

"Oh, no they're not," corrected the actor sarcastically. "This is my last picture on the contract and I wish to hell we could get on with it so I could get back to bootlegging."

Jack said to Alicia, "Let's get on with it."

She clasped her hands together. "Irving, you've come home." Jack guided her through the simple scene for over an hour before they were able to get it on film.

Henry Turk was finally able to cry hoarsely, "Cut! That's a take! Print it! May God have mercy on my soul, print it!"

The cameraman stepped out of the booth, which held only him and the noisy camera, enclosed in the booth so as not to ruin the soundtrack. He was dripping perspiration and gasping for breath. His assistant hurried to him with a towel and a cold glass of wine. "Dear God," he gasped, "who is that no-talent bitch sleeping with?"

"Mr. Roland," cautioned his assistant.

"Well, she's brilliant! Positively glorious! She's going to be a big star! Give me that wine."

Alicia Leddy rewarded Jack Darling with a tongue-in-the-mouth kiss that left his front teeth aching. "You're wonderful," she whispered.

41

"What's your phone number?" he whispered.

She whispered her phone number. And then added, "If a man answers, hang up. It's Mr. Roland."

In the kitchen of Ezekiel Lovelace's bungalow, Herbert Villon said to the coroner, "I want an autopsy on this one. Daddy swallowing acid the way his daughter did is too much of a coincidence."

Hazel Dickson chimed in, "It could also show a depressing lack of originality."

A detective spoke up. "His prints are on the acid jar."

"Acid jar," mused Villon. "Not acid bottle."

"Not bottle, jar," said the detective, Jim Mallory.

"Jar, not bottle," said Villon.

"Jar."

"Oh, for crying out loud," said Hazel. "You boys are almost as funny as Amos 'n' Andy." She doted on the newly successful radio stars. "What about those empty picture frames in the living room?" she asked Villon.

"The pictures are missing," said Villon.

"Now stop kidding around!"

"They're missing, aren't they? So that means they're missing! Maybe there were never any pictures in them, ever. Maybe he had the frames around for an emergency."

"My guess is that the murderer took them."

"Who said Lovelace was murdered?"

"I say Lovelace was murdered because I'm positive his daughter was murdered, and Lovelace was murdered to keep him from talking to me or anybody else."

Villon sat on a chair while studying the corpse. "What did you expect to find out from old Ezekiel?"

She spoke evenly. "Why he thought his daughter might have been murdered."

Villon's eyes traded death for homeliness. "He told you that?"

"When I phoned and asked him to speak to me. You weren't at Dolly's funeral; I was. And I almost got trampled to death for my sins. I saw the grand opera of Jack Darling passionately

42

embracing Dolly's corpse. Oh my dear, it just occurred to me. Supposing when they married she'd decided to adopt his name. Could you just see it on a marquee? 'Starring Dolly Darling'!"

He stared at her glumly. "This is no time for levity, Hazel. Get on with it."

Hazel began pacing as the meat wagon attendants arrived to remove the body. Hazel suggested to Villon they repair to the living room and avoid seeing the distasteful act of removal. Once there, she positioned herself in front of the pictureless frames, which she thought would dramatize her suspicions as to why the unloved Darlings were murdered.

"To continue, he embraced her corpse with the kind of passion that makes me suspect he might be a necrophiliac. Through his heartrending sobs—"

"Spare me the salad dressing."

"Well, they *were* heartrending. In fact, they were damn sincere. That was no Pola Negri slice of ham when she plotzed herself over Valentino's coffin. This was a lover pleading to be forgiven. I mean, run this over in your mind. Theirs was a whirlwind courtship, love at first sight or some such cornball thing. They marry fast, elope to San Francisco, and Jack hasn't told the ferocious Mama Marie. Christ, were he and his sister lucky their mama didn't eat her young. Then suddenly whammo, Jack dumps his darling without so much as a by-your-leave. Now, Herbert, being the movie buff you are, you certainly had to have heard the scuttlebutt that it was Mama Marie who made him unload the tragic beauty."

"So?"

"So I think Mama Marie found out something about Dolly's past that could have been harmful to her darling offspring and, by association, harmful to Annamary."

"Like what?"

"Like what I think is missing from these frames." She held up one of the frames for effect, and then saw something that made her cry "Aha!" triumphantly. "Look at this!" Hazel crossed to where Villon sat on the shabby sofa and held the frame under his eyes. "See? A little scrap of white? Down here in the corner?"

"I'm not blind."

"You dummy, that's the scrap left by a photograph hastily torn from the frame. Torn by the murderer after committing the foul deed."

"Oh, stop talking like one of your blood-and-guts stories. Mallory!"

The detective came hurrying in from the kitchen, followed by the hearse attendants carrying the remains out on a stretcher. "Yeah, Herb?"

"Did you dust this frame?"

"Yes. No prints."

"Not even the old man's?"

"It's absolutely clean."

Hazel wisely said nothing. She let Villon take center stage. He said, "That puts another picture on the case. All right, Hazel, all right. Stop gloating like a whore at a stag smoker. Phone in your scoop and let's get back to town."

Hazel said, "We've got company." She nodded toward the front door, where a small boy stood with his hands in his pockets.

"Hello, sonny," said Villon. "Something you want?"

"Is old Zeke dead?"

"If you mean Mr. Lovelace, yes, he's dead."

"Then I guess the sissy man killed him."

"Sissy man?" Villon and Hazel exchanged glances. "What's a sissy man?"

The boy smiled shyly. "A man who walks like a lady. You know, like my uncle Melvyn. You know?"

Villon didn't know his uncle Melvyn and didn't want to. "Why do you think he was killed?"

"Because I heard the sissy man say, 'I'll kill you.'"

"Those exact words?"

"I think."

"You're sure it was the sissy man?"

"I saw him come out of the house and go to his car. He

walked like a sissy man, like this." He waved his hips from side to side. Hazel found him charming despite his runny nose.

"What kind of car was it, do you know?"

"It was a rich car."

"What's rich?"

"A car I seen on Hollywood Boulevard. That was a rich car. A movie star car."

"Did you recognize the sissy man? Have you see him before? Maybe in pictures?"

"I don't go to the pictures much. But I didn't see his face. I was spying from the back of the house."

"Why were you spying?"

"I always spy," the boy said matter-of-factly. "There's nothing else much to do around here."

"You were spying, but you didn't see his face."

"Well, old Zeke knows I spy." He smiled again. "It's a game we play with each other. Except I'm not to spy when he has a lady in the house." He wiped his nose on the sleeve of his sweater. "I didn't think it would matter if I spied on the sissy man. I saw him go in the house. Then when I heard the argument I sort of thought I better go away because Zeke doesn't like me to hear secrets because I can't keep one and I tell everybody."

"When did you hear the sissy man say, 'I'll kill you'?"

"Just as I was sneaking away."

"You didn't stay away too long, did you?" interrupted Hazel.

"I hid in the grass at the side of the house like I told you, the grass by the porch. That's when the sissy man came running out and got into his car and drove away."

"After he left, did you go into the house?"

"I was going to, but just then I heard my mom yelling for me so I went to see what she wanted. I had to go to the store. I just got back a little while ago and I saw the meat wagon pull up." Hazel assumed in this derelict area he saw lots of meat wagons pull up. "So I hurried over. Is Zeke real dead?"

"As dead as he can get," Villon told him. "Thanks a lot, sonny. You've been a real help."

"Are you a detective?"

"Yes I am."

"Oh. Well, when I grow up, I'm going to be a gangster." He did a fair imitation of a machine gun as he ran away.

"And there departs the future of this country," said Hazel as she reached for the phone to relay her scoop.

Hazel's story made the evening newspapers and the seven o'clock news on the radio. It traveled through the Hollywood community like a fatal virus. Bertha Graze, gnawing at a bar of chocolate, said to her cat, Mephistopheles, "Isn't it nice, darling, to hear something like that instead of the awful sounds of dreams shattering?"

FIVE

"For crying out loud, Annamary, save your histrionics for the camera." Willis Loring was on the floor of their suite at Annawill doing the fifty-eighth of his projected one hundred push-ups.

"You heard the radio. Dolly's father was killed the same way she was and—"

"And the hell with it. The police don't say positively he was murdered; they suspect foul play, that's all—they only suspect."

"When the police suspect, that means they know positively."

"What are you worried about? You didn't kill them." She didn't respond. Willis abandoned the exercise and sat up with his hands clasping his knees. "You couldn't kill, could you, Annamary? Soft, sweet, gentle Annamary. Could you murder two people and then pour acid in their mouths to make it look like suicide? Could you do that, Annamary?"

"Oh, shut up." She was lighting a cigarette. She caught a glimpse of herself in a wall mirror. She didn't look like a killer. But then, what did a killer look like? She had seen photographs in the newspapers of women condemned to death for committing murder, and they all looked dull and dumpy.

Willis was musing, "I think you're capable of plotting a murder, you're clever enough for that. But commit the actual killing? No, not you, Annamary. You're too squeamish."

"I'm not all that squeamish. I married you."

He clutched his stomach, feigning agony. "Oooh, that hurt."

"I thought I hit lower than that. My aim was always shaky."

"I wish I had the talent to think like a detective. How do you suppose they go about figuring out that a supposed suicide is really a case of murder? I suppose it's because somehow the killer slipped up, a slip that is all too obvious to the clever detective. But if detectives are all that clever, why are they always shown as buffoons in the movies?"

"Willis, why do we stay married?"

"I guess because we're buffoons."

"We don't love each other anymore."

"Oh, I don't know. I still get a bit of a twinge when you walk into a room."

"That's sciatica."

"Nonsense! I'm in the best physical condition!"

"We haven't had sex in ages."

"There's more to marriage than sex. There's friendship."

"Which reminds me, Madam Blanche phoned while you were out playing tennis or whatever it is you do when you say you were playing tennis. Your account's long overdue. My dear, over eight hundred dollars? Where do you find the energy?"

He was on his feet and pacing. "Listen to me. Seriously. Supposing we're really finished in pictures. What do we do? How do we face the future?"

"With the sound advice of Mama and our business manager. Mama says our contracts with Alex Roland are unbreakable. And you still have your offer from Joe Schenck."

"He's interested in you, too. I forgot to tell you."

"I don't want to produce my own pictures. Oh God, I've been acting since I was a kid of three. I deserve a rest. I *need* a rest."

"You've been resting for almost a year now. How much longer can you go on resting?"

"How much longer can we go on with this marriage?"

He was headed out of the room. "This is where I came in."

Jack Darling was walking Alicia Leddy to the studio commissary. They were giggling with their heads together like school children until something caught Alicia's eye. "Say, who's that battleship headed for the executive offices?"

Jack followed her gaze. "That's no battleship. That's my mom."

48

"Oh."

Marie Darling was positively under full sail as she walked with an ominous-looking determination toward Alexander Roland's kingdom. There were no drawbridges to cross, no sentries to challenge her, no crossed lances to bar her from entering. There were receptionists and secretaries, all of whom over the past decade had learned to dodge the slings and arrows that threatened to come whizzing out of Marie Darling's mouth at any provocation. Now Marie barreled into the building while Alicia expressed admiration and envy of the awesome exhibit.

"She looks mad."

"Are you always given to understatement?" Jack guided her into the commissary.

Marie steered herself into Alexander Roland's office, past Roland's weakly remonstrating male assistant, a failed interior decorator named Jason Cutts. Roland looked up from a memo he was reading and his eyes narrowed into slits. "I don't see your name in my appointment book, Marie."

"That's because you've been avoiding my calls." She slammed the door shut behind her and marched to a chair opposite the Great One's desk. "Do you really think you can get away with it?"

Roland was lighting a cigar. "I don't know what you're talking about."

Marie held her handbag tightly clutched on her lap. "We've been associated for over ten years. We've had our ups and downs and disagreements and battles and lawsuits, but it's all been very profitable. My kids made you millions."

"Likewise, I'm sure."

"I'm not going to let you lower the curtain on them. I know what's going on with you and the other Jew big shots. I know about that meeting in Mayer's office."

His face reddened as he raged, "How in the hell—"

"I also got friends in high places, Alex."

Roland showed a trace of a smile. "Especially one friend with a crystal ball."

"That's for me to know and you to find out." She pointed a

beefy finger with menace. "I want you to start lining up talkers for Annamary, Jack, and Willis."

"They're washed up."

"Like shit they are!"

"Okay, so Schenck wants them. Schenck's desperate. United Artists needs pictures. They need stars. Who've they got? Chaplin? He makes a picture every five years. Pickford? She's done her first talker playing a southern whore. How do you think that's going to go over with the audiences who prefer her as a perennial teenager with long curls?"

Marie said coldly, "It's going to go over big. I saw *Coquette* at a screening and she's wonderful. You forget she trained on the stage. Mary'll quit when she's good and ready, like my Annamary."

"And what about Fairbanks? Who does he choose to write his first talker? William Shakespeare, may God have mercy on him. And Schenck's sister-in-law, Norma Talmadge. Did you see her talker *New York Nights*? You could cut that Brooklyn accent of hers with a reaper."

"Norma's different. She doesn't care anymore. Peg, her mother, is as shrewd as I am. She salted away millions for Norma and her sister Connie. And Norma's screwing young Gilbert Roland; she doesn't give a damn about anything else. Well, my kids give a damn, damn it!"

"Kids!" snorted Roland. "Annamary's thirty-five, Willis is over forty, and Jack hasn't drawn a sober breath in years." He rolled his chair back with a ferocious shove and shouted, "I don't want them on this lot!"

Marie was out of her chair like a ball shot from a cannon, clutching his lapels with fingers of steel. "You stinking son of a bitch! You'll never break their contracts. They're ready to play, you be ready to pay! Every penny and that's millions!"

"I'll blacklist them in every studio in the world! They'll never work in pictures again!"

"Oh yes they will! And right here at Diamond! And you're going to pay them every nickel you legally owe them!"

"Don't you threaten me!"

50

Marie backed away from him, her face magically transformed into an astonishing mien of ladylike serenity. "I am not threatening you, Alexander. I am simply stating facts. By the way, I understand your wife is thinking of making a comeback in talkers. Nice girl, Helen. Good actress. Good woman. Too good for you. By the way, have you told her about this latest . . . 'find' of yours . . . what's her name? Oh yes. Alicia Leddy . . ."

"You bitch."

"My stomach's rumbling. Must be time to eat. Tomorrow, after lunch. Shall we say two o'clock? I'll expect to meet you here and decide on the first talkers for my kiddies. By the way, what are those ugly discolorations on your face? Bed sores?"

Bristling with rage, Roland waited until she left the room, then shouted into the intercom, "Jason!" He overrode Jason's meek "Yes, sir." "That twat who took notes at the Mayer session. Call Mayer and tell him to fire her. She's one of Bertha Graze's spies!"

In his puce-and-orange striped private office, Jason Cutts did not do as he was told to do. First he gave the switchboard a number, and when he heard a familiar voice cooing at the other end, he said briskly, "Well! Have I got something for you to die for! His holiness has ordered me to phone the prince of darkness at Metro and tell him to fire the twat that took notes at the ecumenical council. And Mama Marie just got through strafing him and slashing below his belt, which I'm sure she'll relay to you herself in good time. Is that enough for now?"

"Oh, that's just lovely," cooed Bertha Graze into the phone while demolishing a bar of chocolate-covered halvah. "And by the by, keep your ears open for any byplay involving Dolly Lovelace and her father's suspected murders. I've been getting a lot of bad vibrations all day."

In the studio commissary, Jack Darling and Alicia Leddy sat with Rita Gerber, Alicia's traveling companion on the Twentieth Century Limited. Rita was telling them, "I no sooner get out to the Fox lot than they tell me they're lending me here to Diamond to do a musical with Lotus Fairweather and Donald

Carewe. They're both so old they'll have to photograph them through sheet metal. And me in a musical! I'm as melodious as a bull elephant in heat! Who's that prancing to the hot food counter?"

Jack recognized Jason Cutts, Alexander Roland's assistant, and identified him. "He's a very nasty fairy. Around the lot he's known as 'Stinkerbell.'"

Alicia demurred. "Oh, I think he's darling. He's been so helpful advising me on decorating my duplex. He's covered the walls with the most unusual prints of characters from the *Arabian Nights*. You know, like Ali Baba and the forty thieves and Scheherezade and"—she was blushing, much to their surprise—"you should see the positions they've gotten into."

Rita asked, "Ali Baba and Scheherezade?"

"No, Ali Baba and the forty thieves. I think it's time I got back to the set."

"What's the hurry?" asked Rita. "I'd like to get to know Jack here better."

Alicia stood up. "I better get back. We're a week over schedule and it's only supposed to take four weeks to shoot but now it's three weeks already and I suppose that costs Mr. Roland a lot of money."

"Hundreds of thousands, kiddo," advised Jack.

"Oh my! Mr. Roland might kill me!"

"If he has to," agreed Jack. After extracting assurances from both of them that they'd phone her, Alicia hurried back to soundstage 6.

"Got a cigarette?" Rita asked. After they both lit up, she asked Jack, "I'm sure you heard about your former father-in-law's murder."

"I'm sure even the deaf, dumb, and blind have heard of it."

"I used to know Dolly a long time ago."

"No kidding?"

"Before she went into pictures. We modeled dresses for Worth."

"With a figure like yours, I don't doubt you."

"I was real sad when I read about her suicide. But now they say she might have been murdered. You got any idea why?"

"If I did, I'd be sitting in an office in police headquarters, spilling what I know."

"You mean they haven't brought you in for questioning?"

Jack was studying the smoldering end of his cigarette. "No, they haven't. As a matter of fact, now that you mention it, I'm a little surprised they haven't. I suppose they'll get around to all of us." In response to her questioning look, he added, "My mother, my sister, her husband. But we had no reason to kill them. I certainly didn't. You must have seen the picture of me . . . holding her."

"It made me cry."

"Did it? Did it really? I think most people found it repulsive."

"I thought it was touching. But then, I cry when I read *The Five Little Peppers*."

"I don't think I'll ever love again the way I loved . . . the way I love Dolly. We had something real special together, something that doesn't happen but once in a lifetime. My lifetime, anyway. Hers too. I know that for sure. I've had lots of affairs and I'll go on having lots of affairs but it won't be like it was with Dolly. You don't know what I mean."

"Sure I do. You and Dolly lived my dream. I'm jealous. I want with somebody what you had with Dolly. But, gee, she was certainly something. Her father used to come and pick her up every day after work."

"No kidding?"

"Every day, rain or shine. Great-looking guy he was. I could have gone for him myself. All year round, even in the winter, he had this gorgeous sexy tan. You know what I mean. I mean you knew the man."

"Sure, but out here, there's nothing unusual about a tan, so I guess I didn't really notice. Anyway, whether men are sexy or not doesn't interest me. I'm strictly for the girls."

"Yeah," she said with a smile, "I been warned you're a lady-killer."

"You have? When was this? We only met an hour ago."

"You passed me on my way to Alicia's set."

"And I didn't notice you?"

"I guess not."

"I'm noticing you now. How do you like it out here?"

"I wish I knew. I been on this mess for eight days now and they say it's got six more weeks to go. I play Lotus Fairweather's kid sister. Granddaughter would be more like it. They're spending a small fortune on this turkey. They're shooting in this new two-strip Technicolor"—Jack let out a low whistle—"and they got about a hundred dancers and singers in costumes that cost so much they'd give the Secretary of the Treasury indigestion. Baby, if anything happens to screw up the works on this one Mr. Roland might have to hock his Diamond."

"It couldn't happen to a more deserving rat." He thought for a moment and then drenched her with charm. "You're so pretty, and you have such a sweet personality. How come you're still single?"

"I'm not. We haven't lived together for years. He's a very sick guy."

"That's too bad. What's the matter with him?"

"He suffers from chronic failure."

"Is that why you quit him?"

"I quit him because when I started getting some good parts on Broadway, my success went to his fists. He used to try knocking me around until one day I flattened him with a frying pan. As soon as I can get the time off, I'm heading for Reno."

"When are you free for dinner?"

"What about Alicia?"

"I'm not interested in eating Alicia."

"Anyway, she's got her hands and her bed full with Alexander Roland." She mentioned the name of a New York actor. "I been seeing him a couple of times."

"You don't sound very enthusiastic."

"Weell . . ." She drew the word out like a strand of chewing gum. "He's only here a couple of months and already he's going Hollywood."

"In what way?"

"He's taking tennis lessons, for instance."

Samuel Goldwyn was waving his hands impatiently as Sophie Gang wished this story conference would draw to an end. Stretched out on the couch with his eyes closed was Goldwyn's latest writing captive from New York, Ben Hecht. Hecht, with Charles MacArthur, had written a big Broadway smash, *The Front Page*, a few years earlier, but he had accepted Goldwyn's offer on his own. MacArthur preferred to remain in New York with his wife, the brilliant Helen Hayes, who had just given birth to Mary, their first child.

Goldwyn was speaking with a pained expression. "Her lawyers tell me I owe Vilma Banky one more picture, so I have to honor the contract, and everyone in this business knows I'm an honorable man." Sophie's face turned beet red as she tried to keep from choking. "But that terrible Hungarian accent of hers? What do we do with that accent?"

Hecht spoke quietly. "We put her in a convent as a nun who has taken an oath of silence. She never has to speak a word."

"Ben! You're a genius! Positively a genius!"

"Trouble is, I don't know anything about nuns or convents."

"So what? So you go to a convent and talk to the Mother Shapiro! I mean, when I did that movie where Ronnie Colman looked for somebody in a church—"

"*Sanctuary*," said Sophie, wishing she could go somewhere and find some for herself.

"Who gives a damn!" exploded Goldwyn, "It didn't make any money. But to find out what goes on in a church, I had my rabbi phone Saint Mary's, and he spoke to the rectum."

Hecht stifled a yawn. He was bored with Goldwynisms. He was sure Sam had a writer who wrote them for him daily. Goldwyn was too shrewd a showman and too wily a businessman to swim in an ocean of malapropisms. But on the other hand, when he was negotiating Hecht's contract and professing to be bleeding copiously from the writer's greedy demands, he pleaded, "Ben, stick with me and this will be the pinochle of your career."

Now he heard Goldwyn yelling, "You're not paying me any tension! You're half-asleep!"

"No I'm not, Sam. I think better with my eyes shut. It's the way I like to sit in a movie house, too." He moved to an upright position, filled his pipe with tobacco, and then torched it. "Sam, forget about Vilma Banky for five minutes and let's talk about the murders of Dolly Lovelace and her father."

"Why should I waste my time! Let the police talk about them!"

"Oh, they're doing a lot of talking about it. I've got a news writer friend, Hazel Dickson—she's very thick with Herbert Villon."

"Who's he?"

Sophie Gang provided the information. "He's the youngest chief inspector in the business. He's in charge of the investigation."

"Did I ask for you to put your two cents in?"

"No, but I was just longing for the sound of my own voice for a change."

"It's a very interesting case, Sam," said Hecht. "Did you know the girl?"

"Of course I knew her! I'm a legend! I know everybody! The only ones I don't know are the ones not worth knowing! Isn't that right, Sophie?"

"Me hear no evil, me see no evil, me speak no evil."

"Who the hell asked for a speech?" To Hecht he said, "I was at her funeral, wasn't I?"

Hecht said, "Everybody goes to everybody's funeral in this town. Not out of respect, but out of curiosity."

Sophie said, "The honest ones go to make sure they're dead."

Sam wheeled on her. "Don't you have to go to the toilet or something?"

"I just went!"

"Go again!"

"Why?"

"To make sure!"

"I knew old man Lovelace in New York." Hecht had nailed their attention. "He worked as a stagehand. In those days, Dolly was working as a model at one of those high-class, overpriced salons on Fifth Avenue. The old man watched her like a hawk. Used to pick her up after work. It's hard to figure how she got away to make it into pictures. He was a knockout of a looker. Fairly tall, built solid, and sported a tan all year round. Never knew of a wife or any other member of the family. Ezekiel used to drink in the same bar I frequented on Eighth Avenue. Sometimes he talked to me, sometimes he'd take his beer to a table in a remote corner and sort of mumble to himself. You know, Sam, I think he was in love with his daughter."

Goldwyn was aghast. "Are you suggesting I make such a dirty picture?"

"I'm not suggesting anything. I think the old man had a deep dark secret that made him overprotective of his daughter. I think that's why they might have been murdered. You see, I was always questioning in my mind the old man's tan. I began to wonder if maybe there was some colored blood in the family."

Sophie Gang said, "My cousin Jenny married a half-breed."

"What's the matter with her?" asked an astonished Goldwyn. "She couldn't find a whole one?"

Sophie Gang asked Hecht, "This writer friend of yours . . ."

"Hazel Dickson."

"Right. Have you told her your theory?"

"We had breakfast together downtown this morning. I told her then. She thinks that's why some photographs might have been stolen when the old man was slain."

With his chronic impatience, Goldwyn said, "I didn't see nothing in the papers about no missing pictures."

"You probably will pretty soon. So anyway, back to Vilma Banky and the convent. So here we have Vilma as Sister Nellie Nausea . . ."

"I want the whole kit and caboodle of them in for questioning," Herbert Villon was telling Jim Mallory, who was jotting down names on a pad. "The three Darlings and Willis Loring. Sounds like a vaudeville act."

Villon tapped a memorandum on his desk. "The coronor was sober when he made these tests?"

"I swear on my wife's grave."

"She isn't dead." The detective merely smiled. "So there were traces of poisoned cookies in their stomachs. You searched Ezekiel's kitchen thoroughly?"

"Fine-tooth comb. No cookies. As for Dolly's house, it had been cleaned out thoroughly after the funeral."

"I want you to talk to her neighbors." Mallory nodded. "See if she had any visitors the day she committed suicide. We know the old man had one visitor, the so-called sissy man, if we can trust a snotnosed kid who spies for a hobby. Who knows? Maybe we turn up a visitor of Dolly's who arrived with a box of cookies and got her to eat one. Maybe sissy man tempted Ezekiel with a chocolate-covered graham cracker."

"I like the ones with the raspberry jelly inside."

"You ain't been poisoned, you dummy!" He reached for a copy of *Screenland* magazine and flipped the pages. "Now, here's a cutie I'd like to slip a little something to. She's just been signed by Harry Cohn at Columbia." He held up the magazine for Mallory's attention. "Now, ain't this here Barbara Stanwyck something?"

SIX

◆

In the vastness of the hygienically white kitchen of Annawill, a black empress named Hettie McLeod sampled one of her own freshly baked tollhouse cookies. Her husband, Dakota, reached for one too and was rewarded with a slap on his hand.

"What's the matter with you, woman? You got enough cookies there to supply a troop of Girl Scouts."

"The doctor says you got to lose fifty pounds and you gonna lose them fifty pounds or you gonna lose *me!*" Dakota recognized the fire in her eyes; he had seen those conflagrations often enough. Hettie continued munching and lecturing. "One day soon the phone's gonna ring and it's gonna be our agent telling us it's our turn up at bat again. We gonna be back in pictures because they's talking and they ain't no better-talking black actors around here then you and me! Look at that Lincoln Jefferson whateverthehellhisnameis that got himself signed up at Fox. Now he calls himself Stepin Fetchit! Stepin Fetchit! The toady! Well, he's starring in something called *Hearts of Dixie!* And can he talk? Why, you can't understand a word he says. But my friend Prunella, she's in the picture, she tells me they scream themselves silly watching him in the rushes. Stepin Fetchit indeed!" She began demolishing another cookie and then mused aloud, "You know something, Dakota?"

"What's that?"

"I think we's too refined."

"Well, hell, woman, we got an education. We got high-school diplomas!"

"That's damn right and that's what's damn wrong. Here's what we gotta be doing." She began humming "Alabamy Bound" and, with her right hand elevated and batting the air, she did a combination of a shuffle and a strut. "Yassa, boss, heah ah cums. Heah ah is, yo' faithful Mammy, Hydrangea. Yassa—"

"Stop that!" raged Dakota. "We ain't shantytown niggers, damn it, and we ain't never gonna imitate them. Woman, we come a long way in this world."

"Oh, sure we have," she said sarcastically, "me the queen of the kitchen and you kowtowing to Mr. Sagging Muscles upstairs!" She mopped her perspiring brow with a kitchen towel. "Three years ago we were getting top money in pictures for our kind and then what happens? Well? I'm asking you? Then what happened?"

"Don't remind me. All of a sudden, not even an offer to play a bootblack. Ah, the hell with it."

"The hell with what?" The question came from the Darlings' British butler, Erskine Simpson-Thwaite, as he entered from the servants' quarters wearing his elegant uniform. ("How about us!" Marie Darling loved to crow. "We got the only hyphenated butler in Hollywood!")

"The hell with trying to get back into pictures."

Erskine said with a haughty sniff, "Only simpletons and retardates want to be in flickers. Don't you realize how well off we are? We're paid top dollar every two weeks. Our living quarters are the best in the community. We eat well, we dress well, and the sons of bitches occasionally treat us with a soupçon of civility. What more could you ask?"

"A good part in the next Janet Gaynor talker," said Hettie wistfully.

"Janet Gaynor? She has a voice like an unoiled hinge. And that thing that plays opposite her . . . um . . . what's his name again? Oh yes . . . Charles Farrell. He looks like a sufferer of chronic constipation. They won't last. Nothing lasts in films. I know." His voice and his face darkened. "Carl Laemmle brought me from England twenty years ago when I was a mere lad, a youth enveloped in a cloud of innocence." He struck a pose while Dakota and Hettie exchanged looks of boredom. They'd seen the performance too often. "They were offering me the world. I had starred in the West End in my first and only production. *I* trod the boards with Ellen Terry and Sir Herbert Tree. Like the fool I was, blinded by the stardust they flung in my eyes, I came to this godforsaken cultural desert to appear in two-reelers. *Two*-reelers. I made dozens of them. I appeared with Lon Chaney, and Harry Carey, Betty Blythe and Priscilla Dean . . . and then ten years later, at thirty-one years of age, I'm told I'm too old to play college boys. Look at me. Look at my face. Do I look a day over twenty?"

"Honeybunch," said Hettie through a hysterical cackle, "you don't look a day over fifty, and you know it. You better stop sniffing all that happy powder you keep snitching out of Mr. Jack's private stock, or you're going to grow old out there in that cold, cruel world of the unwanted."

Erskine favored her with a look intended to wither, but Hettie was bending over at one of the six stoves examining another batch of cookies. Dakota gave her a loving whack on the behind and Erskine poured himself a cup of coffee while muttering under his breath the futility of dealing with inferiors.

In the library, Marie was on the phone excoriating Detective Jim Mallory. "If your Mr. Villon would like to question myself and the members of my family, Mr. Gallery—"

"Mallory."

"Whatever the hell it is, he can get himself behind the wheel of a car and drive himself out here. Around here we don't go to the mountain, Mr. Ignoramus—"

"Mallory."

"Don't interrupt! The mountain comes to us!"

She slammed the phone down.

"Mama, my nerves!" cried Annamary, who was seated at a desk flipping the pages of a magazine.

"The nerve of those sons of bitches expecting *us* to come downtown to answer some questions."

Willis Loring had been pouring himself a sherry, but the hand holding the decanter froze. "Was that the police?"

"That was indeed the police!"

Annamary lost interest in the magazine as her brother came strolling through the French windows, the doors of which were ajar in hopes of luring a breeze. "Police? Police? Did I hear you say police? If that's a sherry you're pouring, Willis, one for me too, please."

Annamary spoke. "What do they want?"

"They want to ask us questions about your brother's late wife and father-in-law," boomed Marie.

"What kind of questions, Mama?" Annamary looked twelve years old.

"You'll know when they get here and ask them."

"They're coming here?"

"Well, we sure as hell ain't going there. Now listen, you three, we got more important things to talk about. I had it out with Alex Roland . . ."

"I saw you storming across the lot, Mom," said Jack with admiration.

Marie ignored him. "I warned him he fulfills every term of your contracts or he pays up in full and through the nose."

"He's having money problems, Mama," said Jack matter-of-factly as Willis brought him his glass of sherry.

Marie was interested. "You know that for sure or is it some piece of gossip you picked up?"

"What I picked up was Alex's new service station, Alicia Leddy and a friend of hers, Rita Gerber. We lunched at the commissary."

"I thought I told you to stay away from the studio!"

"Mama, I'm bored up to here." He indicated his neck. "Alex is behind schedule on at least half a dozen pictures, three of them in that new color process, and you've heard how expensive *that* is."

"The son of a bitch, it serves him right!" She paced slowly to the French windows. "If it wasn't for the commitments and the money he owes us, I'd sing in high C to see Alex Roland going broke."

Willis snorted. "Fat chance! He's been on the edge of disaster lots of times, but he never topples over."

Jack said, "Maybe that's because there was nobody behind him to give him a little bit of a push."

Mama Marie commanded center stage. "I gave him an ultimatum. Tomorrow afternoon he comes up with a talker for each of you or he settles with me financially and we move over to Joe Schenck at United Artists."

"Joe doesn't want me, Mama," said Jack plaintively. "Where do I move to?"

"Don't you worry, baby. You're gonna make a comeback, a real big comeback. We'll be on top of the world for as long as we want to be."

In Herbert Villon's office, Jim Mallory looked sheepish as Hazel Dickson laughed snidely. "You have to hand it to Marie Darling, and you might as well because she'll take it anyway. What an old battle-ax. Well, Herbert? Do you send the paddy wagon for them or do you swallow your professional pride and go storm the citadel?"

"Your prose ripens as fast as you do."

"Don't be mean, Herbert. I think it's really funny. That woman's an original. She makes the rest of those tough Hollywood mamas look like marmalade."

Jim Mallory finally spoke up. "What do we do, chief?"

Herbert arose and crossed to a mirror and spoke while examining his reflection. "I've always wanted a look at Annawill. There's no time like the present. Have a car sent around."

"Can I come too?" asked Hazel coyly.

Villon rewarded her request with an obscene gesture.

Helen Roland, Alexander Roland's wife, sat in Gloria Swanson's magnificent living room, waiting for the fabulous actress to finish pouring their cups of tea. Gloria looked at her guest and displayed her two perfect rows of ivories as she asked, "How do you take it? Milk? Lemon? Brandy?"

"Lemon would be fine," said Helen, her voice a pleasant contralto. "What do you think, Gloria?"

"About what?"

"About my trying for a comeback."

"Why not? You have a lovely voice. Christ knows you're prettier than ever. Your figure's great, and why the hell did you leave pictures in the first place?"

"Alex wanted me to. It didn't matter. I wasn't missed."

"Ah now, come on, you still get fan mail, don't you?"

"Yes, some of my old faithfuls still keep in touch."

"Have you discussed this with Alex?"

"He doesn't care what I do. He's got a new girl friend."

"Oh, thank God you know about this one." Swanson laughed. "You know how awful I am about secrets!"

"I'm glad for anyone that keeps him out of my bedroom." She laughed. "Poor silly bastard. Struts about like he was a young rooster."

Swanson put her cup and saucer down and chose a cigarette from a platinum case. "Why'd you marry him in the first place? You were never in love with him."

Helen watched Swanson lighting up. Even that ordinary gesture had star quality. "Well, it was at the end of my romance with Jack Darling. I realized Jack never had any intention of marrying me, and here was Jack's boss showering me with unwanted attention. I married Alex to get back at Jack." She sighed. "You know . . . the best-laid plans. Glory, would Joe Schenck consider my doing a film for UA?"

Gloria sent a smoke ring to its doom in space. "Do you have anything in mind you'd like to do?"

"Yes. I'd like to do the life of Dolly Lovelace."

"Ye gods, are you *mad*?"

Helen folded her arms. "It's a hell of a story. And there's plenty I know that could add some more spice to it."

"Isn't it spicy enough as it is? I mean my God, sweetie, now that her father's been murdered, and I suppose you've heard the rumor all over town that he was really a Negro."

"I've heard everything there is to know. I've gotten it from Lolly Parsons and God knows what Bertha Graze is spreading with her trowel. I want to play Dolly Lovelace. I'm the right age, I'm years younger than Alex."

Gloria said pragmatically, "Alex is fine for a first husband. You should be looking around for number two. Take me. Joe Kennedy and I can't go on forever. He's got political ambitions and there's enough gossip about us as it is. He'll never divorce Rose to marry me because he's too damn Catholic. And then there's all those kids. So I've got my eyes peeled for husband number four."

"Glory, got any theories as to why the Lovelaces were murdered?"

"Sure, doesn't everybody? Number one theory is the Negro angle. A black passing for white on the silver screen? Wow, what a story that would have been had it broken while Dolly was still alive. They were killed to shut them up. Dolly was a wreck when Jack told her he was dumping her. She was desperate. She was all over town making all kinds of threats about Jack and his mother and drippy Annamary. I mean, isn't *she* the cat's pajamas! And I'm sure you've heard Dolly was supposedly having it off with Willis Loring?"

"She wasn't!"

"She was." Swanson giggled. "Mama Marie smuggled herself into a screening of my talker. I'm told she sat dumbfounded in her chair at the standing ovation it got at the end." Swanson broke out into the film's theme song, "Love (Your Magic Spell Is Everywhere)." Then she stopped in midsong and said, "I've done it, Helen. In *The Trespasser* I've licked the talkers. They won't be calling me Gloria Swansong like that bitch Hedda Hopper predicted."

"Alex calls her 'Garbage Mouth.'"

"The hell with her. Let's see what we can do to get Joe Schenck lathered up about you making a comeback. You're sure Alex wouldn't set you up in one himself?"

"He would but I won't. Besides, he's up to his ears in money troubles."

"Oh, not again."

"He's overloaded and underbudgeted. He's been signing up talking talent without even testing them. He's loaded the studio with an army of clinkers. He needs some money-makers fast."

"If he goes under, I won't shed any tears. You know how I loathe him."

"You don't really."

"Oh, yes I do. Now more than ever. I loathed them all. Look at what they're doing to so many of our friends. They're destroying careers and lives without so much as a how-do-you-do. Aileen Pringle was over last night and you know what a smart cookie Pringie is. Even she's given up. She's taking supports, anything she can get."

"I didn't know she was broke."

"She's not. But she's hurting in here." Swanson indicated her heart. "She's not being asked to parties anymore. Betty Compson highhatted her at the club on Sunday. She no longer gets preferential treatment at her favorite restaurant. And *she* speaks beautifully."

"She always did. I don't understand what's going on."

"The boys are ganging up to rid themselves of the high-priced ones. They're getting these nobodies from Broadway and London for a fraction of silent stars' salaries. Look what the Warners are doing to Monte Blue and Jack Mulhall. Putting them into quickies to wind up their contracts. Trying to humiliate them into quitting. They've got Blanche Sweet in a movie and she's not even getting any billing!"

"Now, that is the lowest!"

"Yet, on the other hand, look at Bessie Love. Couldn't get a job for years and all of a sudden she can play a ukelele and sing, if you can call it singing, and she's even dancing. And she's a smash talker hit in *The Broadway Melody*."

"But how long will it last?"

"How should I know? I'm a star, not a philosopher." She shoved the tea tray aside. "How's for a martini! The sun's going down."

Erskine Simpson-Thwaite ushered Herbert Villon and Jim Mallory into Annawill's imposing reception room. "Who shall I say is calling?"

"Chief Inspector Herbert Villon and Detective James Mallory," said Villon.

66

"May I take your hats?" asked the butler haughtily.

"Will we get them back?" asked Villon. Erskine knew when he was beaten and left them cooling their heels.

Mallory examined the room while whistling between his teeth. "And this is only the reception room."

In the main parlor, Marie draped herself on a sofa while Jack sat at the piano running his fingers lightly over the keys. Willis and Annamary shared a love seat. They had heard the door chimes and knew it was the police. The butler had been instructed to wait a few beats before conducting the policemen into the main parlor.

In the kitchen, Hettie said to Dakota, "Must be the cops."

"They'll get nothing out of Mama."

"They'll get plenty out of Mama. But nothing they can use. You know Mama. She'll tie them up in knots. Stay out of them pots, Dakota. Let the dinner stew in peace. The police won't."

Mama Marie's gracious smile was patterned on that of Queen Mary of England as Villon introduced himself and Mallory. They accepted the seats and refused the drinks they were offered. Willis Loring asked, "Would you prefer to third-degree us individually?"

"This isn't a third degree, Mr. Loring. We're just looking for some assistance in what we suspect to be two murders. Mr. Darling . . ."

"Yes?" Jack spun about on the piano stool and seemed on the verge of asking, "Anyone for tennis?"

"You were married briefly to Dolly Lovelace."

"That's right." He laced his fingers together. "Soon after our marriage we found we were incompatible."

"Yet that was quite an emotional display with her corpse at her funeral."

"Just because we didn't get along didn't mean I stopped loving her. I love her now. I always will. But we couldn't live together."

"I have information that suggests you left her because you found out she had black blood."

"That's a lie!" shouted Mama Marie, no longer Queen Mary of England.

"Mama, please," pleaded Annamary while clutching the strand of pearls around her neck like a lifeline.

Villon continued, ignoring Marie's outburst. "That kind of news could lead to scandal and possibly ruin your career. Both your careers, I suppose, were at stake."

"I would never have abandoned Dolly because of a scurrilous lie." Jack looked noble and brave and gallant as his brother-in-law suppressed the urge to blow a raspberry.

Villon said, "Our theory is that Dolly and her father were murdered to keep them quiet."

"How dare you!" Mama Marie was on her feet and waving a fist at Villon.

"How dare I what?" asked Villon with a quick look at Jim Mallory. The detective was enjoying the scene immensely.

"How dare you insinuate we had Dolly and her father murdered!"

"I didn't insinuate anything of the kind."

"Oh yes you did! I'm on to your filthy cop tricks!"

"You are? Which filthy cop tricks?"

Mama's hands were on her ample hips. "Have you got a search warrant?"

"What do I need a search warrant for? We're only here looking for information. What's all the fuss about?"

"Mama, sit down!" Annamary startled even herself with her awesome tone of voice. Marie sat.

"You refused to come to headquarters and, rather than issue warrants and embarrass you—that action would certainly have made headlines—we very nicely came here to you."

"You came here to make capital of three great stars of the silver screen! You cops are always out looking for headlines!"

Jack said, "For crying out loud, Mama, will you let them ask their questions so we can get it over with?" He had crossed to the bar and was pouring himself a whisky. To Villon he said, "If there was Negro blood in Dolly, she never told me, and that's the truth. When we married I was having problems, and I don't have to tell you what they are. Drink, dope, women, a fading career. Dolly was a fool to have married me. She was on a

68

skyrocket to stardom. The truth is, I married her to try to bum a free ride back to the top."

"You shut up!" yelled Marie. To Villon she said, "Don't you believe any of that hogwash."

"It's the truth!" shouted Jack.

In the kitchen, Erskine, Hettie, and Dakota, grouped around an open window, could hear most of what was going on between the family and the police. Hettie commented, "If she had black blood in her then she was too damned good for that bum!"

Jack downed the whisky in one gulp and poured another for himself. Annamary leaned forward in her seat and addressed Villon. "Mr. Villon, we are not murderers. We are actors. I loved Dolly as though she was my own sister and I was very sad when she and Jack split up." She couldn't resist adding, "I know my husband adored her too."

His face beet red with embarrassment, Willis murmured something that sounded like "Arrumph" while Marie wondered if the cops knew about her late husband the pickpocket.

Villon said, "Miss Darling, I think you are misreading me. I never insinuated that anyone in this family is a murderer. In truth, you haven't given me a chance to finish. You're all on the defensive for no reason that I can understand."

Mallory looked at Villon with tacit admiration. He was handling them brilliantly. He was prepared to do battle with Marie Darling because he had been forewarned by Helen Dickson that the old woman's favorite target was the jugular. He also understood that solidarity was the family watchword. Villon was convinced that there wasn't anyone in the world not capable of murder whether premeditated or driven to it emotionally. He remembered at least two occasions when he himself had to be restrained from killing.

Villon said to Marie, "Have you ever visited Ezekiel Lovelace at his home in Inglewood?"

"What for? Why should I visit him? I never even met him."

"Really? Now, isn't that strange? Didn't he attend the wedding?"

"He wasn't asked."

Villon's eyes moved from Marie to Jack. "Didn't Dolly want her father at her wedding?"

"Well, actually no, she didn't. You see, she was afraid of him."

"Do you know why?"

"Well, back in New York, where they came from, he was very stern and very strict with her. She couldn't go anywhere or do anything without his permission. She worked as a model for Worth—you've heard of Worth?" Villon nodded and thought, *Condescending son of a bitch.* "He used to be there at the end of every work day, waiting for her. He was suffocating the poor kid."

"How did she get away from him?"

"She ran away while he was out of town with a show. He was a stagehand. Several people in films had noticed her when she modeled. I mean, that astonishing beauty, the way she walked, it was so, well, it was so feline."

Jim Mallory hoped Jack wouldn't burst into tears; his voice was getting highly emotional.

"She was a sure bet for films. Whether she could act or not, she was a sure bet." He was indeed fighting tears. He regained control and continued. "Well, she turned out to be a pretty good actress. I was nuts about her. Anyway, he tracked her down because of her pictures; that was a cinch, of course. He came out here, but by then she wasn't afraid of him anymore. She was becoming an important star at Diamond Films, and Alex Roland—he's the head, you know—he was not about to jeopardize a gold mine. I think Alex frightened Ezekiel . . ."

"Oh, tell the truth," said Marie impatiently. "They paid him to keep away and the miser salted it all away and lived in that filthy hovel."

"I thought you never visited him?" Herbert bit off each word and aimed them at her like arrows.

"I didn't, smartass. Dolly told us how he lived and where he lived and I'm sorry they're dead but where he's concerned, I say good riddance to bad rubbish. He was a terrible father."

"He wasn't her father," said Villon. "He was her husband."

SEVEN

Jim Mallory would never tire of describing the tableau that followed Herbert Villon's startling revelation. Annamary's gasp, Willis Loring's quizzical expression, the indescribable look of hatred on Jack's face as he stared at his mother, and Marie's face, freshly quarried marble. This he stored in his memory bank as Villon continued.

"It was Ezekiel who had the colored blood in him. His mother was a black woman, New Orleans creole. Ezekiel's father took her out of a cat house and married her to spite his family, which has nothing to do with my case." He addressed Jack. "When she married you, Dolly became a bigamist." Marie was his tongue's next target. "You knew that."

"The hell I did!"

"The hell you didn't. I know the private operator you hired in New York to track down Dolly's background when your son told you he intended to marry her. Unfortunately, by the time you got your information, they were already married. So instead of telling your son his new wife was a bigamist, for reasons of your own you decided to twist the facts and nail Dolly as a black woman instead of revealing it was her other husband who had the black blood. Well, what the hell, Mrs. Darling, either way if the word got out, it would have been one hell of a scandal."

"It still could be," said Marie, "so you two cops keep mum about this, you hear? I got friends in high places. I could make it hot for you."

"Mrs. Darling, there are two things you never do to me. You

71

never serve me boiled fish and you never threaten me in any way or at any time. And so, ladies and gentlemen, I now have several reasons why the Lovelaces were targeted for murder."

While Villon was speaking, Annamary went to her brother, knelt at his side, and put her hands over his, which were lying limply on his lap. Jim Mallory remembered her doing it exactly the same way when she costarred with Eugene O'Brien in *The Cinderella Girl*.

The next ten minutes were occupied with Villon questioning their whereabouts at the time of both deaths. Willis Loring could supply golf dates, tennis appointments, and a manicure. Annamary was sweetly vague and Villon decided that about the only thing she could ever kill was somebody's appetite. Jack confessed to alcoholic hazes, discreetly omitting the probability he might have been blacked out with either heroin, opium, or morphine. Mama Marie said, with a magnificent look of defiance, "I don't even remember what I did half an hour ago."

In the kitchen, catching snatches of what was going on with the police, the group at the window couldn't contain their delight.

"Bigamy!" exhaled Hettie. "Ain't that a honey." She nudged Dakota in the ribs. "They ain't no other Mrs. McLeod in the vicinity, is there, precious?"

"Not so I's noticed," said Dakota.

Erskine Simpson-Thwaite left their company to retire to his bedroom, where he phoned Bertha Graze.

Nibbling on a maraschino cherry, Bertha chirruped her gratitude to the butler and told him to drop by anytime and pick up his reward.

In the police car driving back to headquarters, Jim Mallory said, "My hat's off to you, chief. You had them cornered and up a tree."

Villon responded with a flat voice. "Jim, they're actors."

"Oh," said Mallory, and kept quiet for the remainder of the drive.

Back in the main salon of Annawill, Marie was doing her best to quell the rebellion that erupted after the officers left. "So I

72

didn't tell you the truth," she snarled at Jack. "It won't be the first time. And as for you two ingrates"—meaning Annamary and Willis—"you owe me what and where you are today. I'm not afraid of any cops, I'm not afraid of anybody. They got nothing on us and they'll get nothing on us."

"Mama," said Annamary sternly, "you lied to the police!"

"Everybody lies to the police!"

"You have too been to Ezekiel's cottage. You forget I was there when you twisted Dolly's arm to get his address."

"I should have twisted her neck."

Jack grabbed his mother's wrist. "Why did you see her father? I mean . . ."

"To pay him off, that's why!"

Tightening his grip, Jack continued, "Are you sure you didn't visit him the day he died?"

"Jack, you're hurting me! Let go of my wrist, you damn kid!" She slapped him hard with her free hand. As he reeled back, she rubbed the aching wrist. "What's gotten into you kids?" Willis was enjoying the scene immensely. "Don't I have enough to worry about without you two turning on me!" To Willis she said, "Pour me a gin."

"Why, of course, Mama. One gin coming up. With a dash of bitters, perhaps?"

Erskine entered. "You're wanted on the phone, Mrs. Darling." Marie thought she'd heard the phone but, what with all the racket in the room, she wasn't sure.

"I'll take it in the library." She snatched the glass of gin from Willis before he could finish pouring and made a grand exit. There was gin slopped all over the bar.

"What a mess," said Willis.

"What a mess," echoed Annamary. She wasn't referring to the spilled gin.

In the library, Marie was expecting a cerebral hemorrhage as she held the receiver to her ear.

"Are you there?" Bertha Graze asked.

"I'm here." Marie sipped some gin.

"Do you think I'm being unreasonable, dear?"

73

"No more than usual, Bertha."

"Can I expect you sometime tomorrow?"

"I've an appointment with Alex Roland tomorrow."

"Yes, I know. At two o'clock."

Marie held the cool glass against one of her throbbing temples. "You know just about everything, don't you, Bertha?"

"My crystal ball, darling. It sees all, it knows all, but it sometimes doesn't tell all. Why don't you come by after your date with Mr. Roland?"

"Sure," said Marie, and then replaced the phone in its cradle. She stared into her glass of gin; although a poor substitute for a crystal ball, it suggested something. She went to the kitchen, where she confronted the three servants. "Okay, I want the truth. Which one of you is on Bertha Graze's payroll?"

In Sam Goldwyn's office, Sophie Gang was sharing some gossip with her boss. "Over at Universal they hear Carl Laemmle is thinking of turning the studio over to Carl Junior."

"Well," said Goldwyn, "I'm not so surprised. He worships his son. Ever since he was a little boy, he placed him on a pederast."

Sophie bit her lip and then referred to her notes. "Could we use Jack Darling for anything?"

Goldwyn tapped on the desk with a pencil. "Who's asking?"

"I got a feeler from Jason Cutts"—Goldwyn had a look of distaste on his face at the mention of the name—"in Roland's office."

"Poor Alex. Marie must have him squirming."

"His creditors have him squirming."

"Them too. It won't be so easy for him to unload the Darlings and Willis Loring. When Marie grabs you by the balls, she don't let go until you sing 'The Star Strangled Banner.'" He leaned back in his chair, yawned, rubbed his eyes, and then stared ahead at nothing. Finally he spoke. "Jack Darling. Such a nice boy once. Nice actor. Good box office for a while."

"Maybe there's something for him in the Irish story," suggested Sophie.

"I'm not so hot for the Irish story, though Fox has brought over a cute kid from Ireland. You know her name . . . Maureen O'Solomon."

"O'Sullivan."

"That's what I said, didn't I?"

"Yes, Mr. Goldwyn."

"You know, actually, Jack could play the leprecohen. Isn't that an idea?"

"That's a very good idea, Mr. Goldwyn."

Goldwyn beamed with self-delight. "Not bad at all. We get Jack and the O'Solomon girl and maybe Victor McLaglen and you know who would be good for the milkmaid? Colleen Moore."

"Mr. Goldwyn, she's just done a talker with an Irish background."

"You're sure?"

"It's called *Laughing Irish Eyes*."

"So what? I happen to know she's soon going to come cheap. First National isn't picking up her option."

"Oh, how sad." Sophie's feelings were genuine. Everyone in the industry liked Colleen Moore. "She's made so much money for them."

"Face it, Sophie, her time is passing. As a flapper, she was hot stuff. But the flapper is finished. So what do you do with her?"

"But she's such a good actress. Don't you remember how wonderful she was in *So Big*?"

"I remember things I long ago forgot." He was lighting a cigar. "You think I like dropping Vilma Banky? She's also a good actress, but what can you do with her in the talkers?" He shook his head sadly. "So many. So many destroyed. Some were good friends. You think I like it when Frances is planning a dinner and she says to me, 'Is it all right to invite Eleanor Boardman?' And I tell her, so far it's all right. Louis B. Mayer is putting her in a couple of talkers. She can talk, but she hasn't got the talking magic. Take my Ronnie Colman, mark my verbs. He'll be bigger in talkers then he ever was. That voice gives him a new kind of sex appeal. You saw how the women reacted when we previewed *Bulldog Drummond*."

"Yes, it was wonderful."

"Even the men like him. That's very important. Before they never even noticed him. Ronnie will go on forever. I'm going to see that he reaches the acne of success." He contemplated the ceiling and then, in the swiftest transition since Jekyll and Hyde, shouted, "And then you know what's going to happen? I'll make him so successful that when the time comes to renew his contract, the ingrate will hold me up for hundreds of thousands of dollars. He'll demand the right to choose his own stories and the right to accept outside assignments at his full fee without a nickel to me. How dare he!" He jumped to his feet. "How dare Ronald Colman do this to me after all I did for him! Oh God, how I hate actors! They steal the bread from my mouth. Take a memo to Ronald Colman. 'You ungrateful bastard . . .'"

Loyalty in Hollywood was as rare as lean hot pastrami. Talking pictures set off a tidal wave of destruction. No earthquake would do the damage of the talkers. Marriages were in ruins. Friendships went up in flames. Families disintegrated. Even in Hollywood's two great houses of prostitution, Madam Blanche's and Madam Frances's, former film greats were being given short shrift. Such steady patrons as Norman Kerry, Lloyd Hughes, Wheeler Oakman, and cowboy stars Tom Mix and Hoot Gibson were finding the house bedrooms suddenly full, and "Why not have a drink while you're waiting." And the wait could be hours, unlike the days when they'd be ushered swiftly into the arms of a waiting whore. At Madam Frances's, the Broadway and London crowd were now receiving preferential treatment. Seated at her bar were two New York favorites, Robert Ames and Robert Williams, both to be dead of heart attacks within the next two years.

Robert Ames asked Robert Williams, "By any chance did you see my last play?"

"I hope so."

Metro star John Gilbert, whose talking debut had been a disaster, was at the farthest end of the bar drinking alone. British actor John Loder, newly arrived in Hollywood, had always admired him and decided to tell him so.

"Mr. Gilbert, my name is John Loder. I'm a great admirer of yours. I just arrived from London and—"

"Sure you've just arrived from London. And what are they paying you? A couple of hundred a week? Well, you listen to me, you limey bastard. I make ten thousand a week and they're going to pay it to me for the next four years. My contract is tighter than this"—he made a fist—"and they can do anything they want to humiliate me. For ten thousand a week, I can swallow anything. Mike! I need a refill."

Loder was chagrined. "I'm sorry. I only—"

"I know. I know, kid. Mike, give the kid a drink. What are you having kid, a pink gin? That's all they ever seem to drink in London is pink gin and beer they should pour back down the horse's throat." As Mike poured a pink gin for Loder, who would have preferred scotch whisky, Gilbert rambled onward. "Don't mind me, kid. I'm used to the Hollywood knife. It's happened before. Greta did it to me, used me to help prove she preferred men, but ha ha ha, she stood me up at the altar. Now I'm married to Ina Claire and when I ask her for a little nookie, she says, 'Oh, go to Madam Frances, dear, they're so much better at it than I am.' So why did I marry her in the first place? Because I didn't marry her in the first place. I married her in the second place but I'll divorce her in the first place. Snotty Broadway bitch. She'll never make it in pictures."

"She has a beautiful voice," said Loder, and then regretted having said it.

"She's too fucking old, young man. Say, what's your name?"

"John Loder."

"Who you with?"

"Paramount."

Gilbert eyed him boozily from head to toe. "You won't last a year."

Loder's face reddened. "I've only signed for six months."

"They've got Clive Brook, you know. That limey'll get first pick of the good parts. You'll get the giblets. Still, he's past forty. And me. Look at me. I'm not yet thirty . . ." His voice faded away. He stared into his drink. John Loder was forgotten.

Madam Frances took Loder by the arm. With a warm smile, she said, "Welcome to my palazzo. You were recommended by. . . ?"

"William Powell."

"Ah! Dear Willie! I thought he might have forgotten me since he's been courting Carole Lombard."

"He tells me you have a girl who dresses up like Mary Pickford. I've always dreamed of sleeping with Mary Pickford."

"So does Douglas Fairbanks," she said wryly. "Yes, my Mary Pickford is available. She's on the third floor in the Puce Room."

"Um, er, Bill said she . . . um . . . what's the American expression . . . 'goes down'?"

"Assuredly. Not as often as an elevator but more often than the Lusitania. Let me take you to her."

Jack Darling wandered over to the bar. He was one of Mike the bartender's favorites. Mike hoped the actor wasn't on Madam Frances's down list. "Scotch and water, Mike."

"Good to see you again, Mr. Darling," said Mike as he filled the order. "It's been a long time. How's the family?"

"They're all right, if you like them." He was looking around the room. "What's become of all the regulars, Mike? There was a time when I came in it was half an hour of greeting everybody before I could get down to some serious screwing."

"Yeah, it's not like old times anymore. We don't even have no more of them old-time orgies. You know, with guys beating the girls with whips or chaining them to the bedposts and making them scream for mercy. Gee, them was the good old days." He leaned forward and lowered his voice. "Now look at this new blood we got coming in here. I mean they're real in-again-out-again Finnegans. Wham, bam, thank you ma'am. Some of the girls say they don't even know if these guys are in bed with them or taking a census. You ain't looking so good, Mr. Darling. It ain't uh, you know, them rumors about your ex-wife and her father, is it?"

"Mike, you don't want to make me forget that I like you, do you?"

Comedian Harry Langdon came in, saw Jack Darling, and, grateful for the sight of a familiar face, joined him at the bar. Shyly, he touched Jack's arm. Jack recognized him and smiled, "How goes it, Harry?"

Harry wrinkled his nose, which made his obscene baby face even more repulsive. "Well, I still have my house, but not for long. First National bounced me. My girl friend left me for a new producer named Emmanuel Katz and now she doesn't even talk to me."

"Katz got her tongue?"

"My agent doesn't take my calls. When I walk down the street in Beverly Hills, little boys throw rocks at me and dogs give chase and nip at my ankles, but other than that I'm in the best of health and determined to make a comeback. Mike, can I have a sloe gin fizz or is my presence an embarrassment?"

Bertha Graze was entertaining two of Louis B. Mayer's biggest male stars, William Haines and Ramon Novarro. Haines had been a silent star for over five years, as had been Novarro. The studio was capitalizing on his true nature as a brash wisecracker in his first talkers while Novarro, due to his Mexican accent, was set for a series of Latin musical adventures. His beautiful singing tenor worked to his advantage and his first talkers, *Devil May Care* and *In Old Seville*, would bring him renewed popularity. Unlike him, Haines's brash-young-man performances would soon prove obnoxious and tiring and, in time, Mayer would find an excuse to slice them from the studio roster. All this Bertha predicted with the assurance of a cat cornering a mouse.

"You know, boys," Bertha told them as she stared into the crystal ball, "you're not Mayer's favorites."

Novarro bristled. "He never like me since he found out I was Rex Ingram's protégé." Ingram had been an MGM director, married to actress Alice Terry, who condoned his occasional flings in the hay with young actors. Ingram particularly liked the handsome and muscular young Novarro and gave him several

79

important roles, which led to his being selected as actor George Walsh's replacement in the title role of *Ben-Hur* four years earlier.

"Protégé! Ha!" roared Haines. "You can sure speak plainer English than that."

Bertha looked up from the crystal ball. "You two better stop visiting that male brothel up in the hills; Mayer has some private dicks around taking photos of everybody going in and out. Think of those morals clauses in your contracts."

Haines paled, then found his usual bravado. "Ah, Mayer wouldn't dare drop me. The Thalbergs are two of my best friends and it's Irving who really runs the studio, not Louis."

Bertha said smugly, "A word to the wise should be sufficient." Then she leaned back while reaching into a plate of nauseating-looking goodies. "Now, if I were you two, I'd play it safe for a while. It just so happens I know a couple of young boys who are friendly and agreeable and for a reasonable price"—she paused to pop a date confection into her mouth—"will offer you their services. They're fresh in from the sticks and dying to meet movie stars."

"Bertha, you rascal," simpered Haines. "How young?"

"Very. They're prime cuts. I can send them around to your place in about an hour or so. What do you say?"

"Send them both to Bill's. Not my place. I live with my mother. She doesn't understand these things. She's very religious."

"Yeah," said Haines, "she's got housemaid's knees from kneeling in front of the Virgin Mary in Ramon's private chapel." Haines then asked, "Say, Bertha, what's that dirty grapevine of yours buzz about the murders of Dolly Lovelace and her father?"

Bertha was tempted to tell them the father had really been a husband, but there was still tomorrow and her meeting with Marie Darling and the sizable sum she expected in return for her silence.

Bertha stalled. "Oh? Have they been officially declared murdered?"

Haines informed her, "That's what Hedda Hopper tells me."

"That bitchy gossip," said Bertha while selecting a chocolate mint. "She ought to be writing a column like Lolly Parsons, she's so frequently misinformed. How come you're so chummy with her?"

Haines grinned. "Because she's so chummy with Louis B. and I need all the friends at court I can get."

"The frigid bitch. It's a wonder she ever managed to give birth to a son. It must be the first and only time that spit worked. Well, gentlemen, let me get cracking on these young men for you."

"Now, just a minute," said Novarro seriously. "They're of age, right? I'm not taking any chances."

"Of course they're of age," said Bertha. "Would I pull something dirty on you?"

Erskine Simpson-Thwaite sat in the furnished room on Cahuenga Boulevard he'd rented hastily after the McLeods had fingered him as Bertha Graze's informer. His suitcases lay unpacked on the floor. "Damn bitch," he muttered to himself, "dismissing me without so much as a by-your-leave. No severance pay. No references. How the hell do I get a job in this town? I'm too old to peddle my ass the way I did when I got my deal with Universal." He stood up and walked the incredibly short distance to his solitary window. "Bertha will help me. She'll have to help me. And she owes me money. Owes me money! Ha! Some fair swap! It cost me my job! What a cushy job too! Oh, Erskine Simpson-Thwaite, why are you such a foolish lad?" He found some coins in his pocket and went downstairs to use the hall telephone. Bertha answered and he told her his plight.

Bertha asked Haines and Novarro, "Either of you in the market for a trustworthy valet who's smart as a whip? He's just been bounced by Marie Darling."

Haines snickered. "You mean the one with the hyphen?" Bertha nodded. "Mmmm, let me think about it."

Bertha assured Erskine there was a good possibility of immediate employment for him and Erskine reminded her he'd be by the next day for the money due him.

Erskine went back to his room with a lighter heart and began unpacking. He didn't think the residents of Annawill would miss the ashtrays, the cigarette lighter, and some of the good silverware, all of which he intended to pawn should the going get rough. After all, it served that rotten old harridan right for not paying him some severance. Gaily he whistled "Only a Rose" and wondered who had murdered Dolly Lovelace and her father.

After Haines and Novarro left, Bertha phoned the two boys, who were thrilled at the prospect of meeting two celebrated movie stars. "And listen," she warned the boy who had answered the phone, "when they ask, and I assure you they're going to ask, you tell them you're over twenty-one, you hear me?" She smiled. "You two are going to make a lot of money in this town. There's lots of fairy boys coming in from New York and London and we'll get them while they're hot."

Over dinner in a popular restaurant on the Santa Monica pier, Herbert Villon was telling Hazel Dickson what he felt she ought to know about his adventure at Annawill. Hazel absorbed the information with a small smile, knowing from experience that Villon had carefully edited the narrative before relating it to her. He told her nothing about Ezekiel Lovelace being Dolly's husband.

"Are you trying to tell me the old gorgon didn't give you what-for at daring to insinuate she and her kiddies could be murder suspects?"

"Oh, there were several small tornados but nothing I couldn't handle."

"You really believe she didn't know Ezekiel, never met him?"

"You know better than that, Hazel baby," he said while spooning lentil soup into his mouth. "The one that confuses me is Annamary."

"She's not very bright. She's got cottage cheese between her ears."

"Don't be too sure about that. At one point she dropped that airy-fairy-Mary façade of hers and let go a quick blast at Mama that made my ears stand up."

"Oh, really?"

"She's even prettier when she's angry."

"What about Hairbreadth Harry, the husband?"

"Now, if you want to talk about a dimwit, there's your likely prospect."

"Don't kid yourself. His is the best act of all. He let Mama do all the work and she's made him a star and a millionaire. I don't know whether you heard this or not, but on the sly he's been buying up a lot of empty lots around here and Malibu and farther up the coast."

"What's he going to do with them? Grow flowers?"

"No, sell them to the county when they decide to put in some highways."

"Ha!" Soup dribbled down the sides of his mouth and Hazel told him to wipe it away. Villon said, "It'll be years before they get around to putting in any highways. The city's so corrupt they'll do nothing until some politicos are assured of an unhealthy cut."

"That ain't what Hedda Hopper told me."

"Damn it, where does that woman get her info?"

"Beats hell, Herbert. She can't act for shit, but they keep her busy because she knows too much."

"One of these days she might get herself murdered."

"Don't bet on that. She's too useful to everybody. So what next, Hawkshaw?"

"Well," said Herbert as the waiter removed his soup plate and replaced it with the pot roast special, "the next murder should help clarify things."

It was the rare time that Hazel found herself at a loss for words. She didn't even dig into her shrimp casserole but let it cool as she waited to hear more from Herbert.

"Yep, Hazel, there's murder in the air. I smell it. Dolly and her father were one thing, two isolated killings that are bound to have a bigger meaning once some other killings take place."

Hazel finally found her voice. "You're kidding, Herbert. I mean, fun's fun but what makes you think there's more to come?"

83

"Remember the Renaissance?"

"Oh, sure," said Hazel with a wry expression. "I had a ball. In fact, it was so small, I had two."

"Lots of killings in that Renaissance. Well, we're having a Renaissance of our own, and I predict there's going to be some killings. There's a human time bomb out there ticking away, and it's soon going to detonate. And when it does, run for the hills."

"By God, Herbert, you've sent a chill up my spine."

"Be grateful. I'm sure that doesn't happen very often."

"You know what you can do." Herbert was too engrossed in his pot roast to respond. "And by the way, how come you didn't tell me you know Ezekiel was really Dolly's husband?" Herbert began choking on his food. Hazel smiled. "Hedda Hopper knows all and tells all. I also slip her a few bucks every now and then." Herbert was gulping some water. "I sent it out on the wire this afternoon. It'll be in all the morning papers."

"You didn't."

"Don't be stupid, of course I did. It's my job. And I've scooped every paper around the world."

"I promised Marie Darling to keep it buried. Oh, my my my. I think the next victim just might be myself. Mama Marie is sure as hell going to plan to kill me."

EIGHT

♦

Marie Darling shook with rage as she held the morning newspaper in trembling hands. "I'll kill that bastard! I'll kill that son of a bitch of a cop!" Hettie had warned Dakota to brace himself against the fury of her wrath when she read the headline, but this was even worse than Dakota had expected. "I'll have him drawn and quartered and after that I'll have him tortured!"

Annamary came hurrying into the breakfast room, her hair neatly tied with a pink ribbon, a delicate negligee over her blue satin pajamas. "What is it, Mama? What's wrong?"

Marie held the newspaper up so that Annamary could read the headline. Annamary's comment was a surprisingly simple, "Well, that's that."

"Is that all you can say? Now the whole world knows Jack was married to a bigamist!"

"So what? Jack wasn't the bigamist."

"I thought I could trust that man Villain."

"Villon."

"I prefer my pronunciation." She turned on Dakota. "Don't just stand there! Pour the coffee!" She stared at her poached eggs. "Ugh. They look like shriveled tits. Take them away!"

"Yes, ma'am," said Dakota, sweeping them off the table and crossing with the plate to the sideboard for the carafe of coffee.

Suddenly, Marie chuckled. "This'll kill Bertha Graze."

"I wish it would," said Annamary as she buttered a thin slice of raisin wheat toast.

"Where's Willis?"

Annamary shrugged. "Tennis. Golf. Horseback. Swimming. Screwing. Choose one from column A."

"He told me you asked him for a divorce."

"That's right."

Marie watched Dakota filling the coffee cups. "There's to be no divorce."

"It's my life, Mama."

"Your life is my life and there's to be no divorce. I'm seeing Alex Roland after lunch and I'm positive we'll come to arrangements for your first talkers. To divorce Willis now would supply Alex with the kind of ammunition that could be fatal to my negotiations."

"Why? The publicity would be terrific. A big shot in the behind to both our fading careers."

"Your careers are not fading. Certainly not yours. You'll always be America's Darling!"

"America's Darling has gotten too old to be America's Darling any longer. Dakota, is there any of that ham left over from last night?"

"There sure is," he said brightly.

"I'd like some. And the coffee could be hotter."

"Ham and hot coffee coming right up." He was delighted to get back to the kitchen and tell Hettie about the divorce.

From upstairs Jack whined, "Mama? Where's Erskine? I can't find my jodhpurs!"

"I threw him out on his ass yesterday!"

"Why? Damn it, why?" He came hurrying down the stairs while tying the sash of his bathrobe.

"Because he's been feeding Bertha Graze everything he knows about us, that's why!"

"Who's going to dress me?"

Annamary's fist connected with the top of the table. "You're a big boy now, dress yourself!"

"Annamary," crooned Jack, "I prefer you demure. Oh God am I hung over."

"Wait till you see the morning paper. It'll split your head wide open." She handed it to him. He read the headline.

"Now I'm a laughingstock! Mama! I'm a laughingstock!" He was on the floor with his head cradled in her lap.

Marie patted his head. "There there, baby, eat something, you'll feel better. We all need our strength. I'm tilting at the dragon today, and that's going to take a lot of energy."

"He's been peddling me around town, Mama."

"What do you mean?"

"I heard it at Madam Frances's last night. He's trying to get loan-outs. He's tried with Goldwyn and with Darryl Zanuck at Warners for a Rin-Tin-Tin movie."

Marie shrieked and Annamary dropped her toast. "My boy supporting a dog star? Is there no end to that monster's insults!" She pushed Jack away, got up, and stomped across the room to a telephone. She barked the number of the Diamond Studios and, when connected, demanded Alexander Roland.

Jason Cutts picked up the phone in Roland's office. "Yes? Just a minute, Mrs. Darling. I'll see if he's in."

Roland, who had just endured an agonizing hour with his accountants, was spoiling for a fight. He grabbed the phone and said in his nastiest tone of voice, "What do you want?" Jason could hear the salvos of buckshot intended to shatter Roland's eardrums. He was surprised by the stoicism with which his monstrous employer accepted Mrs. Darling's abuse.

"And what's more, you dirty swine," Marie yelled, "I'm going to make you eat dirt!"

Very calmly, Roland said, "Marie, your son, your daughter, and your son-in-law will never work for Diamond Films again. Sue and be damned. You and your family will never pass through the studio gates again." He handed the phone to Cutts. "Slam it down."

Marie yelped and then stared at the dead instrument in her hand with a mixture of horror and amazement.

Jack hurried to her. "What's wrong? What did he say to you?"

Dakota returned with Annamary's ham and a fresh carafe of coffee but wisely kept a low profile when he saw Marie Darling sink to the floor and begin howling like a wounded animal. Annamary was frightened. She was sure Marie was having a fit.

"Mama! Mama! Don't, Mama, don't!"

Jack shouted at Dakota, "Brandy! Quick!"

Dakota hastily dropped the plate of ham and the carafe on the sideboard and hurried to the bar.

Marie gasped and sobbed and choked and puled, and between sound effects she beat the air with her fist. Then she attacked the floor. By the time Dakota returned with the brandy, Marie was exhausted, spent, a pathetic figure whose tearstained face looked as though an army of vagrants had marched across it. Then she slapped the brandy out of Dakota's hand. Dakota reared back, not knowing what next to do until Annamary waved him away.

Annamary whispered hoarsely to Jack while she took her mother into her arms to comfort her; it was a rare occasion for their roles to be reversed. "I have a feeling we're finished, Jack."

"We are? Are we really?" He walked away from the women and ascended the stairs, back to his room, his lips moving but no sounds emerging from his mouth.

In Alexander Roland's office an hour later, Jason Cutts announced Mrs. Roland was in the outer office. Roland indicated for Cutts to send her in and Helen Roland breezed past Jason like a pleasantly scented zephyr. When Cutts left, closing the door behind him, Roland asked brusquely as Helen settled into a chair that faced his desk, "What do you want? It better not be money. There's going to be a lot of belt tightening around here. I'm going to be chopping heads, Helen, lots of heads."

"I'm going back to work."

"You're not!"

"Now there's all the more reason for me to. You're in financial hot water and Joe Schenck has offered me a film at United Artists."

His eyes narrowed suspiciously. "How come all of a sudden?"

"I haven't slept with him. Gloria Swanson arranged it for me."

"You've been off the screen too long. They've forgotten you."

"Joe doesn't seem to think so."

Roland leaned across the desk. "If you go back to work, the whole industry will know I'm on my back."

"The whole industry already knows, and you know they know. I'm going back to work because I'm tired of doing nothing. We have no children and we never will from what my doctor tells me, so I need to do something, and charitable works have never been my long suit. I'm telling you now because I wanted you to hear it from me and not from Hedda Hopper or one of those other contemptible leeches who suck up gossip like vampires."

"Are you sure he's not stringing you along? He'll do anything to please Gloria now that she's big again and bringing in profits."

"He wants me to play Lucrezia Borgia."

"Typecasting."

"Don't be unkind, Alex. Not now. Not ever. Whatever you've done, you've never been unkind to me."

"Why didn't you tell me you wanted to go back to work? I would have found you something."

"You mean *tossed* me something, if anything at all. I wouldn't accept the crumbs you feed Laura Gates and Tessa Main, two fine actresses wasted on secondary roles. What's the matter with you and the rest of those gangsters? You used to know how to build stars and market them profitably. Pictures begin to talk and suddenly the whole sad lot of you don't know how to make pictures anymore."

"I don't need any lectures."

"No, you need adrenaline. What's become of the spark, Alex? The dynamo that used to turn out forty to fifty pictures a year and more than half of them big box office winners. Look what you're doing now because you don't know how to handle the talkers. Talkers! Talk talk talk until one begins to ache for the charitable affliction of deafness. If they're not talking, they're singing. And they're paralyzed. They don't move. Movies are called movies because they moved. Talkers don't move, they talk. My God, how I've come to loathe perfect diction."

"Don't cross me off, Helen. I've got seven pictures in production now and I know at least four of them are winners. They've got to be!"

Helen pitied him. She said warmly, "They will be, Alex. I'm sure they will be."

"Would you like to have lunch with me?"

"I wish I could, dear. I really would like to. But I'm lunching with Frances Marion. She's doing my screenplay." *My screenplay.* How wonderful those words sounded to her. *My screenplay.*

Alexander Roland smiled for the first time in weeks. "Helen, all of a sudden you look ten years younger and more beautiful than ever. Why don't I take you out tonight? Someplace quiet, like we used to do back in the old days. What do you say? Would you like that?"

She recognized the cry for help. "Of course, Alex. I'll have cocktails waiting when you get home." She crossed to him and kissed his cheek. *Charitable works have never been my long suit.* And here she was, dealing from strength.

Bertha Graze glared at Erskine Simpson-Thwaite as her teeth mashed a caramel to a pulp. "Haven't you seen the morning paper? It's the headline, you silly simp. 'Dolly Lovelace Was a Bigamist.'"

"Well, what about it? I gave you that information yesterday in good faith. You owe me!"

"I don't pay for useless crap. Now get out of here."

"You've got to pay me. I need the money. Mrs. Darling refused to give me my severance. I'm hard up. I need the money!"

"If you'd stayed away from the track and the sniffing, you'd be a wealthy man."

"If if if—I don't need any of your ifs. You owe me and you're going to pay me!"

She stared and chewed and then crossed to a sideboard. She opened a drawer, found a roll of bills, peeled one off, rolled it into a ball, and flung it at him. "Here's a fiver, sucker. Go buy yourself some jelly beans."

"One of these days, Bertha, somebody's going to kill you!"

"Oh yeah? Says who? You know where the door is. Use it."

Erskine's eyes spoke volumes of hatred. He picked up the crumpled note, his eyes never leaving her face. Almost obsequiously, he backed out of the room. Then he turned and hurried out the front door. Bertha Graze sank back onto the divan. Damn it, she thought, this means Marie Darling won't be around to make her contribution. Who the hell could have leaked the story to Hazel Dickson? She snapped her fingers. That bitch Hedda Hopper, that's who. Hmmm. Now what can be done to stop Hedda Hopper?

In soundstage 6 at the Diamond Studios, the cast and the crew sat around reading, noshing, and gossiping while Henry Turk, the director of *The Bride Wore Sneakers*, was trying to get Alicia Leddy, his leading lady, to cry. After an hour of coaxing, pleading, and swearing by Turk, Alicia Leddy stamped her foot and said, "I'm sorry. I just don't cry easily!"

Turk pleaded, "Make believe your mother died!"

"I'm an orphan."

"Make believe your dog died!"

"I don't own one."

"How about your pussy?"

"Don't be vulgar."

Two middle-aged women extras sat to one side quietly conversing. One knitted as she chatted; the other did some crocheting. The knitter, Carrie O'Day, said, "Have you been getting many calls lately?"

The crocheter said, "I get a lot but I don't take them all. When I need a little extra spending money and don't want to bother my son for it. Mind you, he's very generous with me, bless his heart, and he loves it that I do extra work because he's so starstruck himself. Believe it or not, only yesterday he was a guest at Annawill."

"You don't say!"

"It's the truth. He met the whole gang of them. Annamary and Jack and Willis and the mother and he says he put the fear of God into the lot of them."

"Och, then he's a man of the cloth, is he?"

"Oh no, nothing so awful. He's with the city government," said Maggie Villon. "He's the chief inspector of police."

"No!"

"Indeed."

"Well, aren't you blessed." Then she said with pride, "My son's an architect."

"No!"

"Indeed! He designed three buildings in downtown L.A. Two are under construction now."

"Isn't that wonderful. You must be very proud of your son's erections."

They heard Alicia Leddy scream. "How dare you slap me!"

"Cry, damn you, cry!" Turk was as usual tearing at his hair.

"You go to hell!" Alicia Leddy, with incredibly dry eyes, walked off the set.

The film's producer, Isaac Sherry, pleaded with Turk, "Go after her. Get her back. Apologize! Alex Roland will have a fit, he'll can all of us! We're behind schedule! We're over budget!" To the ceiling he sobbed, "This talker needs a miracle!"

Turk said, while lighting a cigarette, "So open it in Lourdes." Then, as he exhaled some smoke, he said, "You know this script was written for Annamary Darling. It was supposed to be her first talker. But then Roland met this Leddy chippy in New York, fell for her, and here we are. No Annamary, no tears, no picture. I think I'll commit suicide tonight."

While the future of Annamary and Jack in talking pictures looked decidedly bleak that morning, Willis Loring was not in fact golfing, playing tennis, swimming, or screwing. He was with his agent in Joseph Schenck's office at United Artists signing a three-picture deal. Schenck offered them cigars and a drink while the agent, Myron Clapp, rubbed his hands together—less for warmth than out of greed—and said to the actor, "Willie boy, this is one smart move we made."

As he poured the drinks, Schenck said to them, "I've got a great adventure script, boys. Willis, it'll put you over big in talkers. You play a white hunter in Africa who is searching for a treasure believed to be hidden somewhere in a cave in Kilimanjaro."

"Where's that?" asked Willis.

"It's not a where, it's a what. It's a mountain."

"Oh, wonderful! Do we go on location?"

"What for?" He gave them their drinks. "We'll use the Selig Zoo animals right here in L.A., and they got a mountain over at Metro we can borrow."

"When do we start shooting?" asked Willis eagerly.

Schenck looked at a wall where presumably a date was written in invisible ink. "We'll start preproduction immediately and we should be ready to roll in eight to ten weeks. I'd like to get Henry Turk to direct because he's fast and he's on the nose."

Clapp advised him, "He's weeks behind schedule on that turkey he's doing for Alex Roland."

"That's not his fault. It's that dumb kid Alex put in the lead. She can't cut it. He should have fired her after seeing the first day's rushes. But not Alex." He shook his head sadly. "Alex Roland should admit he's made a mistake? Never." He said to Willis, "Annamary should be playing that part. It was written for her, you know."

Willis was surprised. "Are you sure?"

"I'm always sure. That's why I'm a millionaire."

"Wait till Mama hears this."

"You know what? You two are the first to know. I'm bringing Roland's wife back to pictures."

Myron Clapp's eyes widened. "Helen Roland's making a comeback?"

"Helen Orling," corrected Schenck. "Helen Roland is a producer's wife. Helen Orling is a star. I'm going to give her a lavish spectacle, the life of Lucrezia Borgia, and this is one time I predict poison will be a box-office bonanza."

Greed once again clouded the agent's eyes. "Does she have an agent?"

"As a matter of fact, she hasn't," advised the mogul. "Would you like me to put in a good word for you?"

"Joe, I'd be in your debt eternally."

"That's what I had in mind."

*   *   *

A few hours after her collapse, Marie made a remarkable recovery and ate an enormous lunch. She dined alone in her bedroom because her children had other engagements, or so they said. After lunch, Marie welcomed Marcus Tender, the family lawyer, a man who had served them for over a decade and who, for a lawyer, was surprisingly trustworthy. Together they laid out a strategy to legally storm the walls of Diamond Films and bring Alexander Roland to his knees. With a clenched fist, Marie said to Mr. Tender, "I won't rest until that man is destroyed."

"If he's as financially strapped as I hear he is, your lawsuit could be the final nail in his coffin."

"Coffin, hell! I won't rest until I see him burned at the stake! I want to smash him, grind him under my heel. I want to cut off his privates and serve them raw to a savage dog." The lawyer shuddered. He hadn't witnessed such ferocity since he tried to buy off his mistress the previous Thanksgiving.

Willis Loring had no idea they'd be in the library when he came home and sought a stiff glass of bourbon before confessing his defection to Joseph Schenck.

"Come on in," boomed Marie. "This is a historic occasion. We're suing Alexander Roland for fifteen million dollars plus expenses." Willis went pale. Marie told him about the awful events that transpired during his absence in the morning, and he found the courage to tell her he'd done his deal with Joseph Schenck.

"You fool! You idiot! You moron!" She continued with an amazing display of vocabulary that more than impressed Marcus Tender. "How dare you go behind my back and shove the knife in to the hilt. Oh my God, how it hurts! I can feel it burning!"

"Control yourself, Mama. Joe Schenck phoned me early this morning to tell me Alex confided last night at a bridge game that he wasn't honoring our contracts. He urged me to come sign a deal and I got hold of Myron Clapp and that's that, we signed the deal."

"Myron Clapp is aptly named, the diseased little vermin."

"He got me excellent terms."

"Now just a moment, you two," the lawyer interrupted. "One

thing has nothing to do with another. Willis can sign a dozen deals, but legally, Diamond Films is still liable to live up to the terms of our ironclad agreements. In fact, this deal with Schenck is a blessing in disguise. It will help our case immeasurably."

Marie viewed the lawyer with suspicion. She had had an affair with one once, but she still didn't know the difference between a habeas corpus and a corpus delicti. "How?"

"It proves that Willis is still a very valuable and desirable commodity. He has been signed by a prestigious organization. And I assume it's a fairly lucrative deal."

"Very," said Willis. "Not as much as Diamond guaranteed me, but in these troubled times, with so many old stars walking the plank, I'm still rolling in clover."

Marie chewed it over for a few moments and then decided to buy it. "Okay. I'll go for it. Did Schenck say anything about Annamary?"

"Marie, this is going to really shock you."

"He doesn't want her."

"No no no, nothing like that. This picture Roland is shooting with his sweetie pie in the lead—"

"It's in terrible trouble. Everybody knows that."

"It was written for Annamary."

"What?" The windows rattled and the doors shook and the lawyer asked Willis for a glass of whiskey to steady his nerves. "The slimy lowlife lied to me. He said he had nothing for Annamary. Why . . . why . . . I'll bet he had a script for you, Willis, and for my Jackie baby and . . . and . . . Marcus! We're suing him for *fifty* million!"

Henry Turk stood outside the door to the cozy bungalow that Alexander Roland had built for Alicia Leddy to use as a dressing room. He tapped the door gently. "Alicia? Alicia dear? It's me. It's Henry Turk, your director. I've come to apologize, Alicia. I'm sorry I slapped you. I didn't do it out of anger or frustration or a dread feeling of impotence that frequently comes over me when I'm working with raw newcomers; I did it to try to help you cry." Stone-hearted bitch, he felt like shouting, I'll bet you never cried in your life, I bet you're an orphan because you ate your parents. He rapped a bit harder on the door. "Come on now, Alicia. Let's get to work and finish this god . . . this movie. It's costing a fortune. Every second the camera doesn't roll costs a dollar, and dollars have a tendency to add up." He rested his head against the door, weary, fed up, despairing, wondering if he'd have a better time baking bread in a monastery. This was how Alexander Roland found him.

"What's the matter with Alicia?" demanded Roland.

Henry Turk explained the situation. Roland showed neither sympathy nor understanding. He banged on the door with his fist and shouted, "Alicia, come out and go back to work or you'll never work in talkers again!" His anger mounting, he rattled the doorknob and the door swung open.

Alicia Leddy sat at her dressing table, her face bloated, her tongue purple and bulging out of her mouth. It was after the initial shock of realizing she was dead that Alexander Roland saw the scarf twisted and knotted tightly around her neck. He had given her the scarf as a little surprise the previous Sunday during a brief cruise on his yacht. She had said nothing when he gave it to her. Now, he suspected, she didn't really like it.

NINE

♦

Hazel Dickson, from the moment she'd first met and become infatuated with Herbert Villon, had respected his sleuthing methods. But now her admiration for him had intensified. He had predicted another murder, and here was the corpse. Alicia Leddy wasn't a pleasant sight, although a mortician would soon sort her out and to some extent restore her beauty, but she was proof positive of Villon's prescience. Gabriel Twist, the coroner, was humming softly, "A Pretty Girl Is Like a Melody," as he delicately examined the corpse.

"She didn't put up a struggle," said Twist. "No skin under her fingernails."

"In this town, few girls put up much of a struggle."

"Shut up, Hazel," said Villon, and two of the other newsmen in the room snickered. They didn't annoy Hazel. Neither one of them was sleeping with Villon.

"The carotid veins in her throat are crushed. Offhand I'd say those did her in. I'll know better when I cut her open."

"Time of death?" asked Villon.

"Roughly I'd say about an hour or so, maybe a smidgen more."

Villon asked Henry Turk, who was sitting on the couch with Alexander Roland, "How much time elapsed before she left the set and you came to apologize?"

Turk, distraught over Leddy's murder, stammered, "Maybe fifteen, maybe twenty minutes."

Villon continued, "And how long after you found the body did you phone us?"

Roland spoke up. "Maybe a minute or two. Once I realized she was murdered, I phoned you people immediately."

Villon asked the director, "Were you and Miss Leddy on good terms?"

Turk exploded. "I could have killed her!" Then, embarrassed, "Whoops—that isn't the way I meant that!"

"I'm sure," said Villon. His tone of voice wasn't very comforting.

"Expensive scarf," contributed Hazel. "I priced one like it at Bullock's."

"I gave it to her," said Roland. He added quickly, "The scarf, I mean. I gave her the scarf." He told Villon about the trip on the yacht the previous Sunday.

Villon said sharply, "I want you reporters and photographers out of here." There were rebellious murmurs. "You got your story, you got your pictures, now wait outside." He emphasized Hazel. "You too, Hazel."

She stared daggers and said under her breath, "Just wait until the next time you ask for seconds." She led the exodus from the room.

As Henry Turk lit a cigarette, Villon directed his attention to Alexander Roland, who seemed mesmerized by the corpse's obscene face. *Only last night, it was only last night I made love to her* . . . "Mr. Roland?"

"What? What?"

"I asked you a question."

"I'm sorry. I didn't hear it."

"I asked is it true you were having an affair with the actress?"

"Yes."

"Was your wife aware of this?"

Roland's voice went up an octave. "I'm sure my wife had nothing to do with this."

"I didn't say she did. I asked if she was aware of—"

"She might have been. She probably knew. She has enough good friends who could have told her. Mr. . . . Villon? Yes, Villon . . . my wife is a very remarkable woman." He didn't tell Villon he had only this morning come to realize that. "Although she's quite a wonderful actress, she doesn't make scenes. She's Helen Orling, you know."

"I know."

"She's making a comeback," said Roland, for want of anything else to say. "I'm very proud of her."

"Were you and Miss Leddy still on good terms?"

Roland's face hardened and Henry Turk was stunned by what he heard him admit to the detective. "I made love to her most of last night and I left her singing in the bathtub this morning. If I was going to murder her, I could have drowned her. It would have been simpler than creating this abominable sight." That was Jim Mallory's cue to cover Leddy's face with a towel.

"And you, Mr. Turk?" Villon looked amiable.

"What? What about me?"

"You just said you could have killed her."

"That was just an expression, you know what I mean? She's been hell to work with. I've worked with some pretty awful, mean-spirited, temperamental bitches like Mae Murray and Pola Negri . . . but this Alicia Leddy took the cake. She was impossible. She couldn't do anything right. She couldn't walk, she couldn't express an emotion, and I spent all morning trying to make her cry. I mean, when you tell Lillian Gish to cry . . . jeez . . . it comes pouring out, real genuine tears." He indicated the corpse. "But this ignorant klutz—"

"Shut up!" shouted Roland.

Villon overrode him. "Oh no no no. Keep talking, Mr. Turk. I love the sound of your voice. Your evaluation of Miss Leddy may be cruelly harsh and brutally judgmental to Mr. Roland, but to my ears it's a Brahms rhapsody."

Henry Turk wondered if Villon had recently escaped from a state asylum. The other detective, Mallory, was smiling. That disturbed Turk more than Roland's outburst. Turk said hastily, "Look, that's just a professional judgment as her director. She was a perfectly nice girl otherwise. I can't think of anybody who hated her." Only the entire company, but what the hell, the kid deserved a more favorable epitaph. "Look, Mr. Villon. Because of her we're weeks behind schedule, we're thousands of dollars over budget . . ."

"I didn't know the budget was a director's concern."

"Are you kidding?" Turk was truly aghast. "A director comes in over schedule and over budget and right away in this town he shoulders the blame. The phone doesn't ring as often as it used to. It could wash me up. Look what it's done to Von Stroheim. Poor Erich has had to go back to acting in quickies to earn a living, and he's a genius."

"And you're not?"

Turk was lighting another cigarette. "I'm great at kidding others, Mr. Villon, but I never ever kid myself. I'm a good, competent hack. Not as good as some, better than most, and I've survived successfully for a long long time. To be perfectly blunt and to be perfectly honest, it was up to Mr. Roland to have replaced Miss Leddy weeks ago when he was informed she was absolutely hopeless. He saw it for himself in the rushes. Sorry, Alex . . ."

"It's all right, Henry." He meant it. "I'm not blaming you. Everybody in the industry knows it's not your fault. Well, there goes over four hundred thousand dollars up in smoke."

Turk said quickly, "We could reshoot her scenes in less than two weeks. Annamary Darling would be wonderful and she works fast. Why don't we—"

Roland thundered, "Not now . . . later." To Villon, he asked, "Is there anything else? I must get back to my office. There's a great deal to be done about this crisis."

Villon asked, seemingly from out of nowhere, "Isn't the picture insured?"

"Hmmm?"

"Mr. Roland, isn't the picture insured?"

"All films carry a certain amount of insurance. I don't know how much there is on this one. I want to consult my accountants. That's one of the pressing reasons I wish to get back to my office. I'll be there if there's anything else . . ."

"That's about all we can do now."

"I need Mr. Turk," said Roland.

Villon asked Turk, "When you came to the dressing room, you didn't notice anybody leave or hanging around?"

"No, not . . . wait a minute. There were a couple of extras sitting nearby gossiping. One was knitting and the other I think was crocheting or something. They were middle-aged. I remember them from the luncheonette scene I managed to shoot the first thing this morning."

Villon instructed Jim Mallory to round them up. Then he dismissed Turk, who accompanied Roland back to his office.

Villon followed them outside, where Hazel Dickson waited for him along with the other newspaper people. "Inspector Villon," she rasped a bit sarcastically, "have you a statement to make about any further developments in this case, other than the discovery of the corpse?"

"Yes. I can't stand your hat."

Sophie Gang was providing Sam Goldwyn with all she had found out to date about the murder of Alicia Leddy. Hers was one of the better grapevines in Hollywood. She was famous for having predicted the gender of Dolores Costello's expected baby even before the actress knew she was pregnant. "So far the only two suspects the police seem to have are Henry Turk—"

"Don't be crazy."

"And Alex Roland. She was strangled with a scarf he gave her."

"Phooey. No grand jury would indicate him with such circumcision evidence."

"Much as he liked her, Alex liked saving his studio more. I hear the insurance just about covers the losses he's been suffering because of Alicia Leddy's incompetence."

Goldwyn torched a cigar and then leaned back, contemplating nothing in particular. "Alex does have a pretty terrible temper. But then, so do I. So do all of us. But murder somebody. Tell me Sophie, what am I capable of murdering?"

"The English language."

"Me? Me murder the English languish? Who do you know has a better respect for words than I do? Huh? Tell me. Me who has hired such great writers as Rupert Hughes and Maurice Maeterlynx . . ."

"Maeterlinck."

"So I said different?" His eyes were slabs of granite. "So what's with Ann Harding? She did her costume fittings for *Condemned*?"

"She has to lose some weight. Her dresses are a little snug." She thought for a moment. "My God, you don't suppose she's pregnant?"

Goldwyn waved the suggestion away. "Don't be crazy. She told my wife when she sleeps with her husband she always uses a diagram. Now what are we doing about Jack Darling?"

"What do you want to do?"

"Didn't we say yesterday maybe we should do something with him? I always liked him, even when he was a snot-nosed kid. Does he talk?"

"Sometimes you can't shut him up."

"I mean for films. Can he talk good?"

"I don't know. I don't know if he's ever tested."

"So let's have him in for a test."

At Diamond Studios, Villon and Hazel were having coffee in the commissary. Hazel was questioning Villon about the murdered actress. "Enough about her throat. How much acid around her mouth?"

"None."

"You suppose the killer ran out of it?"

"Different killer."

"Oh go away."

"Different killer, I'm telling you."

"You mean to tell me there's no connection between Leddy's murder and the murder of the Lovelaces?"

"I didn't say there was no connection, I'm just saying it's different killers." Hazel waited. She stirred her coffee though it didn't need it. "The Lovelaces were poisoned. Leddy was strangled. Murderers stick to the same modus operandi."

"You're so positive."

"Look, murderers have this much imagination and no more."

He made a small space between a thumb and an index finger. "Murderers are really very monotonous. I've never heard one tell a joke."

Hazel clucked her tongue rapidly. "Murder is no laughing matter."

"I'm telling you, Hazel, stranglers do not poison and poisoners do not strangle." He sipped his coffee and made a face. It was bitter and tepid. "Studio coffee, yuck. Shoe polish." He pushed the cup and saucer aside. "I think the next one will be different."

He enjoyed the startled expression on her face. "*What* next one?"

"The next murder."

"*What* next murder?"

"How do I know? But there's going to be one—has to—unless I can nail Leddy's murderer within the next couple of hours, and I doubt if I will because I've got no eyewitness. Unless Jim Mallory rounds up those two old ladies Henry Turk saw gossiping near Leddy's dressing room. And even if he does, they might not have noticed anyone because when two women are gossiping, war could break out and they'd be too busy yentaing to notice." He was studying a cuticle. "There's going to be another murder or two or so because whoever murdered Alicia Leddy didn't murder her because he or she disliked her. She was murdered because of Alexander Roland and the precarious financial situation of this studio. Somebody wants to destroy Diamond Films."

"Or Roland needs the insurance to cover his losses."

"That's my girl." Villon smiled. "That's when I'm proud of you. Either way, it's all connected to Alexander Roland."

"So maybe he murdered her after all."

"Nah. Men like Roland, if they need somebody murdered, they don't soil their own hands. They can always get somebody to do it for them. You know as well as I do this town is loaded with dozens of killers for hire."

"Of course. They're known as agents. And what the hell do you mean you don't like my hat?"

*   *   *

Jim Mallory had found Carrie O'Day and Maggie Villon and was escorting them to Villon's table. Hazel laughed. "Well, will you look who Mallory's found. Your very own mother! How are you, Maggie?"

"Never better!" she said with a small wave of a hand.

Villon stood up and hugged his mother. "What are you doing in the studio?"

"Me and my friend Carrie were working extra, but the company's been dismissed. Isn't it tragic, that poor Leddy girl. And her first picture too. Usually they get killed after the picture's been released, not before it finishes shooting." She said to Hazel, "I love your hat."

"Ha!" trumpeted Hazel.

Villon asked the women if they'd noticed anyone near Alicia Leddy's dressing room at what he approximated to be the time of her murder.

"Henry Turk," said Mrs. Villon.

"Just Henry Turk?"

"He's all I saw, Herbie."

"Now, hold on, Maggie," said Carrie O'Day. "What about the musketeer?"

"The musket . . . oh hell, yes. There was this man dressed as a French musketeer wearing a domino mask I think it was. But he's probably from the stage next door. That's where they're shooting that musical with Lotus Fairweather and Donald Carewe. They've been working for days on this masquerade party scene. I heard one of the assistants say it'll probably break the studio, something like that." Villon sent Jim Mallory to the adjoining soundstage in search of the masked musketeer.

Hazel said, partly to herself but loud enough for Villon to hear, "So Roland's got another loser in the works."

"He's got more than that," said Mrs. Villon knowledgeably. "Well, you know how it is, dear," she said with a sweet smile. "When you work in a studio, you hear all sorts of gossip." Then abruptly and sternly she said to her son, "You're pale and you've lost weight. Why haven't you been eating? They pay you enough, don't they? Hazel, why isn't he eating?"

"Well, you see, Maggie, there's this series of corpses that are sure to kill even a glutton's appetite . . ."

Jack Darling was strutting about the rear terrace of Annawill with an airy bounce. "So Sam Goldwyn wants me for a voice test tomorrow! Ha! Ha! How about them apples."

His mother was beaming as she stirred a Sazerac with an index finger. "Sam's always been a loyal friend, bless him. He says he's got a great part for you in another gentleman thief picture he's got lined up for Ronnie Colman. He's going to have to give you costar billing. No child of mind gets listed under the title."

Annamary, who was reclining on a lounge trying to cool herself with a bamboo fan, cautioned, "Don't kill it, Mama. Jack isn't snowed under with offers. If the word gets out Goldwyn's interested, then a lot of other producers will hop on the bandwagon. Be smart, Jack, start practicing 'How now brown cow' and 'Peter Piper picked a peck of pickled peppers' and costar billing be damned."

Cornelius Upland, their new butler, emerged through the library's French doors. "Sorry to interrupt, madam"—his facial tic didn't seem to annoy any of them—"there's a certain Alexander Roland calling."

Marie was astonished and delighted. "In person?"

"Oh no, madam, I'm so sorry." The tic's twitching accelerated, making him look as though he were flirting. "He's on the telephone."

"Ha and ha and ha," said Marie to her children. "So Marcus has had the papers served already. Good old Marcus. Bring the phone out here, Upchuck."

"Upland, madam."

"I'm so sorry. Bring it out here . . . and take your time about it." She was sitting up like a ferret about to pounce and destroy its prey. Annamary was hypnotized watching her husband prowling around the trees and bushes of the estate's arboretum, carrying a hunting rifle and practicing to be a white hunter. She hadn't seen such enthusiasm on Willis's part since the first time they ever slept together. She was vastly impressed. He's going to make good in the talkers, she was thinking. And I'm glad for him. If he succeeds, my conscience will be less troubled when I take the train to Reno.

Marie was gloating as she sipped her Sazerac and Jack was prancing about reciting "The Boy Stood on the Burning Deck," a childhood memory, enunciating each word with exaggerated clarity. Upland returned carrying a telephone. He plugged it into the wall and then set it down on the table next to Marie. He handed her the receiver. Marie counted to ten and then spoke.

"Marie Darling here." Each word dripped with acid.

"Just a moment," said Jason Cutts. "I have to interrupt his conference."

"Well, make it snappy," said Marie icily. "I've got calls coming in from Adolph Zukor and UFA in Berlin."

It was for over an hour that Alexander Roland's conference had consumed his time and his patience. The conferees included Henry Turk, Diamond's accountants, and two of the studio's shrewdest lawyers. They had convinced Roland to swallow his pride and attempt a peaceful overture to Marie Darling, and offer Annamary the lead in *The Bride Wore Sneakers*. Jason buzzed Roland. Roland stared at the phone as though to lift it might mean instant electrocution. He hated Marie Darling with a passion that would have inspired envy in Jack the Ripper. He cleared his throat and spoke into the phone.

"Marie, I want to apologize for my rudeness this morning. I've been under a terrible strain." He spoke rapidly, not giving her a chance to interrupt. "And we've suffered a terrible tragedy here. I don't know if it's been on the radio or you heard it elsewhere, but Alicia Leddy was murdered."

"How awful," said Marie. She sounded as though she were admiring a piece of jewelry. With her hand over the mouthpiece, she told Annamary and Jack about Alicia Leddy. Annamary was genuinely shocked and Jack made a mournful whistling sound.

"Marie, I'm up against the wall. I'm in terrible trouble. But I think we can save the movie. Henry Turk's directing and he says he can redo Leddy's scenes in under two weeks. Marie, I want to settle with you. I want Annamary to replace Alicia Leddy. Now let me finish. I'll not only live up to our contract, but I'll give her a bonus and I promise you before the picture is finished, her second talker will be lined up and ready to shoot within four weeks."

Marie finally had a chance to speak. "Jack has found a script he wants to do." It was the first Jack had heard of this. "It's got a great title. *Margin for Terror.* I got my hands on it a couple of weeks ago and three studios are bidding for it. It's a great part for Jack. He plays a lady-killer, a young Bluebeard. I want you to get it for him. It can't miss. You better hurry, Alex, because Sam Goldwyn wants Jack for Colman's next one after *Condemned,* and you can call Sam and verify that yourself. Willis has signed to do three for Joe Schenck, but you're still to guarantee me in writing he'll do the three he's owed under his Diamond deal. Then you can tear up those papers my lawyer served you."

It was the first that Alexander Roland had heard of it. "I haven't been served with any papers by your lawyer." He looked at his lawyers. "Have you had any papers from Marcus Tender?" They dueted no. He told this to Marie.

"That incompetent sunnuvabitch! That lowlife rattlesnake!"

"Marie!" shouted Roland. "The hell with him! Do we have a deal or don't we!"

Marie was famous for her chameleon moods. "Alex, I'm glad we're in business again. I want Annamary to have her suite back, repainted and redecorated. The same for Jack and the same for Willis when he returns to the lot after doing his jungle movie for Joe Schenck."

"What jungle movie? You mean that chestnut about a white hunter looking for lost treasure? Don't let him do it! Doug Fairbanks turned it down and so did George Bancroft and even poor old Harry Carey who needs a break desperately has turned it down in favor of some jungle quickie at Metro, he said the script was so awful." Marie shrieked for Willis, who came trotting on the double, assuming someone was dying of a heart attack. "Get him out of it! Whatever you do, Marie, don't let that be his first talker. I've got a foreign legion movie that's perfect for him. It's better than *Beau Geste* was. Warner Baxter is begging me to get Bill Fox to lend him to us for it. Marie, do you hear me?"

"My God, yes. Give me some time to scheme! Leave it to me. You know I can handle it." And how he knew she could handle it. "Willis! You're too sick to start that movie for Schenck! You're joining the foreign legion for Diamond. What was that, Alex? Yes, yes, I'll bring Annamary to the studio right away." Annamary bolted upright while placing the bamboo fan aside. "You know she's no trouble with costume fittings. Who's the male lead? Who? Arnold Holt? Oh God, Alex, he must be sixty if he's a day. Ah, the hell with it. Everybody's eyes will be on my baby. She'll wipe the screen with Holt. Hang up so we can get started!" She hung up. "Baby, baby, I've done it. I've done it! You're replacing Alicia Leddy in *The Bride Wore Sneakers*. Hmmm. We'll have to change that title. Come on, we've got to get it to the studio. Come on, you two"—she waved at her son and her son-in-law—"come on! We're returning to Diamond in triumph!" All the scene lacked was an orchestral background of "Pomp and Circumstance." "Upchuck!" shouted Marie. "Bring the limousine to the front door!"

Bertha Graze was on the phone with William Haines. "But, darling, as I just finished explaining to poor Ramon, those boys fooled me too! I had no idea they were under eighteen. You have to admit they looked older than that. Now don't be a fool, Billy boy, you have to give me the money to give to them or they'll go blabbing it all over Hollywood. Ramon's already on the way here with the cash. You know he keeps a lot on hand for emergencies in the strongbox under his mother's bed." Her voice coarsened. "Listen, Haines, if Louis B. Mayer hears of this indiscretion, you're through in pictures." Haines said something nasty and then told her he needed time to get the sum she requested. "All right, dear, just as long as I get it by tomorrow morning."

She hung up the phone, chomped down on a bar of chocolate stuffed with almonds, and pondered who she'd select as her next blackmail victim. The phone rang and she said sweetly, "Bertha Graze here. Why, hello dear. Yes, I heard the radio. Poor Alicia Leddy. Helen Roland must be relieved. Oh yes, I know Helen doesn't have a vindictive bone in her body, but still, they do say a woman scorned could be a vessel of wrath." She gave her mouth a rest as she listened. Then she gasped. "Annamary's replacing Leddy?" She listened again as a sly smile began to emerge. "Well well well. So the Darlings reign at Diamond once again. How marvelous. Come around tomorrow for your money, dear. I can see we're going to work together marvelously, Upland."

TEN

Detective Jim Mallory, with the aid of an assistant director, combed the set of *Daughter of the Casbah* but could find no musketeer. The A.D. kept reminding Mallory, "I tell you there's no musketeer on the costume manifest. Maybe he's working some other set."

"This is a masquerade party, right?"

"This is one mess of a masquerade party, buddy."

"Who's the hunchbacked old lady over there drinking the Coke?"

"That's our leading lady, Lotus Fairweather."

"Oh. Who's the dwarf standing next to her?"

"That's our leading man, Donald Carewe."

"Those two are the stars?"

"Yeah, but they sing real good."

"What's the name of this turkey?"

"Daughter of the Casbah."

"What's a Casbah?"

"I think it's some kind of a melon."

"Daughter of the Melon?"

The A.D. said wearily, "Mister, I only work here. Now, will you take my word for it, we got no musketeer."

Jim Mallory found Villon and Hazel walking toward the executive building and reported there was no musketeer.

"I didn't think you'd find him," said Villon.

"Then why'd you send me hunting for him?"

"In case I was wrong."

110

Hazel asked, "Do you think that might have been Leddy's killer?"

"Your guess is as good as mine."

An automobile horn warned them to move aside. The Darlings' limousine snaked past them. Hazel recognized the human cargo on the backseats. "Well, as I live and breathe, it's Marie Darling and company. I always figured if she buried the hatchet with Alex Roland, it would be in his skull."

Villon said, "Henry Turk wanted Annamary to replace Leddy. I guess he convinced Roland."

Alexander Roland emerged from the executive building to greet Marie and her stars. He had been alerted by the guard at the gate that their limousine had arrived. Upland, doubling as chauffeur, held the back door open and Roland reached in to assist Marie from the vehicle. His cheek sideswiped hers, and when Annamary moved into his outstretched arms, he kissed her with genuine affection.

"Touching," commented Hazel, struggling to keep a straight face.

"I hate to tell you where it grabs me," said Villon. Marie espied Villon and her morning anger at him resurfaced. Confronting him, she said venomously, "You promised not to blow the lid off Dolly's bigamy. How dare you cross me up?"

"I didn't."

"Bullshit!"

"I broke that story, Mrs. Darling." Hazel feared no woman.

"And who are you?" blazed Marie.

"Hazel Dickson, reporter."

"Reporter," scoffed Marie. "There are three things that can walk under coffee tables without injuring their heads—dachshunds, politicians, and reporters." She pivoted around and returned to her group, who were being ushered into the building by Roland.

"Charming," said Hazel. "I'm sure she sleeps on a bed of nails. Comfortably."

"This is obviously no time to try and have a chat with Alexander Roland."

"I thought you said all you had to say back in Leddy's bungalow."

"Oh no, he was in a rush to check on the picture's insurance and I decided he'd be no use to me until he got his priorities settled. I suppose he thinks he's in good shape now that he's got Annamary to replace Leddy. I wonder how he managed it."

"He couldn't have sold his soul. He doesn't own one."

"You're a hard woman, Dickson. I'm going back to the bungalow for another look around."

"I thought you already gave it a thorough going-over."

"It wouldn't hurt to go through it again. You don't have to join me if you've got better things to do."

"You don't get rid of me that easily, Herbert." She smartly fell into place between Villon and Jim Mallory and they walked briskly to the murder scene.

One could almost feel the heat of activity in Alexander Roland's office. Ethel Swift, the costume designer, arrived to escort Annamary for her fittings. After the customary hugs and kisses and squealings they were accompanied to the wardrobe department by Henry Turk, who was reading a script of *The Bride Wore Sneakers* aloud to Annamary while on the trot. Willis, realizing he was along only for moral support, wandered over to soundstage 5 when he heard Jason Cutts say they were filming a masquerade party with lots of pretty extras. Marie and Jack remained behind with Roland so Marie could tell the mogul the plot of *Margin for Terror*. Listening, Jack remembered it was a script she had commissioned several years back, which for one reason or another never made it to the screen. Marie was a good story-teller and the plot held up well. It would need dialogue and Jack decided he would write that himself. Roland agreed with Marie that Jack as a Bluebeard type would be an excellent transition from his plethora of country yokel roles. Roland elaborated for them a new physical look for Jack to go with the role: slicked-back hair, a pencil-thin mustache, a goatee. He decided Jack would be surrounded with a supporting cast of women recently brought from the East and from London. Jack studied

Roland as the rhetoric flowed from his mouth like a destructive flow of volcanic lava consuming anything in its wake.

Jack had never liked him. In the five years that he had starred for Roland, he always felt he was making films not because of his talent but because Roland felt he had to use him to keep Marie from defecting with Annamary and Willis. Jack had never reached his box-office potential as predicted by Marie. He was popular enough—his films mostly made a profit—but he hadn't reached the superstar status of his sister and his brother-in-law. Haggling over casting rights for Jack, his mother and Roland reminded him of two spitting cats on a backyard fence clawing at each other with arguments. He knew they thrived on this unbecoming behavior. It was part of the moviemaking game. Constant disagreement, constant discord, constant jockeying for position. In the end, he knew, they would compromise and then retreat to their corners, waiting for the bell to announce the start of the next round.

"I should phone and cancel Goldwyn," said Jack.

"That can wait," snapped Marie.

"I don't think it should," insisted Jack. "It was generous of him to consider me when no one else in this town cared."

Jason Cutts entered and interrupted. "Mr. Roland, Jay Mack in insurance."

"Excuse me," said Roland to the ceiling as he picked up the phone. "Jay? What's the story?" He listened. "What the hell do you mean we aren't sufficiently covered?" Roland found a handkerchief and wiped the beads of perspiration forming on his forehead. He realized Marie's eyes were drilling into his face. "Jay, I'll call you back in fifteen minutes. I'm in the middle of a conference." He hung up.

Marie barked, "Isn't there enough to cover Annamary?"

"This has nothing to do with Annamary," he lied. "I've got six other pictures shooting. This transition from silents to talkers is a killer. Do you know what it's costing to soundproof the stages? The recording equipment? New lighting boards to accommodate the new film we need to record sound waves? It's brutal, I tell you, brutal. And the banks want their pounds of flesh. The hell with it. I'll go with *Margin for Terror* as Jack's first talker."

"I want to write the dialogue and direct it."

Roland groaned. "Now, come on, boy, you'll have enough to do adjusting to the new sound techniques. Write the dialogue, okay, but act *and* direct? Impossible!"

Jack stood up, truly the boy on the burning deck. "I direct too or I'm going to Sam Goldwyn."

Roland fought hard to refrain from telling him to go to hell. He'd never liked the young man, whose presence on the lot he had endured to keep Marie happy and not chance losing Annamary and Willis. He found Jack to be unclean and perverse, and never could understand why a clever, promising youngster like Dolly Lovelace had ever consented to marry him. Dabbing at his brow, he urged Marie, "You've got to make him listen to reason. Talkers aren't easy. The microphones are stationary and it's up to the cutters to try to give the films some movement. Marie, please. I've agreed to just about everything you've wanted but this is going too far."

"Jack, dearest," said Marie in the tone of voice she'd used to get him to leave Dolly Lovelace, "Alex will let you direct your next picture, won't you, Alex?" Roland pursed his lips but said nothing. "I have to agree with him. It's important you concentrate on your acting this time. You'll have words to memorize. You never had to do that before."

Roland chimed in. "It's a whole new crap shoot, Jack. It's not like the silents when you could move your lips and say nothing and to hell with the lip readers. We shoot longer scenes now, and it takes concentration to know your lines and your moves and the location of the microphones. And that's not all. There's no more of that staying up and playing into all hours of the night and not worrying about what time you arrive on the set the next morning. In talkers we arrive at the studio no later than seven A.M. and stay until God knows what time. Listen to me, Jack, we're all of us underequipped. We don't have enough sound equipment yet and not enough technicians have been trained. That's why we're shooting around the clock. We have to shoot when we can use the equipment."

Jack crossed one leg over the other. "I've got it all worked out in my head. I'm going to revolutionize the talkers. I'm going to show you how to make the microphones mobile."

Roland's blood was boiling. He pushed his chair away from the desk and was on his feet pacing and punishing the air with his hands. He might have been drying nail polish. "*He's* going to revolutionize the talkers. *He's* going to show us how to make the microphones mobile. You some kind of a Houdini you can make the damn things float through the air?"

"I'm going to put them on fishing rods."

Roland screwed up his face. Marie looked from one to the other. Was this really her Jack talking? Had he thought of this all by himself? He who had yet to master the new dial telephone.

"It'll work," persisted Jack. "And I want to write the dialogue because I don't want too much of it. Just because pictures are talking doesn't mean they have to talk you to death. And you won't have to suffocate the camera operator by enclosing him in a booth with the camera to muffle the noise. You can shoot silent and add the sound later, so the camera can become fluid again. What I'm telling you, Alex, is that I plan to unchain the talkers."

Roland went back to his chair. After a moment's thought, he said, "I'll think about it. I have to discuss it with the technicians. Oh my God, all this and there's a murderer on the loose."

"Of course," said Marie, "that poor Leddy girl."

"She was strangled with her scarf," said Jack.

"How awful! But why?"

"Who knows?" said Roland. "It seems to me murdering her was totally pointless. She had no known enemies, she wasn't in Hollywood long enough to acquire any."

"Tell that to the marines. The minute you step off the train in this town you've got enemies. Dolly used to say she had enemies she'd never been introduced to. There, you see? Why should she have been murdered? Because she was a bigamist? Because everybody spread the rumor she had black blood? Don't shush me, Mama, you were one of the worst offenders and you're not even ashamed of yourself."

"How dare you talk to me like that!" Marie bristled. "I did what I thought was right for you and I haven't done so badly either, damn you! You should be grateful you're sitting in this office and being given the opportunity of a whole new career!"

"That's right," said Roland, wishing he could be rid of the two of them and talking to Jay Mack in insurance.

"Ahhhh, you both make me sick!" Jack shouted and stormed out of the office, slamming the door shut behind him.

"I don't know what's gotten into him lately," raged Marie. "Ever since Dolly's death, he's a changed boy."

"He's no longer a boy, Marie."

"Well, whatever he is, he's changed, and I don't like the change one bit!" The chameleon's tone softened. "Oh, let him direct the movie, you can assign someone you trust to be with him through the shoot."

Roland clasped his hands together and leaned across the desk. "I can't afford to take any risks, Marie. I'm up to my ears in trouble. You know it. Of course you know it. Everyone in this damned place knows it, and they're all gloating. The vultures are circling and waiting to pick at my carcass." He pushed himself back. "Well, they're going to have a long wait. I'll sleep on it, Marie, I'll tell Jack tomorrow." Grudgingly he added, "Those ideas of his are interesting. They're bold and maybe that's what the industry needs. Ah, who the hell knows. Christ, Leddy's family. I wonder if anyone's notified Leddy's family." He buzzed and Jason Cutts came hurrying in.

After hearing what was on Roland's mind, Jason told him Leddy's agent was in touch with her family. "He also wants her full week's salary. A deal is a deal. Well, that's what he said!" He fled as Roland flung a pencil at him.

Marie stood up, preparing to depart. "I'd better see what's happening with Annamary in wardrobe. You really like *Margin for Terror?*"

Roland nodded. He was staring ahead, glassy-eyed. Marie left and when he heard the door close, he emitted an agonized sob. "Alicia," he whispered, "poor Alicia."

Erskine Simpson-Thwaite sat in a booth in the Hollywood Brown Derby restaurant with actress Hedda Hopper. "I hope you know I'm not picking up the tab," he warned her.

"Oh, all right, Ernie, we'll go dutch."

He was aghast. "I can't even do that!"

"Ah, damn it, I'll do it but don't order expensive."

"Well, after all, you *did* ask *me* out."

"You phoned me, I didn't phone you. Where are you living?"

"In this dreadful boardinghouse. I've been all morning registering with agencies seeking a new position, but it seems everybody's firing their butlers these days."

"Yes, you boys are becoming as obsolete as title writers. That uproar you hear is the tightening of belts around the waist." A bitter woman who had never achieved the success as an actress she fantasized as her due, Hedda had a sharp, acrid voice. She'd been married to a great stage star and monologist, DeWolf Hopper, the father of her son, but after the divorce she had sought a career in films. Stardom eluded her but she was serviceable playing aunts, bitchy sisters, elegant society women. She had managed to cultivate several powerful friends, among them Louis B. Mayer, who saw to it that she was fairly steadily employed at MGM. She augmented that income by gathering and selling gossip to the highest bidder while dreaming of having her own syndicated gossip column some day.

Erskine was excoriating Bertha Graze. Hedda agreed with him. "Bertha's heading for a fall," predicted Hopper. "She's gotten too brazen and cocksure. She's made a lot of dangerous enemies."

"I hope she gets hers, and I hope she gets it soon."

"What have you got for me?" The waiter brought them menus. When he departed, Erskine spoke.

"Willis Loring had an affair with Dolly Lovelace while she was married to Jack Darling."

"Affair, dear, or a quickie when Jack wasn't looking?"

"It was more than once. I know that for sure."

"Well, I'll put it under my hat. Dolly's fresh news until they come up with her killer."

"What about all these murders all of a sudden?" asked Erskine, looking and sounding like somebody's maiden aunt. "Do you suppose there's a connection between the three of them?"

"Like what? Leddy was newly arrived in town. I doubt she ever got to meet Dolly or her phony father."

"She met Jack Darling." Hopper was interested. "Yesterday at the Diamond studio. I overheard him on the phone telling a friend he'd met this hot dish and lunched with her and a friend."

"Who was the friend?"

"He didn't mention a name. But I gathered it was female and an actress working on the lot."

"Okay, Ernie, that's worth working on."

He asked eagerly, "It's worth the lunch, isn't it?" He was pathetic and her heart of steel almost softened and buckled.

Instead she glanced at the menu and said, "Let's both have the special. It's the cheapest." She signaled the waiter, who hurried to the table, took the order, and then left. Erskine was gently blowing his nose and Hedda looked at him with pity. She said, "Where did it all go wrong, Ernie? You had it all going for you twenty years ago."

"I had it all going, and how swiftly it went. Do you suppose I might have a chance in the talkers? After all I began in the theater. I worked with Ellen Terry and Beerbohm Tree. Don't you think my voice is still good?"

She was lighting the cigarette she had jammed into a holder while he was whining pathetically. "Your voice is fine."

He brightened and gathered steam. "I could play butlers perfectly, couldn't I?"

"Perfectly."

"Hedda, you couldn't possibly put in a word for me with Louis B. Mayer, could you?"

A busboy brought them rolls and butter. Hopper said, "I'll see what I can do."

Erskine Simpson-Thwaite attacked the basket of rolls ravenously. Hopper cursed herself for having committed herself to this lunch. A swift phone call would have sufficed. Anyway, Jack Darling had known Alicia Leddy. That ought to be worth something to the loathsome and loathed Mrs. Louella Parsons.

With Jim Mallory in tow, Herbert Villon had finally gotten his audience with Alexander Roland. He had managed to get Hazel Dickson to return to her office with a promise of dinner that night. Alexander Roland appeared to have aged since Villon had interrogated him at the murder scene. He must have had a rough time with the Darlings, Villon guessed. And now Villon was compounding the damage by telling the mogul he suspected there would be fresh murders in the offing.

"You know, Mr. Villon," said Roland, "I'm having a perfectly terrible day. You don't mind my confiding in you like this?"

"Not at all," said Villon agreeably, wishing the man would tell him more, a lot more.

"My actress is murdered when there's still three weeks of shooting left to do and my insurance people now set off a load of dynamite under my butt by telling me we don't have sufficient coverage. You know, Mr. Villon, I find myself surrounded by idiots. Then I have an actor who has yet to talk on the silver screen tell me that not only does he intend to write the dialogue for his first talker"—he underlined the next sentence with a mocking magnanimous gesture—"but he also means to direct it." Villon reasoned he was talking about Jack Darling. "Now, you come into my office to tell me that your scientific mind informs you there just could be a few more murders. Is this a reasonable deduction on your part, Mr. Villon, or is it some sort of intuition you are employing—or are you merely amusing yourself by trying to scare the shit out of me?"

"Mr. Roland, on the surface, Alicia Leddy's murder appears to be cruelly and tragically pointless."

"Meaning some maniac said to himself this morning or maybe yesterday or God knows when, 'I think I'll strangle Alicia Leddy because I've got nothing better to do'!"

"Actually, Mr. Roland, that's how a lot of killings do occur.

Pointless, meaningless, motiveless. But in Leddy's case, I think she was murdered to cause you harm."

Roland's voice was rising. "You're back to my wife again!"

"Not at all. Please don't jump to conclusions. I disciplined myself a long time ago not to jump to conclusions. Detection, Mr. Roland, you must believe me, is ten percent looking for clues and ninety percent thinking. You also hope for a lucky break, and those have happened to me too. But in this case, I think Leddy was killed because the killer wanted it to cost you money."

"He must have a very benevolent fairy godmother because his wish has been granted. It *is* costing me a hell of a lot of money."

"But it isn't going to break you."

"Whose side are you on?"

"I'm dead serious."

Jim Mallory thought, And Alicia Leddy is seriously dead.

"I think the murderer is out to break you. He, or possibly she, is out to bring Diamond Films to ruin."

Roland was flabbergasted. "But *why*?"

"That's what I'm trying to find out. Who wants to destroy you and your studio?"

Roland exhaled. "Well, off the top of my head I can think of half a dozen competitors. I admit we're a pretty ruthless bunch. Do you know at this very moment William Fox of Fox Films and Louis B. Mayer of MGM are conspiring to gain complete control of Mayer's company? Do you realize this man is willing to sell out to an archrival because he's mad at the men in his New York office who give him orders? It will fall through, but it is a perfect example of the treachery that goes on in this industry and will continue to go on long past our time. So *you* tell *me*, Mr. Villon, who wants to destroy me?"

"You might give it some thought."

"Don't be stingy, let's give it a whole *lot* of thought." He tilted his chair slightly and looked out the window at the activity below. Scenery being hauled from workroom to soundstage, costume racks trundling along the road, actors and actresses, technicians, hustling from stage to stage. He never ceased to wonder at how he enjoyed knowing he was responsible for it all. He also knew if he had to give it up, he would die, slowly but surely. He sighed and directed his attention back to Villon. "A lot of actors who were big in silents and are now on the skids I'm sure would love to ruin me. But why just me? Why not Zukor at Paramount and Jack Warner and the others who helped put the grease under the skids?"

"Someone who has a really powerful hatred."

Roland shook his head from side to side, pondering Villon's ugly statement, and then asked, "It couldn't just be some run-of-the-mill maniac on the loose?"

"It could, but I don't think so. The person who murdered Alicia Leddy realized it would cost you a lot of money to replace her. Maybe the killer reasoned he'd forced you to shut down the movie altogether. Maybe the killer didn't bank on the fact you'd be lucky enough to get Annamary Darling for a quick replacement."

Roland sat bolt upright. "My God! You're not suggesting Annamary's life is now in danger!"

"Mr. Roland, Dolly and Ezekiel Lovelace were murdered over the past couple of weeks. They had links to the Darling family."

"But they had no link to Alicia Leddy, did they?"

"I don't know. If there is, I'm going to try and find it. What other expensive pictures do you have in production?"

"My big musical, *Daughter of the Casbah.* I'm a half a million in the hole on that one already!" He mentioned two others, and Villon and Jim Mallory exchanged looks emphasized with raised eyebrows.

"How big a studio police force do you have?" asked Villon.

"I don't know the exact numbers, but it's a sizable payroll. Believe me, it's a very sizable payroll. I wish I could pare it."

"I'd beef it up, if I were you."

"But to do what?"

"Triple-check strangers wandering around. Triple-check security at your gates. Keep an eye out for suspicious-looking characters."

"Just about everybody in a studio is a suspicious-looking character!" exclaimed Roland.

"I'd especially tighten the security on whatever soundstage Annamary Darling is working on. Don't give me that look, Mr. Roland. Better to exercise overcaution then to have your people underguarded. I also suggest you increase the security at your home."

"Yes. Yes, you're right. Perhaps you've heard my wife—she's Helen Orling—is making a return in talkers. Yes, I'm certainly going to add more protection for her right now." He buzzed the intercom and barked a series of orders to Jason Cutts for increased security. When he finished, Villon and Mallory moved to leave.

Roland stood up and walked them to the door. "Well, Mr. Villon, thank you for a terribly pleasant chat." He opened the door for them. "Let's not do it too often."

ELEVEN

"This sort of thing never happened when I worked for the Shuberts," trilled Lotus Fairweather nervously on soundstage 5. "I toured for them in *Blossom Time, The Student Prince*, and *Rose Marie*, but never once was a member of the tour murdered." She had conveniently forgotten her own near-assassination by a Chicago critic. "I'm so frightened, Donald. I refuse to sit in my dressing room unaccompanied."

"There there," soothed her costar, Donald Carewe. "Why would anyone want to mark you for death?" Except me, you clumsy bitch, upstaging me at every opportunity.

She looked around the set with apprehension. "Do you realize the murderer might be among us right here? He might be one of the spear holders or one of the Nubian slaves or—"

"Stop wringing your hands," cautioned Carewe. "It looks very stagey." He studied the frightened woman whom he had known for a good many years. He was there that day so many years ago when she had finally admitted she was thirty years old. Now her eyes were darting around like sparrows caught in a tornado. Her skin was flushed and her mouth reminded him of a blob of congealed blood.

"I can't work under these conditions, I just can't. I want to go home. They should let us all go home." She hurried in search of the director.

In the commissary, the usual hubbub of voices was now a cautionary hum. Alicia Leddy's murder was the topic of conversation with the return of the Darlings and Willis Loring running the murder a close second. Willis Loring's visit to the *Daughter of the Casbah* set had borne fruit. He had captivated Rita Gerber and they were now sharing a pot of tea and a plate of biscuits.

Rita Gerber had her hands clasped under the table trying to stop them from shaking. "I don't mind admitting, Mr. Loring—"

"Willis."

"Yeah. I don't like your Hollywood. I don't like what's going on around here. Murder! Christ, I can't stop shaking."

"Have a sip of your tea."

"It's too hot. She and I came out on the same train."

"She? You mean Alicia Leddy?"

"She was so innocent. Just a kid, honest. I think she was maybe eighteen or nineteen years old. Snuffed out just like that. The stars of this turkey I'm in are demanding bodyguards."

"You should too."

"I'm only a supporting player. And borrowed."

"It's a good sign if they're borrowing you."

She brightened. "Oh yes?"

"That means the word's out that you're promising."

"As what?" she asked suspiciously.

"As an actress."

"How would they know? This is my first assignment."

"If you were signed directly from a Broadway play, that means you've got something a bit more special then the others already out here."

"Sure. Goose pimples." She sipped her tea. "It's okay now. The way I like it. Your brother-in-law liked her too."

"The girl? Jack knew the girl?"

"He met her this morning. Right here. I introduced them."

"When did you meet Jack?"

"Today. We sort of got to talking. I like him. I usually like them tall, dark, and handy. But Jack's got something different. He looks like he needs mothering."

Willis was amused. "You might be right. His mother was always stingy with her affections."

Rita looked at her wristwatch. "I wonder if I should be getting back to the set. It's beginning to get dark out there. I don't want to be walking around the lot in the dark. It's creepy and spooky—too many places somebody could hide and then come jumping out at me."

"I'll walk you back to the set."

"Oh would you? Gee, you're a peach!"

In Bertha Graze's apartment, a young actress named Thelma Todd was admiring the paisley shawl artistically draped across the grand piano. "This is real paisley, isn't it?"

"Oh yes, my dear. A gift from an old admirer. My father." She was walking about the room slowly, chewing a nougat and switching on some lamps. "Now then, shall we get down to your reading? Who did you say recommended me, dear?"

"Charley Chase."

"Oh yes, the comic at Hal Roach Studios. So he recommended me, did he? How nice considering I gave him a very dark reading."

Todd had positioned herself at the table holding the crystal ball, directly across from Bertha. The lamp behind Bertha caused her face to reflect a satanic cast. The movement of her jaws made Todd think of a shark about to pounce. She asked, "What's a very dark reading?"

"Well, dear, it's what happens when the crystal ball suddenly goes dark in a spot. That could be very troubling."

"Something bad in the future?"

"Usually."

"Like what?" She was nonchalantly lighting a cigarette.

"All sorts of things." Bertha wondered who, if anyone, was Todd's lover. She loved to jolt a client by telling them the days of a current affair were numbered. "The dark spot could mean a death in the family, an option won't be renewed, a miscarriage, small annoyances like that."

"Could it mean murder?"

"It certainly could. Why do you ask? Do you know something I should know?"

"Did you by any chance get to read Alicia Leddy?"

"Why, no, I didn't. I never met the poor thing."

"I did. I met her at a party last week. Funny . . ." She exhaled smoke, which settled briefly around Bertha's head like a slipped halo. "She couldn't get over her luck in starring in her first talker, and who could blame her. But you know, she had this strange premonition that something would go wrong with the movie."

"From what I've heard, *she* was what was wrong with it. It was all over town Henry Turk was going crazy trying to get a performance out of her. Alex Roland should have dropped her weeks ago. But she was his girl and I don't have to tell you the rest. Now, let's see what I can see." She closed her eyes and passed her hands over the sphere while mumbling something that sounded like "ubbledeeoooogoooo." Thelma kept her eyes on the crystal ball, hoping it wouldn't divulge anything pornographic. This former grade-school teacher had a taste for sexual low jinks she didn't learn in the halls of academe. Bertha rested her hands at her sides, opened her eyes slowly, and stared into the ball.

"Ahhhhhh."

"What do you see?"

"I see a tall man."

"Is he dark?"

"He is dark."

Thelma said coyly, "I like them tall, dark, and handy."

"He's in your apartment."

"Where?"

"The bedroom's a safe guess."

Thelma smiled warmly. "Do you think he's going to attack me?"

"No."

"Shit."

"You're having a disagreement."

"Sweetie, you don't need a crystal ball to tell me that. Everybody in this town knows that Toddy rarely gets along with her men. Can't get along and can't do without."

Thelma wasn't aware Bertha was stalling, trying to unlock from her vast store of memory something she might have heard about the actress that she could now elaborate on. "You knew Dolly Lovelace?"

"Yes, I did. I was in a couple of her pictures. Don't tell me you predicted her murder?"

Bertha was home safe. Dolly Lovelace. Thelma had thrown her the ball and Bertha now carried it gracefully as she popped a Jujube into her mouth. "She had a very dark spot and it was a real big one." Their eyes locked. "She laughed at me. She didn't believe me. Within a month she was dead."

Thelma shuddered. "I was at the funeral. I was almost crushed to death. My pal ZaSu Pitts rescued me, she pulled me under a pew with her. And that's when the coffin fell over and Dolly's body came out with arms outstretched like she was begging to be brought back to life. And the next thing you know Jack's hugging her and kissing her and it was so awfully macabre and disgusting and ZaSu thought it was so romantic. She has her problems too."

Bertha gasped and then clasped a hand over her mouth. Thelma stubbed the cigarette out in an ashtray. "Come on, come on, don't horse around with Toddy. What do you see? It's a dark spot, right? Come on, out with it. I can take it. I ain't afraid of anything. I've worked with Alexander Korda."

"Goddamn it, I see *me*." She was wiping the crystal ball with her handkerchief.

"How did you get into my act?"

"I see myself! And the paisley shawl. It's around my neck and choking me!"

"Ah, stop kidding around, Bertha. That's an awfully large paisley shawl." On the other hand, Bertha had an awfully large neck.

Bertha left the table. The room shook as she crossed to a window that overlooked her backyard. "I shouldn't have seen myself in your reading."

"Maybe some cosmic wires got crossed," reasoned Todd.

"They shouldn't have. This is the first time we've met."

"Maybe we knew each other in another life. Do you believe in reincarnation?" Bertha didn't answer. She was deeply troubled. "Say, listen," Thelma tried. "Maybe this is a first! Maybe we're both sharing that dark spot. Ha ha ha! Wouldn't that be funny?"

Lotus Fairweather was frightening everyone with her predictions of doom on soundstage 5, probably the only Cassandra in existence who could hit a high C. Instead of shattering glass, she was shattering nerves. Several of the personnel had seen Alicia Leddy's body carried to the meat wagon. Rita Gerber was wondering where she could procure some sleeping drafts, foreseeing rejection by the arms of Morpheus. Willis Loring had decided to hang around the set after escorting Rita back from the commissary. There were so many pretty girls in various stages of undress, a smorgasbord of feminine pulchritude. He saw Jack Darling deep in conversation with a sound technician who seemed to be impressed by whatever lines Jack was feeding him. Donald Carewe was basking in the knowledge that the brothers Shubert back in New York wanted him to star in a tour of *The Desert Song*, which they wanted to send out quickly before Jack Warner released his singing talker starring John Boles.

Carewe's agent had reached him in his dressing room. "Listen, kiddo, we better grab this offer. Your *Casbah* thing is already being fitted with a black wreath. Sorry, kiddo, but I can tell from the rushes the movies ain't for you." Carewe was a practical man who had a wife and four children back in Great Neck, Long Island. The Shuberts didn't pay the best but they paid better than most and their tours were guaranteed because they had a monopoly of theaters across the United States. Onscreen, his image magnified a hundred times, he was too old to be playing leading men. Onstage, with heavy makeup and footlights and overheads, he could still look younger. And Sigmund Romberg's score was lovely. He could sing "One Alone" to perfection. Then his stomach turned a somersault at the thought that the role of Margo, his leading lady, might be offered to Lotus Fairweather. He hurried to a phone and called his agent.

"No Lotus Fairweather as Margo," he warned his agent, "because I'll kill her if she's doing it."

This was overheard by a grip who relayed it to a carpenter who relayed it to an electrician who passed it on to an assistant director who orbited it toward Jason Cutts who promptly informed Alexander Roland who demanded the immediate presence in his office of Donald Carewe who entered the office smiling obsequiously while entertaining the absurd fantasy he was about to be offered a five-year contract without options and almost had a heart attack when an outraged Alexander Roland demanded to know why Carewe had threatened Lotus Fairweather's life.

Detective Jim Mallory occasionally came up with an intelligent suggestion for Herbert Villon. It was therefore announced on all the soundstages that the police would be in the murdered actress's bungalow dressing room for the next hour or so and would appreciate any information that might be useful in the investigation of Alicia Leddy's murder.

Rita Gerber engaged the service of an assistant director to accompany her to the bungalow through the maze of threatening shadows that now covered the studio like a menacing shroud. They passed Donald Carewe returning from his audience with Alexander Roland, muttering imprecations against the gossipmonger who had tried to implicate him in the future death of his leading lady.

"Sounds like he's going crazy," said Rita to the A.D.

"That's possible if he's been in this town longer than two weeks."

When they arrived at the bungalow, Rita said, "Gee, kid, I don't think I can go in there."

The A.D. laughed. "Afraid of ghosts?"

Villon had heard them and opened the door. "Do you want to see me? I'm Chief Inspector Villon."

The A.D. said, "Miss Gerber wants to see you."

Villon smiled his most charming smile, erasing all of Rita Gerber's fear and apprehension. "Won't you come in, Miss Gerber?"

She said to the A.D., "You wait for me."

"Okay, okay. I'll be right here. But don't take forever. It's beginning to look like we'll be shooting most of the night."

Jim Mallory stood up when Rita Gerber entered ahead of Villon. She sat in the chair he offered and then her eyes panned around the room.

Jim Mallory was armed with pencil and pad and waited patiently for Villon or the actress to say something. Villon asked, "What's your full name, please?"

"Rita Gerber."

"Did you see anything that happened around this bungalow?"

"No. It's nothing like that. It's just that I had coffee this morning in the commissary with Alicia and Jack Darling."

Villon said, "Darling was here this morning?"

"Like I told you, sure. We sort of got to talking and he said when he has nothing to do he comes to the studio to learn more about how they make talking pictures. I think he's a real nice guy. I knew he was on the make, but he's a star, you know, so what could be so bad you give a star your phone number?"

"That depends on your taste in stars."

"I'm sure, but I doubt that I'll ever get to meet John Barrymore. Anyway, Alicia and I came out from New York on the train together and we got to know each other pretty good. I mean she was so young and naïve, fresh out of the chorus from where Mr. Roland spotted her."

"He's a great spotter."

"I kidded her a lot about if you want to get ahead you have to sleep with the right people and she said I suppose you'll never know if they're right until you sleep with them and if they're the wrong ones it's too late already."

"I had no idea she was so profound."

"Neither did she."

"Did she seem apprehensive of anyone she might run into in Hollywood?"

"No, she was afraid of the same thing I am—would we make it out here? So this morning there we were, she starring in a talker and me on loan out for this fat part in a musical turkey which is nutty since I can't sing a note. I was flattered Jack

Darling was buying us coffee. She said he'd helped her do a scene for her director."

"I suppose I can assume he also had Miss Leddy's phone number."

She smiled ingenuously. "Why don't you ask him? He's on my set talking to the sound technicians. I saw him just before I left to come here."

"Did you see Miss Leddy again today?"

"No," she said softly. "Then when I heard she was dead, well, you can imagine how I felt, how I still feel. She wasn't stabbed or anything awful like that, was she?"

"I can't tell you that until I see the coroner's report." Villon had cautioned Hazel Dickson not to use the scarf in her story until he saw the report. It could possibly be a red herring like the acid-burnt mouths of Dolly Lovelace and her husband.

"I can tell by the way you talk it must have been awful." She dabbed at her misting eyes with a handkerchief. "I can't tell you anything else. I better get back."

"We'll go with you." He said to Mallory, "I don't think we'll be receiving any more volunteers. Let's go."

They picked up the assistant director and walked the short distance to stage 5.

Sophie Gang was anxious to get home to her canary, her goldfish, and her invalid mother, but Sam Goldwyn insisted she join him in watching the day's rushes. As they walked slowly to the projection room, Goldwyn was considering replacing an elderly character actress who was having trouble remembering her lines.

"She can't remember a thing. Do you suppose she's suffering from magnesia?"

"She says the director makes her nervous. She's really a very good actress, but face it, she's over seventy. When you're that old, it's not so easy to remember."

"And what's with that crazy ingenue, that Frances Carlisle? I hear she claims her father came over on the *Mayflower*."

"Probably as a stoker."

"And have you any idea why Fitzmaurice is giving everybody

such a hard time?" George Fitzmaurice was the director the character actress said made her nervous. "Here I am helping him move from silents to talkers when nobody else would give him a hello, and he's making so many problems. Doesn't he know his repetition is at stake?"

"I'll talk to him in the morning."

"And how about that Alex Roland! Making an about-face and putting the Darlings and Loring back to work. How dare he snitch Jack from under me!"

Sophie was tired. "You didn't sign Jack to anything. You offered to test his voice."

"Don't put words in my mouth! Well, now Alex has a murder case to deal with. It serves him right the way he's been treating his wife."

"What's Mrs. Roland got to do with murder?"

"How do I know? Maybe we should find her something now that Joe's putting her in a picture. Say, did we sign that blond kid . . ." He snapped his fingers trying to recall the actress's name.

"Florence Britton. We're signing her tomorrow."

"Maybe Ben Hecht's got a good idea there."

"Where?" Goldwyn's non sequiturs always tired Sophie Gang.

"A picture about Dolly Lovelace. It might be right for Miss Great Britain."

Sophie was too weak to correct him. "She hasn't any experience."

"When I get through with her, she'll have experience."

When Villon and Mallory returned to soundstage 5 with Rita Gerber, they had to wait for a musical sequence to finish shooting. They had just entered the stage when the warning red lights flashed and an A.D. shouted "Quiet!" Rita realized she was needed in this scene and hurried to a group of scantily clad girls chained to each other. One of the wardrobe people handed Rita a whip and when the director called "Action!" Rita lashed away with an unbecoming fervor. The whip was a treated strip of cloth that left red welts on the girls' backs. To one side, a sound effects man cracked a real whip in synchronization with Rita's actions. It had been carefully rehearsed and timed so that Rita and the sound man acted in concert.

The orchestra situated behind the camera blasted away mercilessly as Donald Carewe somewhat precariously balanced himself on a stone parapet brandishing a scimitar and belting in his bruised baritone a warning to Rita and a group of dastardly extras in beards, mustaches, and turbans (Villon decided these were slave traders).

> *"Trading in slaves*
> *Depraves*
> *And will lead to your graves . . .*
> *You varlots and knaves . . .*
> *Will suffer from my braves . . ."*

Villon whispered to Jim Mallory, "Lyrics not by Emily Dickinson."

"Oh, is she out here?"

Carewe, they realized, was no longer singing.

"Ye gods," shouted the director, "where is Miss Fairweather? This is supposed to be a duet!"

The stage echoed and re-echoed with shouts of Lotus Fairweather's name when suddenly Rita Gerber emitted a piercing shreik.

An assistant director following Gerber's finger pointing upward to the flies said, "Here comes Miss Fairweather now."

Lotus Fairweather's body came plummeting down and missed crushing Rita Gerber by inches.

Villon drew his revolver and yelled to Mallory, "Up there!" There was further pandemonium at the sight of the two police officers with weapons drawn taking the stairs two at a time as they rushed up to the platforms in the flies.

Jason Cutts had the news from soundstage 5 within seconds and hurried into Alex Roland's office to tell him, praying the news would not bring on a heart attack. What Roland suffered was not a heart attack, but more of a convulsion. Cutts poured him a brandy and Roland downed it in a gulp. He gasped, "The police! The police!"

"They're there. They saw it. They're chasing the killer."

But Villon and Mallory were unsuccessful. Grips and electricians placed variously in the flies had seen nothing. They had heard the *whoosh* of the falling body, but they hadn't heard a scream. They hadn't heard anything else. As they hurried back downstairs, Villon shouted over his shoulder to Mallory, "Get to a phone and get us a backup and don't forget the coroner."

"I never forget the coroner."

As Mallory went in search of a telephone, Villon pushed his way through the wall of humanity surrounding the body. Rita Gerber was off to one side with an A.D. having hysterics and Donald Carewe had hurried to his dressing room to phone his agent and tell him he would probably be available to the Shuberts earlier than expected.

Alex Roland and Jason Cutts came tearing out of the executive building into a waiting car that drove them to the soundstage. Roland had remembered to shout a command to a secretary and tell her to phone his wife with the awful news and let her know it might be hours before he'd get home.

Jim Mallory, after phoning headquarters, found Hazel Dickson at home to give her an exclusive. They were frequently trading favors. Hazel shouted, "You're in my will!" She phoned her scoop to the night editor and then hurried to the Diamond Studios in her trusty Model T.

In the wardrobe department, costume designer Ethel Swift clutched her throat upon hearing of Lotus Fairweather's death and said, "That costume cost a fortune! If she's ruined that costume I'll kill her!"

Annamary Darling moaned and began to faint. Marie caught her daughter in her arms and bellowed, "Courage, baby, courage! Ethel, you got some hooch? Well, get it!"

Ethel opened a wardrobe trunk where she kept a stash of bourbon and falsies and unscrewed the cap of the bootleg booze and took a stiff belt. She then poured some into a paper cup and held it to Annamary's mouth.

Jack Darling entered wardrobe and, seeing Annamary in collapse, hurried to her and began rubbing her wrists. Marie asked him if he'd heard about Fairweather's tragedy.

"Heard about it? I was there! I saw her come down! It was awful! It was just awful!"

Mallory and Villon managed to clear a space around the body. Villon stared at it, lying like a crumpled, shattered doll, arms and legs askew. He heard an extra say, "Just because she was so lousy in the picture was no reason for her to take a dive. I mean come on already, she's got that rich husband back east, don't she?"

Villon knelt and examined her neck. Her face was bloated. Her mouth was agape with her purple tongue protruding. Around her neck, tightly wound and knotted, was a silk stocking.

Villon stood up and Mallory asked, "How do suppose the killer lured her up to the flies?"

"He didn't. He carried her. He killed her someplace else."

"But how did he get the body up there without being seen?"

"Jim, there are lots of ways to get into these soundstages. And anybody who knows his way around could move a dead elephant in here without being caught."

"Oh my God, my God!" Alexander Roland had arrived with Jason Cutts. "Oh my God! Why did she kill herself! Why!" He grabbed Jason's arm. "Hurry, Jason, hurry. Call Jay Mack in insurance!"

TWELVE

"Whaddya mean she killed herself?" questioned an electrician, oblivious to the fact he was contradicting the head of the studio. "Looks like she was strangled with that stocking around her neck."

"Strangled?" Alexander Roland stared at Villon. "She was strangled like Alicia Leddy was strangled?"

Villon heard a sharp intake of breath and realized it was his own. Mallory said nothing. Instead, he busied himself with the help of some studio policemen in pushing back the personnel crowded around the dead woman.

"Mr. Roland?" Roland saw Ethel Swift arriving, followed by the three Darlings. "How did you know Alicia Leddy was strangled?"

"How? What do you mean how? Somebody told me, that's how. I heard it from somebody."

"What somebody?"

Roland screwed up his face trying to remember. It didn't help. "I don't remember. Mr. Villon, I hear so much during a day, what with all my meetings and conferences."

"I want you to try and remember. It's very important that you remember."

Donald Carewe had returned from phoning his agent. Roland espied him and pointed an accusing finger at him. "Him! That baritone! He threatened to kill Lotus Fairweather!"

"Oh please! Not again!" pleaded Carewe. A chorus of voices joined Roland's, those who had overheard and relayed his threat from one to another and finally to Roland.

136

"Oh my God!" shrieked Ethel Swift. "The costume is ruined! Absolutely ruined! Look at those paillettes and those bugle beads scattered all over the floor. I begged the clumsy bitch to take very special care of the costume! Goddamn it, I was going to use it again in the movie about the amnesiac World War soldier, *Over Where?*"

"Ethel, shut up!" shouted Roland.

Villon had confronted Carewe. "Come with me. I want to talk to you."

Carewe babbled with fear. "It's all a mistake, it's a terrible mistake." Alone on the set under the stone parapet, Carewe explained to Villon his remark about Lotus Fairweather's possibly joining his tour of *The Desert Song* and how he felt he couldn't cope with her again. He was sweating profusely and grinding a handkerchief between his damp palms. "You understand, don't you? How could I kill her when I have a wife and four children in Great Neck, Long Island?"

"Where were you when she came crashing down from the flies?"

The baritone's eyes widened, suddenly realizing he had an alibi. "Why, I was standing right here on this parapet. Lotus should have joined me for a duet. We had to stop the scene because she wasn't here with me. And that's when she . . . you know . . ."

"Thank you, Mr. Carewe." Villon walked back to join Mallory, leaving behind him a bundle of shattered nerves. Marie Darling was worrying Roland with her usual ferocity. "My children must be protected! I will not permit them on this lot without armed escorts! My darling Annamary will not commence shooting tomorrow unless the stage is fully patrolled. You! Villain!"

"Villon," corrected Mallory.

"What kind of a chief inspector are you anyway? These murders are taking place right under your nose!"

"That's not where they took place," said Villon.

"Don't quibble!"

Roland tried to placate her. "Please, Marie, there will be more than adequate protection." He was relieved to hear the sound of approaching sirens, hoping they would fortify his promise to Marie.

Marie pointed a finger at the corpse. "And I suppose there isn't enough insurance to cover this thing either!"

Roland's face began to redden. "Please, Marie . . ."

"Please, Marie! Please, Marie!" she mimicked cruelly. "No one ever does anything to please Marie!" She took Annamary's arm. "Come, dear, we're going home."

"But you can't leave now," wailed Ethel Swift. "We're not finished! She has six big scenes tomorrow and we've only fitted four of the dresses!"

"Marie . . . please!" pleaded Alexander Roland.

Villon's backup came hurrying onto the stage followed by Hazel Dickson. Villon wondered how she'd gotten wind of the killing so soon. If she was here, the other reporters and photographers wouldn't be far behind. The next couple of hours had to be unobstructed so that he could question as many people as possible. Who had last seen the soprano and where? He saw Jack Darling with an arm around Rita Gerber in an attempt to comfort her. The girl's shoulders were shaking and her face was a mess. Her mascara had run down her cheeks and onto her chin. The special makeup needed for Technicolor film looked caked and peeling. She was no longer pretty.

Annamary said to Marie, "Stop pulling my arm, Mother. I am not going home until I've finished all the fittings. If we don't do it tonight it will only mean my getting here at the crack of dawn. I've promised to do this film and I'm going to do it right."

"Don't work yourself into a state, dear," said Marie.

"I'm not in a state," replied Annamary angrily. "You're the one who's in a state. You're always in a state. And when will I learn my dialogue? Somebody's got to help me with my dialogue! Where's Henry Turk? Henry! Are you here?" She was told her director was on the adjoining stage setting up for the next day's shooting. "I need to see him. Somebody go get him." Somebody went to get him. Annamary walked briskly out the door trailed by her mother and Ethel Swift.

Hazel was standing near the body staring at the stocking that presumably was used to strangle her. "Silk," she murmured. Villon overheard her.

"What about it?"

"That stocking. It's silk. That's all."

"What are you doing here?"

She knew she must protect Mallory. "Ummm . . . we have a dinner date."

"We do?"

"We do."

"Well, now it's pretty obvious we don't. So why don't you run along home—"

She interrupted him abruptly. "I'm on a story. I'm staying here until I get it all. And especially now that here comes the thundering herd." Her rival reporters were streaming onto the stage followed by photographers.

Villon shouted to Mallory, "Keep this gang back! Hey, you bozos!" he shouted to a group of studio policemen. "Get those reporters and photographers out of here! Get going! Get the lead out!"

"Get the lead out!" echoed Alexander Roland as Jason Cutts returned to his side. "Out with it, out with it. What did Jay Mack tell you?"

Jason was gasping for breath. "He says we're okay. Because it's being shot in color, he doubled up on the insurance."

"Thank God for small favors. Now listen, I want you to draw up a list of replacements for Fairweather. There's that new girl over at Paramount—"

"Jeanette MacDonald."

"That's her. Call them and see if she's available." Jason started to hurry off but Roland grabbed him by the collar. "Stop rushing away until I finish! Jack Warner has a whole harem full of sopranos. Let me see . . . he's got Vivienne Segal . . ."

". . . and Bernice Claire."

"I never heard of her. Who is she?"

"She's a San Francisco girl. They found her there."

"Who else sings?"

"Bebe Daniels sings. And Swanson."

"Swanson forget. She'll cost an arm and a leg. How do you know Daniels sings?"

"She's doing *Rio Rita* for the new Radio Pictures."

"Imagine that! Bebe sings! Her agent offered her to me for next to nothing if I'd give her a break in a talker and I turned him down. Why didn't he tell me she sang, I'd have signed her up on the spot." Cutts remained silent. He knew his boss knew absolutely nothing about musical talent. The man was tone deaf.

Cutts said, "There's a cute young kid at Universal, Jeanette Loff."

"Not opposite Carewe. She'd look like his daughter."

"Mr. Roland, if I may offer a suggestion . . ."

"Go ahead, I'm listening." Cutts almost swooned. Alexander Roland was going to listen to a suggestion—something that happened as infrequently as the summer solstice.

"Since we have to reshoot from the beginning, why not replace Carewe with a younger man; then we could pair the girl with anyone we like."

"What younger men? Who do you have in mind?"

"There's John Boles . . ."

"Not Boles. He's in everything. Somebody else."

"Walter Pidgeon?"

"You call him young? He's almost forty."

"Alexander Gray. Dennis King . . ."

"Now, Gray isn't such a bad idea."

"He's just finished one for Warner. Now if we could team him up with someone like Jeanette MacDonald, together they might go great in a series."

"Operetta stars in a series? Are you crazy? In another year or so audiences will be so fed up listening to all this yowling and howling the singers will be hitchhiking their way back east. Get on the phone and see if you can line up Gray and MacDonald, but don't sound desperate! It'll cost too much!"

"But Mr. Roland, it's all over town already that Fairweather's dead!"

"Already? Already? What has become of decency and fair play?"

Villon, Mallory, and all of their team busied themselves inter-
rogating the cast and crew of *Daughter of the Casbah*. The coroner
had arrived grumpily, having been called away from his dinner.
Before setting to work examining the corpse, he told Villon that
Alicia Leddy had positively been strangled with the scarf, but
her death had not been instantaneous.

An electrician was telling Villon, "Well, she was carrying on
about getting protection, you know, scared stiff because of Alicia Leddy's murder. She kept insisting she be given a bodyguard and said she was going to phone her agent and demand
he get her a bodyguard. So the last I saw her I guess she was
going to her dressing room to use the phone."

"She must have a maid, doesn't she? Aren't all stars assigned a
maid?"

"Only if they don't have one of their own. Fairweather has—
had, you know—that's her over there with the bag of peanuts.
The Chinese girl sitting on the steps."

"Thanks. You've been helpful." The electrician felt as though
he'd been pinned with an invisible medal. Villon was heading
toward Fairweather's maid. Hazel Dickson crossed his path.

"What did the coroner tell you just now?"

"You don't miss a trick, do you?"

"That's why I'm so good." She winked. "Come on, Herb. I'm
on my way to a big hoist in salary."

Villon wondered what it was that had first endeared her to
him. She had ordinary, homely looks. She didn't dress particularly well. He sometimes wondered how she could see, the way
she pulled her cloche hats down so tightly on her head. She
occasionally talked out of the side of her mouth, probably because that's what so many girl reporters did in the talkers. And
she pushed food onto her fork with her fingers. She must have
had an awful childhood.

"Herb!" he heard her say. "Where are you? You're miles
away."

"I wish I was." He told her what the coroner had told him.
"Leddy was strangled by that scarf."

"And this one with a silk stocking and then dropped from the flies. Why didn't anybody hear her scream? I've been asking around and absolutely no one so far heard her scream."

"She was already dead before being carried to the flies."

"So why bother carrying her up there?"

"For the effect, baby, for the effect."

"I don't get you."

"Where's your sense of showmanship? Haven't you seen enough murder mysteries to recognize that shock effect that makes the audience scream? The body falling out of the closet? The body falling through a trap door? The corpse pinned to the library wall with a Ubangi spear?"

"Ubangi?"

"Love to. Your place or mine?"

"Not funny, Villon. Hey, wait a minute. Showmanship, huh? Somebody making a grandstand play." She thought for a moment and then spoke the name with some hesitation. "Alexander Roland?"

"Why not?"

"Roland would screw up his own works? It doesn't make sense."

"It does if you know the tough spot he's in with his whole operation. His empire is very shaky financially. The bankers are calling in their markers. He's got a dozen talkers in release out there, but they're getting little action. He's not as shrewd as Metro with their backstage musicals and thrillers or Warner with his gangster pictures and newspaper pictures. Warner is even cutting down on his operettas; in fact, he's sending some into release without the song numbers."

Hands on hips, Hazel demanded, "How do you know so much about what's going on in pictures?"

"I'm movie crazy, you know that, cutie. I read all the trades. I hang out at Musso and Frank's and the Brown Derby. I've got my ear to the ground. I like to know what's going on."

"Alexander Roland is not the killer type."

"What's a killer type?"

Like a shot, she replied, "Marie Darling."

"That is positively a killer type. In fact, in my books she's a killer's killer."

"Could she have carried Lotus Fairweather up to the flies?"

"I think she's been carrying heavier loads than that."

"Why would she want to kill Fairweather?"

"Who said she did?" He was anxious to get to the Chinese maid. "You're the one who branded her the killer type. To me, she's just another ogress of a show business mother. She's right up there in the rogues' gallery with Mama Gish and Peg Talmadge and a new one in town named Rosie Green whose kid Mitzi looks to make it big at Paramount unless Mama's big mouth gets them both exiled back to New York. Now go ask questions somewhere else. I've got somebody I want to talk to."

Hazel followed him with her eyes, making a mental note to cross-examine him about the Chinese maid later.

The maid continued munching a peanut as Villon introduced himself. "I understand you were Miss Fairweather's maid?"

"She wore dirty underwear."

Villon smiled. He could see he had himself a live one here. "I'm not interested in her underwear."

"You should be. Somebody might have killed her because she was such a slob. Never washed her makeup off before she went home. Next day you'd still see traces of it on her chin and neck. Very filthy. My mother begged me to wear rubber gloves in the dressing room."

"What's your name?"

"Ah Fong Gu. That means 'Little willow in the wind who will withstand the force of a hurricane and the cruelty of a brutal husband as he will have given her a lavish dowry.' Call me Loretta."

"How long have you worked for Miss Fairweather?"

"They hired me a week before shooting." She stared into the bag of peanuts. "That's about five weeks ago."

"You didn't like her, I gather."

"Oh, not so. Only her unclean habits. I felt very sorry for her. She was so old." She made it sound as though old age were an unpardonable sin. He'd always been led to believe that Orientals venerated their elders. "I mean so old for pictures. She knew it, too. She kept saying, 'I'll never make another film after this. I'm lucky I got this one.'" The girl shrugged and flashed a

143

winning smile. "Maybe she was psychic. Maybe she knew she was going to die. She had her fortune told last week."

"Do you know the name of the fortune-teller?"

"That fat one. Just about everybody goes to her for advice."

"You mean Bertha Graze?"

"Yes, that's her. I think she's a load of baloney. Nobody can predict the future."

"I thought you Chinese invented astrology."

"No, we didn't. The Egyptians did. We invented spaghetti. It's true. Marco Polo took it back to Italy with him."

"When did you last see Miss Fairweather?"

"Lying there on the concrete."

"I mean alive."

"Ummm, I guess about half an hour before she came flying down." Villon found her nonchalance about the murder charming and hated himself for it. "She came into the dressing room to use the phone and asked for privacy so I gave it to her. I went to the commissary to buy these peanuts. Want some?"

"No, thanks. They'll spoil my appetite."

"How come? They're more appetizing than that thing over there." She pointed at the corpse.

"Did she have any enemies?"

"How should I know? She didn't confide in me. I was like a piece of furniture to her. You know, utilitarian. 'Loretta do this, Loretta do that, would you scratch my back please?' Do I have to hang around here much longer? I've got two kids who need their supper; my husband works nights."

Two kids! Villon repressed his astonishment. She looked seventeen years old.

"I'm twenty-eight." She might have been reading his mind. The charming smile was back. "Everybody thinks I'm ten years younger than I am. Catch me five years from now and two more babies, I'll look thirty years older. I'll look like my grandmother. Is it okay if I go home?"

"The studio has your address and phone number?"

"They sure do."

He bid her good night and went in search of Jim Mallory, but the coroner stopped him.

144

"Much like the other one," the coroner told him, "except she has broken bones from the drop. Nothing to do with her death. She was dead before she came down. Like Leddy, crushed carotids, couple of bruises indicate some small bones are probably fractured. This one's no chicken, you know."

"I know, and she knew." He left the coronor and resumed his search for Mallory.

Mallory was questioning Willis Loring, who was standing on his status as a star to carp about this invasion of privacy. Unimpressed by the bluster, Mallory nailed every word to Loring's ear. "You were present at the scene of a murder and therefore you are subject to questioning. If you're not happy giving me some answers here we can always retire to headquarters. But the coffee's terrible there."

Villon joined them and recognized a display of Hollywood temperament immediately. Mallory had probably made the mistake of interrupting the actor while he was putting the make on one of the slave girls. "How we doing?" he asked Mallory.

Mallory said with a slight trace of sarcasm, "Mr. Loring is finding it difficult to be cooperative."

Loring said to Villon, "I find all his questions pointless. I was sitting and talking to one of the young extras when the body landed, so you can't suspect me of killing her. I mean I'm a superb athlete and in magnificent condition"—Villon expected him to flex his muscles, but the actor disappointed him—"but I couldn't have made it down from the flies before her body landed. I'm good, but not that good." Villon toyed with suggesting he might have used a stunt double but swiftly decided the actor would not be amused.

"Which one of the girls were you talking to?" asked Villon. Mallory was relieved he had taken over the questioning. Mallory was tempted to lay one on Loring, the man was that obnoxious.

"I don't see her around." He craned his neck in all directions, looking to Villon like an eccentric Hindu dancer. "Her name was Abigail something or another."

"Well, you keep looking for Miss Something or Another and please don't leave this set without my permission."

"Now, you see here!"

"I don't see here because all I see is a dead body and that's the second one today and from the way things look to me there could very well be a third before the night's over. Don't pull any star crap on me, mister. I don't need you for a movie, I need you to cooperate when we ask questions. It's not my fault you were on the lot catting around . . ."

"How dare you!"

". . . I repeat, catting around trying to find yourself a nosh for the night. You egos disgust me the way you prowl around and prey on these kids as though it was your feudal right."

"How very moral of you, Mr. Villon. As a matter of fact, you might be happy to know that from time to time an occasional kid says no." He added with a growl, "You hypocrite."

Villon and Mallory left him lighting a cigarette. Jack Darling was still with Rita Gerber who, fortunately, had repaired her makeup. Villon led Mallory to the couple.

Villon said to Gerber, "I saw how shaken up you were. I'm sorry it affected you so badly."

Gerber's eyes widened. "Affected me! You didn't see it happen! She came diving down at me like a bomb from an airplane! She missed hitting me by inches!"

"Rita might have been crushed to death," said Jack.

Gerber took back the spotlight. "I wasn't all shook up because the old bag bought a one-way ticket. It was realizing I could have been killed. On loan-out, yet!"

Villon asked Jack, "You saw the body drop?"

"I was talking to a sound technician about some ideas I've got." He favored Villon with his famous yokel grin. "They're pretty revolutionary. You see, I'm directing my first talker and I'm going to show Alex Roland how innovative I can be." Villon wondered privately if the young man had invented the wheel but then admonished himself for such a frivolous thought. He needed food. Jack Darling continued, "Anyway, I heard someone say 'Here she comes now' or something like that, and I heard someone scream—"

"That was me," said Rita.

"So I turned and the body came whooshing down, like I said before; it was a miracle it missed killing Rita."

Villon said to Mallory, "The poor killer. He might have killed two birds with one stone." Mallory hoped the others hadn't heard him.

Rita asked plaintively, "What happens now?"

"We keep hunting for the murderer," said Villon.

"I mean with the picture!"

"I'm sure Mr. Roland is at this very moment phoning around for a replacement for Miss Fairweather."

"Do I have to stick around? I'm pooped."

"I'll let you know when you can leave," said Villon in a friendly tone of voice. "I see there's a table set up over there with refreshments. Why don't you refresh yourself?"

Jack and Rita watched the two officers walk away in search of a murderer. When they were out of earshot, Gerber said to the actor, "Are you really directing your first talker?"

Jack said firmly, "I'm directing it," almost adding, "or else."

"Is there a part in it I can do?"

"I don't know. What can you do?"

"If you go home with me, I'll show you."

Villon was waiting while Mallory stopped to light a cigarette. "Do you know anything about this fortune-teller Bertha Graze?"

"Much the same that you do, I suppose. She has a network of spies who supply her with inside info she uses in her fortune-telling routine. She's been suspected of trafficking in blackmail but she's never been nailed, never been brought up on charges. A lot of biggies in town swear by her when they're not swearing at her. She's so obese, the city's considering rezoning her, and you don't want her as an enemy."

"Have a talk with her. It seems last week she predicted Fairweather's fortune."

"You mean misfortune, don't you?"

"That's what I'd like to know."

Mallory looked at his wristwatch. "Maybe I can connect with her tonight, unless you want me to stick around."

"Connect with her. I don't think we can expect any more

147

surprises tonight." They were watching the corpse being removed from the premises, the coroner following in the wake of
the solemn procession like a solitary mourner. "Farewell, Lotus
Fairweather. They'll be putting a tag with her name on it around
her big toe. I hope, wherever she is, she finds the billing satis-
factory."

THIRTEEN

◆

"I'm glad you're here. You shouldn't be. It might be dangerous, but I'm glad you're here."

Helen Roland went to her husband's outstretched arms, accepted his embrace, and kissed him. "I came as soon as I heard the news of Lotus Fairweather's death on the radio. I thought you might need me."

Roland's face darkened. "Helen, somebody's out to get me. It's a conspiracy. Somebody's out to break me." The voice rang defiant. "I am not that easily broken. Would you like some wine? I promised Villon—he's the chief inspector—I'd hang around awhile longer. Then we can go somewhere for dinner. Maybe by then I'll have an appetite." He sat at his desk. "Oh! The wine." He moved to get up. "Do you want the wine?"

"No, no, stay where you are."

"I wonder if it could be Goldwyn."

"Sam? That's impossible. He and Frances are two of our best friends."

"So what does best friends mean in this town?"

"Why would Sam want to ruin you? What possible reason could he have? He's the most successful independent here. He doesn't want to head a major company. He's told us that time and again."

"Talk is cheap."

"Sam isn't."

"Both women killed in the middle of expensive productions. I've got four others shooting. Not as expensive, maybe, but still, they're costing money. Supposing this murderer decides to kill someone featured in those four talkers? Oh boy, could that really destroy me!"

Helen was at the window watching the scene below, Fairweather's body being loaded into the meat wagon. "Maybe it's something else."

"Like what?"

She moved away from the window. "Someone looking to settle an old score."

He snorted. "That's a few hundred suspects right there."

"Don't be so hard on yourself. Not that many people hate you."

"Helen, after all your years in pictures, you're still a babe in the woods. I've got enemies to whom I haven't been properly introduced. There's a faceless army out there who hate people like me. They don't know me, they never met me, they likely never will know or meet me, but they hate me. It's the same with Sam and Mayer and Fox and all the rest of us Brahmins who run a studio. We are men of power, men of incredible power, and power frightens and intimidates people. And out there, there could be one"—he wagged an index finger at her—"just one, crazy enough to come up with such a cockamamie idea as to kill my actresses in the middle of shooting two big productions. I'm not even adequately covered on *The Bride Wore Sneakers*, but I'll dig into my own cash reserves for it."

"I'm a very rich woman in my own right."

"I'll never let you dig into your own right! You earned that money as a star and you hold on to it. Invest. Invest heavily. Nineteen twenty-nine looks like the greatest year for the stock market. You mark my words."

Her voice was tired. "I'm marking."

After a short silence he asked, "You know Annamary is replacing Leddy in the bride movie?"

"Yes. I'm glad everything's settled with the Darlings."

"What's settled?" He was raging. "You know what that crazy son of . . . that crazy Jack is demanding? He wants not only to act and write the dialogue for his first talker, he wants to direct

150

it. Can you beat that, the son of a gun? Wrecked for years by hooch and dope and scandal and now he wants to be the new Erich von Stroheim. Why am I so surprised? Can you tell me? In this town? This town which breeds madmen by the scores? I'm beginning to question my own sanity."

"What are you going to do about Alicia Leddy?"

"What's to do? She's dead!"

"The gossip about the two of you hasn't died."

"I'm sorry I hurt you."

"That sort of pain died a long time ago."

"So what do you want me to do?"

"I think you should give a statement to the newspapers."

"What statement?"

"What a terrible tragedy for a girl at the start of what would have been a brilliant career. That in the brief time she was here you had come to know her well and will miss her, as much as a person as an actress."

"You really want me to say something like that?"

"Yes. You'll be thumbing your nose at them. And it has class."

"How long did it take you to think it up?" he said with a pleased smile.

"I didn't. Gloria Swanson did."

"That one!"

"Alex, they'll never be giving charity dinners for Gloria."

It was that rare exquisite moment when Sophie Gang was enjoying the lap of luxury. She was sharing the backseat of Goldwyn's custom-designed town car with her employer. The radio was offering music by Abe Lyman and His Orchestra. The bar was offering just-off-the-boat bonded scotch and soda with the added bonus of salted peanuts and pretzels. Goldwyn's very handsome new chauffeur was stealing glances at her in the rearview mirror, and though the holiday was months away, Sophie was aglow with Christmas spirit. Her heart caroled "Joy to the World" and maybe there'd be a very special yuletide gift awaiting her when she got home, her invalid mother stretched out dead in bed.

151

She heard Goldwyn saying, "How many times have I told you blood is thicker than waiters? You couldn't pry those Darlings apart with a nail file. Can you imagine letting that pisher Jack both write and star in his first talker?"

"Jack also insists on directing it."

"He what? Who told you that?"

"Jason Cutts. Roland's Jason. We talk a lot."

"You tell him as much about me as he tells you about Roland?"

"I lie a lot."

Goldwyn chuckled and then sipped his drink. "It's a good thing you talked me out of signing up that Lotus Fairweather. You saved me a lot of money and a lot of grief. Still, I liked her. She wasn't kidding herself. She knew she was getting too old for leads. She also smelled a little. I met her husband and her parents in New York the day I tested her." He sighed. "I suppose I should pay my respects to the family of the diseased."

"I'll wire flowers when they announce the funeral."

"Now tell me, what should I do about this here Swede Ibsen?"

"He was Norwegian."

"He was? You mean he's dead?"

"Very dead. Like Lotus Fairweather and Alicia Leddy."

"Now why would Ronnie Colman want to play in a movie from a play by a dead Norwegian?"

"My God, which one?"

"An Enema of the People."

Sophie almost dropped her drink. "I can't remember anyone ever doing Ibsen in films, do you? Unless in his native Norway."

Goldwyn recalled, "Somebody did his *The Dead Duck* or was it the other play about a bird, *Hedda Gobbler?* Ah, who cares. I won't do Ibsen." They rode in silence for a while. Sophie looked at her wristwatch. It was just eight o'clock. From the radio she heard the opening bars of Gershwin's *Rhapsody in Blue* signaling the Paul Whiteman Orchestra radio hour was beginning. Goldwyn said, "I wonder who's out to get Alex Roland?"

"You think these murders are for revenge?"

"What else could it be? Two actresses just arrived from the East? Both starring in their first talkers, and big budgets yet! I can't believe Alex Roland could be such a schmuck. You know," he said cozily, "Frances and I were talking about the murder of the Lovelaces over breakfast this morning. You know Dolly and Frances were real good friends, even though Dolly lost *The Swan* to my Frances. Anyway, you read how their mouths were disfigured by acid? Well, you know something, Frances asked me . . ."

Frances Goldwyn was a great beauty who had abandoned a successful film career when she married Sam Goldwyn. She was a wonderful wife above and beyond the call of duty. She handled Goldwyn with the skill and understanding of the trainer of a Thoroughbred. She was not in love with him, and he knew that, but nevertheless their relationship was warm and intimate.

While pouring coffee for the two of them, she asked Goldwyn, "Sammy, do you remember that movie Willis Loring did a long time ago, when he and Annamary had just begun their affair?"

Goldwyn feigned shock. "They had an affair before they got married? They slept together before the marriage?"

Frances said flatly, "They did more sleeping together before they got married than after they got married. Anyway, do you remember that movie?"

Goldwyn was getting irritated. "What movie? He's made dozens of movies!"

Frances was buttering a piece of toast. "He played a detective and there was this murder in Chinatown. And then there were some more murders. Don't you remember? All the victims had acid burns around the mouth except that wasn't the way they were really killed."

There was an amused expression on Goldwyn's face. "Maybe they ate poisoned fortune cookies?"

"You're close. They ate poisoned cookies, all right, but they weren't so fortunate. Come on, Sam, I remember you took me to a screening when you were courting me."

"And we weren't sleeping together." He refrained from

adding, *And we still seldom do.* "Yes, it's coming back to me. Something with 'revenge' in the title . . .''

"The Revenge of the Hatchet Man," said Sophie Gang.

"That's it! That's it! I can't wait to tell Frances. Sophie, you're a genius. You're indisposable."

"So why don't you give me a raise?"

"All right, so you're not a genius." He closed his eyes and pretended sleep. Sophie caught the chauffeur's eye in the rearview mirror and winked. He winked back. Sophie was feeling a tingle she hadn't felt in years. She hoped there was a sale on wild oats. She was planning to sow a lot of them.

"Sew sew sew," said Ethel Swift mournfully, "that's all I ever seem to do around here!" She was delicately stitching the sleeve of a dress Annamary was modeling.

"Keep quiet, Ethel," said Annamary. "This is one of the most beautiful dresses you've ever designed. I predict it'll make them drool in Paris."

Ethel was so elated she promised herself not to stab the star's skin again with the needle. "You really think so? Well, if I must say so myself, it's got a better line than anything Chanel ever designed."

"It has wonderful style. It makes me look good. I haven't gained weight, have I?"

"Hell no, honey. It's just Alicia Leddy was built smaller than you. That's why I've had to let it out."

"She wore this dress?"

Ethel Swift was swift. "Never had a chance, poor thing. She was to be fitted tonight." She stole a quick glance at Annamary and with relief saw the lie had placated her. "She was built like a small girl. She could never have been right for this dress. You really show it to its best advantage. Hon, there ain't a lot of you in this town who know how to show a dress at its best advantage. Besides you, there's Lil Tashman and Irene Rich and of course Swanson, and with the rest of them it's hit and miss. There." She bit the thread and got to her feet and then stood

154

back to examine the dress from a fresh perspective. "Stand back a little." Annamary moved back a few feet. Ethel clapped her hands. "It's gaaawwww——juss! Absolutely exquisite. Audiences will applaud when you make your entrance!"

They heard applause from behind them. Herbert Villon resisted an urge to take the actress in his arms and marry his lips to hers with an erotic French kiss. "Very very beautiful. A welcome oasis in this desert of ugliness."

Annamary showed something of a smile. "That's almost poetic."

Ethel was fussing with the hem of the dress. "Still on the job, Mr. Villon? Isn't it getting late?"

"Detectives don't punch time clocks. Miss Swift, you must have thousands of costumes here! What do you do about moths?"

"Balls." She added quickly, "Mothballs."

Annamary asked Villon, "Did you want to see me about something?" None of the three saw or heard Marie Darling walking toward them between two rows of neatly hung dresses and costumes.

"Actually, I do. It's really from out of left field. It has to do with this fortune-teller Bertha Graze."

"You mean fortune-hunter!" snapped Marie. "What about her?" She moved closer to her daughter and examined the dress she was wearing as though it were mounted on a slide under a high-powered microscope.

"Her name's cropped up in connection with Lotus Fairweather. Seems Miss Graze has a direct line to almost everyone in pictures."

"She doesn't have a direct line to my family, if that's what you've come to ask."

Villon asked Annamary, "I wonder if Dolly Lovelace ever mentioned consulting her?"

"No!" shouted Marie.

"Yes," contradicted Annamary.

"Well, which is it?" asked Villon, while not missing Ethel Swift's smirk..

155

Annamary said, "I know she saw her at least once, but that was a long time before the tragedy. Why?"

"I was wondering if Graze might have predicted something unpleasant for her."

"You mean the 'dark spot'?"

"Annamary, hold your tongue!"

"Hold your own, it's big enough." Marie clenched and un-clenched her fists.

"What's the 'dark spot'?" asked Villon.

Annamary stared at her own beautiful vision in the full-length mirror in front of which she and Ethel were working. "Bertha supposedly sees it in her crystal ball. It foretells gloom and doom. As far as I can tell, all Bertha sees in her crystal ball is her own grossly obese face."

"So you've seen her," said Villon.

"Believe me, it was only out of curiosity. Bertha saw a 'dark spot' when she was reading Dolly and it upset the poor kid. She told me about it and I scoffed and Dolly told me not to scoff because Bertha had told her a lot of other things that she couldn't possibly have known about. But Dolly wasn't con-vinced—"

Marie interrupted rudely, "Bertha Graze has a network of spies. They're all over the place. Our butler was one of her informants. I fired him, the traitor. She's a blackmailer. A mean, vicious blackmailer."

Villon asked, "Has she tried to blackmail you?"

Marie's reply was an eloquent "Like hell."

"If I may continue," interjected Annamary, "I met Bertha and she gave me an elaborate reading and it was mostly poppycock, but no dark spot. So I asked her was she sure she didn't see a dark spot? Well, you should have heard her. I should be grateful there wasn't one, her dark spots were dangerous and dire and who the hell knows what else. So I asked her how dare she frighten the hell out of poor Dolly. She said she couldn't help it. Dolly had the spot and that was that. Apparently Bertha's spots are unerasable. Does that satisfy you?"

Villon was interested in a costume hanging in a nearby rack and asked Ethel, "Isn't this a musketeer outfit?"

Ethel asked, "Where?"

Villon took the costume off the rack. Gripping the hanger, he held it up for Ethel to see.

"Oh, that one," said Ethel. "It's the wardrobe cliché."

"What do you mean?"

Ethel was having difficulty threading a needle. "It's always being borrowed for masquerade parties or some such."

"Would you know if it was used today for the masquerade scene in *Daughter of the Casbah*?"

"Search me. You'd have to ask one of the wardrobe mistresses. I'll yell for one." She shouted, "Bessie!" She told Villon, "Bessie Shea, she's on late tonight."

A voice nearby yelled, "What do you want?"

"Come over here! On the double!"

Bessie Shea emerged from another aisle of costumes. Over one hand was draped a ballgown, in the other she held a scissors. She was small and fiftyish and proved to be a gusher. She took one look at the musketeer outfit in response to Villon's question and said, "No, that wasn't used. It's not photogenic." Poor costume, thought Villon, career finished while still wearable. "Not in color anyway. But it's been out for a lot of parties." She laughed. "Let me see now. Henry Turk—he's a director here—he wore it to that last thing Charlie Chaplin threw. And let me think—oh yeah—Arnold Holt"—the leading man in *The Bride Wore Sneakers*, the mention of whose name made Annamary wince, though no one noticed—"he borrowed it for Marion Davies's party, and of course Mr. Roland wore it for that shindig at the Goldwyns' beach house a couple of months ago."

Ethel Swift said to Annamary, "It was designed for your brother." Annamary shifted from one foot to the other. "He wore it in that musketeer thing he did here a couple of years ago."

Marie stared at the costume. "What's so important about this rag?"

Villon happily told them, "Someone masked and wearing a musketeer costume was seen near Alicia Leddy's dressing room about the time she was being murdered." It reminded him to speak to Alexander Roland and jog his memory about who told him Alicia Leddy was strangled with a scarf.

Ethel Swift was wide-eyed. "Do you suppose that's the outfit the murderer was wearing?"

"Why not?" asked Bessie Shea matter-of-factly. "Just about everybody else has worn it."

Villon replaced the costume, and Bessie Shea considered that as a cue for her exit. Villon asked Marie, "Are you sure you've never met Bertha Graze?"

"That's none of your damn business!"

"I take it then that you have. Did she see any spots before her eyes when you were there?"

"As a matter of fact, no," said Marie, suddenly quite amiable. "I went there to warn her to lay off my family."

"Why? It seems Annamary and Dolly went to her voluntarily. Mrs. Darling, I think Bertha Graze knew that Ezekiel Lovelace was really Dolly's husband and was threatening to expose the bigamy."

"You can think what you like! It doesn't mean a thing to me!"

Much as he disliked Marie Darling, Villon had to admire her. Grudgingly, but it was admiration. She was a tigress when it came to protecting herself and her young. He wondered if someday soon he might have to cage the creature. "Thank you, ladies. You've been very helpful."

Watching him depart, Ethel Swift commented, "He's really some looker." She heard neither agreement nor disagreement. The fitting continued in an uneasy silence.

"How come you don't like jelly apples?" Bertha Graze asked Jim Mallory.

"They're bad for the teeth." He tried to avoid the unpleasant sight as she began demolishing the glazed fruit, but there were mirrors all over the place reflecting Bertha and her jelly apple in various ugly angles.

"So you want to know about the reading I gave Lotus Fair-weather?"

"That's right."

158

"You know, that's privileged information. Being a cop, you should be familiar with that. You know, like what a lawyer and a doctor knows is privileged information. Like Swiss banks too, you know?"

"I know. Now shall I repeat the question or are you going to start talking?" He wasn't willing to take any bets as to how much truth he'd hear.

"It was a pretty quick reading. I didn't go into much depth. You see, the lady had a certain odor and it was a very hot day and even with six electric fans going full blast, it wasn't what I would exactly call a very pleasant experience." She placed the stick that had held the demolished apple in an ashtray and licked each sticky finger on her right hand. Mallory was the soul of patience. He hoped she wouldn't suggest a short bout of wrestling. "One of the dancing girls in her movie had recommended she see me. Let me see now, yeah . . ." Her tongue was busily engaged working a piece of apple free from a space between her back teeth. It made her look as if she had three puffy cheeks. "She was worried about how the movie would turn out. As I recall, I told her it wouldn't."

"Meaning she might be dead?"

"Oh no no no. Nothing like that. I didn't see a dark spot."

"What's that?" As Bertha explained, Mallory's mouth formed an O but he made no comment.

"Actually, I didn't need to look into my crystal ball to find the bad news. It's been all over town that *Casbah* is a lemon and she was no good in it. There's another one like her, this Carlotta King in John Boles's *Desert Song*. Brutal, I hear, real brutal." She now had an oversized finger in her oversized mouth prying at the offending piece of apple. Mallory was glad he hadn't eaten dinner yet.

"You told her the picture would flop."

"Oh sure. It's best to level with the clients. They know you can't be accurate about everything. But I made her feel better when I told her her marriage would be more solid than ever. She was kind of cute. You see, I always fish around to see if maybe they're having a little hanky-panky on the side. So I

159

asked her, 'Are you in love with a married man?' and she said, 'Why, yes, my husband.' Cute, no?"

No, thought Mallory, but said nothing.

Bertha Graze sighed with relief. She had disgorged the piece of apple. "So she was murdered? Strangled with a silk stocking and then sent into space from the flies without a parachute. Boy, what won't some people think of next?" She was rummaging about in a half-filled box of chocolates. "Damn, the clients are always eating the soft centers." Mallory could see she had no soft center. "Well, what else do you expect me to tell you?"

Somehow, Mallory hadn't expected this visit to be so futile. He persisted. "You're sure you saw no, uh, dark spot, was it?"

"Dark spot."

"You saw none for Fairweather."

"So help me Hannah." Her right hand raised to swear an oath. "As a matter of fact, you want to hear a hot one?" She popped a chocolate-covered almond into her mouth. "I saw one of my own today!" She told him about the incident with Thelma Todd. "Nearly knocked the wind out of my sails!"

"Didn't it frighten you?"

"Well, I have to admit for a couple of minutes there it did. But then I looked at Toddy—that's what we call Thelma—and saw how unnerved *she* was. I mean she runs with a real fast crowd and some pretty questionable hombres, let me tell you. Anyway, I figured there's no such thing as getting crossed dark spots and it was all for her so I didn't even charge her for the reading."

Mallory was wondering if Thelma Todd was doing a movie for Diamond Films at the moment. He asked Bertha if she knew.

"You know something, I don't know what she's up to professionally right now. I could tell you plenty something else, but then, like I said before, that's privileged information. Say, would you like a Baby Ruth to munch on?"

Helen Roland had been studying Herbert Villon carefully. She liked the easy and affable manner in which he asked questions. She could tell that her husband also liked him, even if he might possibly be a suspect in the murders of the two women. Villon was determined to jog Roland's memory, determined to know who had told him Alicia Leddy had been strangled with her scarf.

Alex Roland snapped his fingers. "By golly! It was when I was settling with Marie Darling to have Annamary replace Leddy. Jack was sitting just where you're sitting, Mr. Villon. It was Jack who said she was strangled with the scarf."

"You're sure, now."

"It was Jack. Ask him yourself. There he is walking to the parking lot with that Gerber kid."

Villon went to the window and raised it. "Jack Darling!" he shouted. "Jack Darling!"

Rita Gerber turned in the direction of Villon's voice. "Jack," she said, "it's Villon, the cop. He's yelling for you."

Jack turned, looked up, and saw Villon. "You want me?"

"Very much."

FOURTEEN

Rita Gerber accompanied Jack Darling to Alexander Roland's office. She had no intention of remaining in the street unprotected. Jack parked her with Jason Cutts, then went into Roland's office, where Helen Roland greeted him warmly. Villon interrupted their scene and asked Jack to take a seat.

Villon half sat on Roland's desk, facing Jack. "Mr. Darling, earlier today in this office you said Alicia Leddy was strangled with her scarf."

"Wasn't she?"

"She was. But how did you know?"

"I was on the stage when she was murdered. I'd been helping Henry Turk get her through a difficult scene, or at least a scene that was proving difficult for her."

"Mr. Darling, the fact that she was strangled with a scarf was withheld from the press. Only a few of us knew that was how she died. So how did you know?"

Jack looked boyishly bewildered. "Someone must have let it slip. Jesus Christ, you don't think *I* killed her, do you?" Villon said nothing. Helen Roland looked embarrassed. Alexander Roland could have been holding a straight flush in a poker game. "I had a date to take her out tonight, for crying out loud!" Roland had a slight coughing fit as his mask slipped. Helen Roland smiled. Jack blushed, remembering Leddy had been Roland's girl.

"Do you remember where you were standing when you overheard the information?"

Jack was fumbling for words. "Well, gee, not precisely . . ." Helen Roland was thinking he needed to be chewing on a piece of straw and standing, shifting bashfully from one foot to the other, to complete the characterization of an innocent back-woods youth. "I remember there were two women extras seated nearby and, well, gee, Mr. Villon, there was an awful lot of activity because of the murder and people were talking all around me and I guess it was then I heard it."

Villon knew he had no case against Darling. He might be telling the truth and if he wasn't, Villon had no way of challenging him. "You didn't happen to borrow your old musketeer costume from wardrobe this afternoon?"

"What for?" asked Jack with a nervous laugh.

Villon told him what his mother and Carrie O'Day had seen at the time of Leddy's murder, a masked musketeer near the scene of the crime. Jack denied borrowing the costume.

"I'm sorry I can't be of more help to you, Mr. Villon."

"So am I." Villon was not satisfied. "We'll be talking again."

After Jack left, Alexander Roland suggested drinks and, while he was pouring them, told them about Jack's projected first talker, *Margin for Terror*. "A young modern-day Bluebeard, how about that for a change of image?"

"I think it's a wonderful idea," said Helen Roland, taking a glass of claret from her husband.

"Funny," said Villon.

"What's funny?" asked Roland, handing Villon a bourbon neat.

"Jack Darling as a lady-killer."

Hazel Dickson hailed Jim Mallory as he stepped out of his tired roadster. "You got anything interesting for me?"

"I've been talking to the eighth wonder of the world, Bertha Graze."

"What about?" They were walking briskly to the executive building.

"About dark spots."

"She's got more than spots, she's got blotches."

"Don't you know about Bertha's dark spots?"

"Everybody knows about them. Not even Rinso can wash them out."

"You seen Villon?"

"I'm waiting for him. He's up there with Alex Roland. I'm starving. Let's go get him." They saw Jack Darling and Rita Gerber hurrying out of the building.

Rita asked Jack, "What was that all about?"

"A load of nonsense. Nothing worth discussing." Rita was wondering what had happened in the office that caused Jack's face to age so dramatically. "Not so fast!" cried Rita as Jack gripped her arm and hurried her into the parking lot. When they reached her car, he opened the front door for her. "I'll phone you later, okay?"

"I thought you were going to follow me in your car!"

"I have to have a talk with my mother. Um . . . something's come up about my first talker. You know how it is."

"Not really, but I'm learning." She got behind the steering wheel and flashed him a loving look. "Until later."

She wasn't sure he heard her, he had hurried away so quickly.

Ethel Swift had been called to the telephone, leaving Annamary alone with her mother. Marie said angrily, "How dare you speak so rudely to me?"

"What are you talking about?" Marie was truly bristling. "Well? What's eating you?" She was busy draping a boa around her shoulders, searching for an effect.

"Eating me! I'll tell you what's eating me! Telling me to hold my tongue because it's big enough."

"Well, it is." She flung the boa aside and crossed to a table where she found a silver fox fur.

"And in front of that damned detective. What's gotten into you? You don't seem to give a damn I've finally gotten you a talker!"

"You're damned right I don't give a damn!" She tossed the silver fox aside and continued rummaging among scarves and boas and assorted fur pieces Ethel Swift had laid out for her. "I told you I don't want to work anymore. I'm rich. I want to give it up."

"You'll be bigger than ever in talkers!"

Annamary turned on her mother with a ferocity that took even the formidable Marie by surprise. "I'm a silent picture actress! All of us silent queens became stars because of our faces, not because of our voices. Listen to me. Do you hear me?"

"I ain't deaf! Stop yelling!"

Annamary took a strong grip on her mother's shoulders, her blazing eyes searing into Marie's. "Listen to my voice. Listen to it. It's not much of a voice, Mama."

"It's perfectly fine!"

"You say that because you want it to be perfectly fine. But it doesn't suit the image I created in silents. It's small, it's weak; I should be behind a five-and-dime counter selling toffee."

"Never!"

"I'm only doing this dreadful film with that dreadful actor just to prove to you I'll never make it in talkers. I can coast along for a picture or two like Virginia Valli and Barbara Bedford, but they're finished. I've seen their talkers. They can't compete with the new women."

"Pfah!"

"Come down to earth, Mama. I'm also older than most of them. I'm too old to be playing an eighteen-year-old bride, sneakers or no sneakers. The new actresses have nothing to worry about because the audiences have nothing to compare them to. They're coming on fresh and new with experience in the theater. They can compare me to the dozens of silents they've seen me in. That was a big mistake keeping me in pig-tails and bare feet for so many years, the way it will prove to have been a mistake keeping Jack in tattered jeans and straw hats and playing peek-a-boo with silly little girls out in the pasture. They probably won't boo me off the screen the way they did John Gilbert, maybe they'll be respectful out of loyalty and even love. But we both know better. The fans are fickle, they're like cheating husbands and wives. Always on the lookout for the new thrill, the new sensation. I've got nothing new to offer them."

"You're a great star," said Marie boldly. Jack had entered and was listening. He was affected by what his sister was saying; he looked old and tired.

"That was yesterday. Today I'm a part of movie history. Tomorrow I'll be as forgotten as a one-night stand."

Marie covered her ears with her hands. There were tears in her eyes. "I won't hear this! I won't! I won't! I won't! Your success is all I have to live for!"

Jack stepped between his mother and his sister. "Maybe Annamary's right."

"You're not giving yourselves a chance! At least wait and see how the public reacts. Don't you have the courage to do that?"

Annamary returned to finding something appropriate to throw around her shoulders for a crucial scene in which she would be fighting off the advances of the film's villain. "I'm doing the film, aren't I, Mama. See? I'm looking for something effective for one of my big moments. I do a lot of screaming in that scene. But you know something, Mama? I've never had to scream before. I don't know how to scream. Maybe I'd better hire Laura Hope Crews or Constance Collier or Alison Skipworth or one of those other ladies they've imported to teach us silent stars how to talk." She smiled at her brother. "We should have made tests, Jack. We should have taken time to learn how to produce pear-shaped vowels and to bear down on our consonants."

"Oh, here you are!" Willis Loring sounded like Stanley discovering Dr. Livingstone. "How much longer will you be? I'm hungry. It's way past dinnertime."

"What's the matter, dear? Couldn't you find a diversion for the evening?" Annamary was playing with an ermine scarf.

"Of course I could," said Willis coldly. "But I thought I'd stay at home with you tonight for moral support. Tomorrow's your big day, your first talker."

"And after I have spoken, will you teach me how to walk?"

"Well," he said huffily, "if you choose to be hostile, I can always find a warm welcome at Madam Blanche's."

"Oh God, what a ghastly life I have," said Annamary.

Jack took her hand. "Would you want to relive it?"

"Sweetie, only if I could do the casting."

Jason Cutts had gone home for the night and Hazel Dickson and Jim Mallory crashed the get-together in Alexander Roland's office. Jim Mallory recounted to Villon his interview with Bertha Graze, after which Alexander Roland said, "If anybody in this town needs killing, it's that dreadful woman."

"Someone did try to kill her once, remember?" Helen Roland was the cynosure of the gathering.

"When was this?" prodded Villon.

"A few years back. Come on, Alex, you remember."

"I do? When was this?"

"About two years ago. She was rushed to the hospital, suffering, the newspapers said then, from food poisoning. She recovered but her parrot died."

Villon was fascinated. "What parrot?"

Helen Roland explained, "She used to have a parrot. She was always feeding it the same garbage she eats. So whatever poisoned her killed her parrot. It obviously did not have Bertha's magnificent constitution. It was in the news just once, I think; there was never a follow-up. But as I recall it had something to do with a box of biscuits she received in the mail."

Villon said to Mallory, "Jim, see if we've got anything on that in the files. Use the phone in the outer office." Mallory went to the outer office and made himself comfortable at Jason Cutts's desk while phoning headquarters.

Villon questioned Roland. "Have you had some run-ins with Graze?"

"Some! Some, he asks me! Constant run-ins with her." He turned to his wife, "Tell him, honey! Tell him how many times she's tried to make trouble for my actors. A terrible woman!"

Villon was angry. "Why haven't you brought charges against her?"

"Are you crazy? That woman has this whole town by the little ones. If she ever tells what she knows, Hollywood would be evacuated in under five hours!"

Hazel said, "And there's been only *one* attempt on her life? Fascinating."

When Ethel Swift returned to wardrobe, Willis Loring was gone. Jack took Marie's arm and led her outside.

"I don't know what's gotten into you two! Annamary is *not* right. It's just her nerves, that's all. And how dare you say maybe she *is* right! Don't you want to be in talkers?" She might have been offering him ice cream.

"Mama, I've got to tell you something."

"Now you just wait a minute. I'm not letting you get cold feet too! You're going to do *Margin for Terror* if I have to chain you to the set."

"Mama, I may be in some kind of trouble."

Frances Goldwyn, the picture of serene beauty, poured after-dinner coffee for herself and her husband in the drawing room of their beautiful mansion. Goldwyn returned from the library, where he had taken an urgent phone call. He was lighting a cigar and looked thoughtful.

"Trouble?" asked Mrs. Goldwyn.

"Trouble for Louis Gross." Gross was another independent producer.

"That man is always in trouble. He has no right producing pictures. He's only in it for the variety of women he can try to molest."

"He molested once too often."

"Yes?" There was a charming lilt when she spoke the word. She dropped two lumps of sugar into her husband's coffee and passed him the cup and saucer.

"He's being accused of statuary rape. His own gardener's daughter, can you believe it?"

"Believe it? I can't wait to phone Edna Purviance and tell her."

"I thought you had lunch with her today."

"She canceled."

"You mean at last she got an offer to do a movie?"

"Nothing that lucky. She was auditioning chauffeurs."

"Since when does she need a chauffeur?"

"She doesn't. I had lunch with Helen Roland instead. What's this about another actress murdered at Alex's studio?"

"That one we met in New York, that Fairweather woman."

Frances made a face. "Poor Alex. What a run of bad luck."

"Maybe yes, maybe no. Do you think he could murder anybody?"

"He hasn't got the sensitivity." She sat up straight. "Now really, Sam, you don't think Alex could possibly kill anyone, let alone his own actresses."

"Who knows? That first one that was killed, that Leddy girl, he was sleeping with her. You know that. Helen Roland is one of your best friends. She always tells you who Alex is sleeping with."

Frances was thinking with amusement, she also tells me who you're sleeping with, but let sleeping dogs lie. She said, "The poor thing. She was just a baby."

"So Annamary Darling is taking her place in the picture."

"Helen told me that too."

"Not at lunch! That decision wasn't made until after lunch, I know, because Jason Cutts, Sophie Gang's spy at Diamond, didn't phone her until—"

"All right, Sam. All right, Helen phoned me to tell me."

"With all the phoning that goes on around this place, I should buy stock in the company."

"Sam, you already own stock in the phone company."

"I do? You see how smart I am?"

Frances set her cup and saucer aside. "Sam, have you had a chance to talk to Alex?"

"What for? I don't need anything from him."

"I think there's something terribly sinister going on at Diamond."

"I'm sure the police agree with you."

"It's not just the how of these murders. But the why. On the surface, they seem so pointless. Like the murders of Dolly Lovelace and her father."

"He wasn't her father. He was her husband."

"You're joking."

"Frances, you should know by now that the only time I joke is when I'm serious. Didn't you read the paper today? It was there in black and wide."

"I haven't had a chance to read it yet. I was saving it for later, for when you're snoring." She crossed to the fireplace and positioned herself with one hand on the mantel. "Do you think the four murders have a connection?"

"Everybody in this town has a connection." He exhaled smoke. "You're suspecting something?"

"I don't know. Woman's intuition."

"Women shouldn't spend so much time on their tuition. Listen. Tell me the truth. Why does Helen Roland want to go back into pictures? I think she'll have a tough time in talkers. She's too soft."

"Helen's stronger than you think. She wants to work again because she's bored."

"She should get herself a boyfriend."

"That doesn't interest her."

"Maybe she killed Alicia Leddy."

"She didn't mention it."

In Alexander Roland's office, Jim Mallory referred to his notes as he spoke. "It's much like Mrs. Roland told us. Graze received a box of biscuits in the mail."

"Home-baked?"

"Homicide didn't say."

"What's the difference?" asked Hazel Dickson.

"It's not so easy putting poison in packaged goods."

"Why not, Herb? Supposing it's those Hydrox cookies, the chocolate ones with the white cream in between. You can pry one side up, poison the filling, and then press it back together again." She folded her arms. "That's the way I eat them."

"With poison inside?"

"Oh, so's your old man! I eat a biscuit, lick the cream, then eat the second biscuit." Helen Roland was cringing. "They last longer that way."

Villon said, "Go on, Jim."

Mallory went on. "She told Homicide she ate one herself and fed a couple to her parrot to shut her up. Seems the parrot always put up a squawk when she saw Graze eating."

"It must have been a pretty fat parrot," commented Villon.

"Homicide didn't say."

Villon was hungry. He wondered for the umpteenth time why he ever chose to become a police officer. "Did Graze know who sent the package?"

"She didn't know. It was nicely wrapped for Christmas, with a ribbon and seals."

"Poisoned cookies for Christmas," said Hazel. "It's the thought that counts."

"Quiet, Hazel. So being Bertha Graze, a pig, a glutton, she gets an anonymous package of cookies and rips into them without giving a damn if they might have been doctored. When it's Bertha Graze, that makes sense. What about the postmark?"

"Downtown L.A."

"That's a dead end."

"Graze's stomach was pumped and the result was analyzed. Cyanide."

"Not very original," commented Hazel.

"But can be very effective," said Villon. "Try it some time."

"They do an autopsy on the parrot, or had Bertha eaten it?"

"Also cyanide. Bertha had it stuffed and mounted. It's in her bedroom. Please don't ask me to verify that."

"What kind of an investigation was done? What about forensics?"

"The only prints on the box were Bertha's. She was kept in the hospital for a couple of nights but then she insisted on being discharged. Once she got home, she stopped being cooperative with Homicide. They kept at it for a while but then decided to file it away until the next attempt on her life. If any more have happened, they haven't heard about it."

"Maybe she's hired a food taster," suggested Hazel. "And talking about food, I'd sure like to taste some."

Helen Roland could tell there was something on her husband's mind, and it wasn't food. "What's wrong, Alex?"

Roland spoke to Villon. "Mr. Villon, the way you were questioning Jack Darling. Do you think he murdered Alicia Leddy?"

"He's a suspect."

"But why would he want to kill her?"

"Mr. Roland, I have only one theory about the reason for both murders because it seems to be the only one that makes sense. Whoever committed these murders had nothing personal against the victims."

"How terrible!" said Helen Roland. "How perfectly terrible!" She asked Hazel, "Don't you agree?"

"Perfectly terrible," said Hazel, thinking of the barren state of her stomach.

"Then this is the work of a maniac," said Roland. "He could be planning to kill more people."

"Yes, she might."

"You think it's a woman?"

"Not necessarily," said Villon, "I was just trying to tell you there's an alternative. You suggested it's a man responsible; I'm just saying it could also be a woman."

Roland leaned forward. "I assume it's a man because what woman would have the strength to carry Fairweather up into the flies."

"Marie Dressler," suggested Hazel.

"She's at Metro," countered Roland.

"Marie Darling," suggested Villon.

Roland exhaled smoke. "Marie's a killer, Mr. Villon, but I don't think she could kill."

"Why not? She could very easily have killed Dolly Lovelace and her husband. Killing Dolly must have been a cinch. She was drunk and on drugs at the time. Marie could have fed her a poisoned biscuit and then burnt her mouth with acid. I haven't questioned her gardener yet."

"Assuming she has one," interjected Hazel.

"They have one," said Mallory. "We've checked."

"And there's all varieties of acid in the gardener's shed," said

172

Villon. "As for Mr. Lovelace, she denied knowing where he lives but Annamary contradicted her. Some kid who lives near Lovelace's place says he saw a sissy man leaving it. I place that immediately after his murder. Sissy man could mean a woman dressed as a man, there's a lot of that going on in this town."

"And vice versa," contributed Hazel.

"Marie had a good motive for killing the two of them, to prevent the scandal of Dolly's bigamy."

"But that's out in the open now," said Helen Roland.

"Too bad it couldn't have been revealed before the murders. The Lovelaces might still be alive."

"Mr. Villon," asked Roland, "what do you think is going to happen next?"

"Maybe we should phone Bertha Graze and ask her if she knows."

"She couldn't have done these killings. I mean how could she have gone undetected?" Roland asked with agitation.

"Disguised as a zeppelin," suggested Hazel.

"You're very tired, Hazel," said Villon.

"I'm very hungry and you promised me dinner."

Helen Roland said to her husband, "How about it, Alex? Dinner at a restaurant or do we go home and raid the icebox?"

"No, let's go to Franco's. I'd like to hear some music after a day like this."

Half an hour later, Villon, Hazel, and Mallory were seated in a booth in a Chinese restaurant. After ordering drinks and dinner, Hazel said to Villon, who she recognized was wrapped in his own thoughts, "I'm no cheapskate, Herb. A nickel for them."

"I was just wondering. Fairweather's body comes hurtling down from the flies. It just misses hitting Rita Gerber. Jack Darling says he was there and heard someone yell, 'Here she comes now.' You know, we've never looked to see exactly where from the flies did the body drop."

Hazel groaned. "What difference does it make as long as it made it to the bottom?"

"With a whooshing noise," said Villon.

"How do you know?" Hazel's skepticism was legendary. "You weren't there."

Villon said, "That's what Jack Darling said. He said he heard this whooshing noise as the body fell, barely missing Rita Gerber." The waiter brought their drinks and a bowl of Oysterettes. Mallory was the first to nibble. "I wonder if it's possible . . ." He had their rapt attention. "If it's possible to have propped up Fairweather's body in such a way that it might start slipping into space very gradually, giving the killer time to get back down to the set and establish an alibi."

"I am not going anywhere until I have eaten," said Hazel sharply. "You two can go back to soundstage five and poke around, but I'm eating first!"

Mallory joined the rebellion. "I'm paralyzed with hunger, Herb. Let's eat."

"Oh, I'm in no rush to get back there. It can wait. I don't like keeping the murderer in a state of anxiety."

"Meaning what?" asked Hazel while ravenously watching the waiter place bowls of steaming food on the table.

"I have an idea the killer knows I'm on to him. And he also knows I can't prove a damn thing. I haven't one shred of useful evidence that I can use against him."

Hazel was digging into her plate of food with chopsticks. "You think you can scare him into confessing?"

"Yes."

"Well, sweetheart, I hope you're right. He's killed four times but they can only hang him once."

"He didn't kill the Lovelaces." With which bombshell, he attacked his egg foo young with relish.

174

FIFTEEN

◆

In a secluded booth in Franco's restaurant on Wilshire Boulevard, Helen Roland studied her husband's tired face. They had eaten mostly in silence, and now over coffee and brandies, Roland having lit a cigar, Helen said, "I'm beginning to wonder if making a comeback in a talker is such a good idea."

"Helen, I wish the talkers had never been invented. But they're here and they're here to stay. In the past year of struggling to retool from silents to talkers, to adjust so painfully to a new medium, to participate willingly, but often unwittingly, in the destruction of careers, lives, marriages, God knows what, I'm beginning to come to a serious realization—it's not worth it."

She put her hand over his and said intensely, "Let's get out, Alex. Let's go to Europe and start a new life. Look at Pearl White. She's living like an empress in the south of France. Rex Ingram and Alice Terry swear they'll never come back from France. It's so much cheaper to live there."

"Helen, I'm almost broke."

"But I'm not."

"Please . . ."

"Please, my eye. I appreciate your pride but in your case it positively goeth before the fall. I've made millions. I own two city blocks in downtown L.A.!"

Roland's eyes widened. "Since when?"

"Since long before I married you. It's all money. I can't possibly spend it in my lifetime. We haven't any children, I haven't any family. All I have is you."

175

"You've been shortchanged."

"Well, Alex, our marriage hasn't been as good as others. But still, it hasn't been as bad as most."

"You still love me? Maybe a little bit?"

She smiled and said, "It depends on the weather."

Roland emitted a sigh that weighed a ton. "I don't think I'll ever get out from under. I'm in so deep, I don't know how to get out. That's the truth, Helen, I don't know how to get out."

"Why don't you talk to Sam Goldwyn? He can get out of anything. He's a good friend. He'll help you."

"I suppose you've already discussed this with Frances?"

"She suggested it. Who else can you turn to? Your lawyers? Your accountants? Those monsters in the New York office? You know they're waiting to pounce and tear you to shreds. I mean really, Alex, where are your friends?"

"Most of my friends are either dead or disorganized." He took a sip of brandy. "Exile. Like Napoleon."

"Napoleon didn't have indoor plumbing. Think Alex, think. We could find each other again, fall in love all over again." Her face was shining the way he remembered it shining in the days when he was first pursuing her.

"You think we could bring back what we once had? You think it's that easy?"

"It won't be easy. But we could have one hell of a good time while we work at it. I've never been to Greece."

"Who needs it?"

"And Egypt. I've always dreamed of taking a cruise up the Nile."

"There's a lot of disease and poverty in Egypt. There's also crocodiles."

"The crocodiles are more dangerous in Hollywood."

He was now clasping her hand tightly, having set the cigar in an ashtray. "You really don't want to do this picture for Schenck?"

She replied sincerely, "I really don't. I only agreed to do it out of boredom and loneliness. I thought you didn't love me anymore."

176

"I'll always love you. It's getting old I don't love. That's why those dumb affairs. Ah, hell. What damn fools we are, men like me." He searched her face. "Do you still love me a little bit?"

"Enough to fight for you."

He kissed her hand, gently and tenderly. "Helen, I have to warn you, the worst is yet to come."

"What do you mean? More murders?"

"I don't know about murders. But I have the feeling the past is about to catch up with me, and when it does, it's going to do its worst."

"Alex, whatever it is, we'll be there facing it together."

"I love you, Helen. And nobody wrote those words for me."

"You're not going to leave me down here by myself!" Hazel Dickson ended the sentence on the edge of a shriek.

"Come along, if you like," said Villon affably. "It's a long climb up." Hazel hurried after Villon and Mallory.

The soundstage was still awash with light. Technicians and other personnel were working at fever pitch preparing for the next day's shooting. Jason Cutts had been reached at his home by a New York agent who informed him that Norma Terris and Howard Marsh, the original Magnolia and Gaylord Ravenal of Florenz Ziegfeld's production of *Show Boat*, were available to replace Lotus Fairweather and Donald Carewe in *Daughter of the Casbah*. Jason had phoned Roland at home after he and Helen returned from dinner at Franco's. Roland okayed the casting with alacrity, and the two replacements were routed to the West Coast. They'd be there in four days.

Helen Roland wore a happy smile for her husband when he told her the news. She had never heard of the actors, but then, she was not alone; few people west of New York had heard of them. She heard Alex say, "At least I won't have to scrap the picture. It'll cost less to finish it than to scrap it. At least we can hope for some decent reviews and maybe enough people will buy enough tickets to help us break even. I don't believe your smile."

"I'm happy for you, Alex." It took all her gifts as an actress to make the words sound heartfelt.

"Sweetheart, I'm not going back on my promise. I'm getting out of the studio. We'll leave this lousy town. But when I leave, I want to leave holding my head up high."

"You're right. It's got to be that way."

"I don't want to go down in defeat the way old man Selznick did. I haven't two sons like his David and Myron to swear revenge for what was done to their father. I want to leave clean and with maybe a little respect."

"You're darn right. The south of France will always be there. In the meantime . . ."

"You want to do the picture for Joe Schenck."

"Please don't mind, Alex. It'll give me something to do."

"Yes. Yes. It's not fair to you. Go ahead with it. And sweetheart, you'll be terrific." The thought of her being "terrific" frightened him. She had convinced him he must get out of the movie business now. But what if she had an amazing success? What if she was elevated to a new height from which she had no intention of descending?

"What is it, dear? What's wrong?"

He took her in his arms and embraced her tightly. "Sweetheart, my sweet Helen. Promise me. Promise me. Whatever happens, we get out of here. We get the hell out of here."

He would never know how happy he made her.

"Over here," said Villon. He, Mallory, and Hazel were on a tier that was built more than halfway to the top of the flies. Villon indicated to them a gate in the protective railing. He looked down and could see the spot still chalked in where Fairweather's body had landed. "She fell from here." He opened the gate in the railing.

"Don't!" cried Hazel with alarm.

"Don't what?"

"Don't open the gate! You might fall!"

Mallory instinctively moved closer to Villon to protect him in case he started to go over.

178

Villon told Hazel to be still and moved the gate back and forth, but with an effort. "It doesn't move too easily. Probably hasn't been oiled in months. It was probably built for the easy loading and unloading of the heavy lighting equipment they needed for the silents."

"You think the killer pushed her body through there?" asked Mallory.

"She went through here, I think, although it would have been just as easy to drape her over the rail and then give her a little nudge. Look." He moved the gate back and forth. It wasn't easy. "But put a weight across the gate, and very soon, the force of the weight will cause the gate to give, to start to open slowly. And in the time it takes our killer to run back down and join the rest of the company, Fairweather's body, which he draped across the gate, caused the gate to open slowly, and down she went."

Hazel was quick to pick up on his deduction. "It would have to be someone who knew every square inch of this studio. Someone who between scene setups prowled around and explored all over the place. The prop rooms, the carpentry stage, wardrobe . . ."

Villon took over, "Up here in the flies . . ."

Mallory provided the coda. "And was down there when someone yelled, 'Here she comes now!' and heard the whoosh of her falling body."

Villon said to him, "Jim, I think we can close this one pretty quickly. We've got to locate that sound engineer Jack Darling was talking to when Fairweather was murdered. Maybe he's down there working with the others. It looks like everybody's on overtime. Come on."

The three descended from the flies at a clip, Hazel's cuban heels providing a castanet-like accompaniment, clicking on the cement steps.

"What are you mumbling, Mama?" Annamary Darling was tired and wanted hot soup and a hot bath. She sat between Marie and Jack in the backseat of their limousine making its way back to Annawill from the Diamond Studios.

"Nobagumderlubdick." At least that's what they thought Marie said. Annamary looked at her brother questioningly. He was staring out the window, lost in one of his private worlds where he frequently sought refuge. The chauffeur was staring at Marie through his rearview mirror. He always suspected her of being a private drinker.

Marie laughed.

"What's so funny?" asked Annamary. Then she heard a weird rattle coming from her mother's throat. "Mama? Mama, what is it?"

Marie's mouth had gone all funny. It was the left side of her mouth and, like the left side of her face, seemed to have found a life of its own. There was nothing wrong with the right side of her face and her mouth. But the left had become twisted, distorted, and ugly. The left side of the mouth was drooling. Her left hand was twisted about like that of a spastic, and the fingers were curled in an ugly pattern. She was slumped down, and though she would never be able to tell her children, her left leg was paralyzed, lifeless.

The chauffeur bore down on the accelerator. Through the rearview mirror he recognized Marie Darling was suffering a crippling stroke. Annamary had her arms around Marie, trying to prevent her from slipping to the floor of the car. Jack came back from his self-imposed limbo upon hearing Annamary's hysteria.

"Mama! Mama!" he yelled. "Mama, what's happening to you?"

"It's a stroke!" cried Annamary. "Oh my God, it's a stroke!"

Jack shrieked at the chauffeur to get them to a hospital, but the chauffeur was already heading toward one.

What's all the commotion, wondered Marie. Why is Annamary holding on to me like this? Why can't I speak? What's wrong with my mouth? What's wrong with my left eye? I can't see through it. It's gone black. Who shut off the projector? Why's Jack screaming like a spoiled little girl? Jack Jack Jack you crazy boy you! Naughty Jack! Bad Jack! My beautiful little baby. Did you get it from my side of the family? No, not my side. There were no loonies in my ancestry. Not that I heard of. But your father. It must be your father. I wrote him a letter after you told me what you told me. I wrote him to tell him to get off his ass and do something for you and I hurt I hurt I hurt and I'm going to die. I suppose death is hereditary.

She sighed and shut her eyes. Her body went limp.

Annamary removed her arms from around her mother with a look of repulsion mixed with horror. "Jack, I think she's dead."

"Dead?" His eyes darted from his mother's distorted face to Annamary's ashen one. "She can't be dead. She can't be. Not now. I need her now. She *can't* be dead."

They had arrived at the emergency entrance to a private hospital that catered exclusively to Hollywood's elite. The chauffeur hurried into the emergency room crying the magic name, "Darling," followed by "I think Mrs. Darling might be dead! She's suffered a stroke!"

The emergency room went into action. Staff was alerted over the Tannoy loudspeaker system. Two interns piloted a gurney down the ramp that led from the emergency room. They lifted Marie out of the back of the limousine and onto the gurney while Jack Darling tried to comfort his sobbing sister. A call had been put through to the Darlings' personal physician, Dr. Edgar Sibelius, who, upon hearing the news, rubbed his hands greedily and improvised plans in his head for a new wing for his already overwinged house.

Two nurses helped Annamary into the hospital waiting room and a third gave her a sedative. Jack had his brother-in-law paged at Madam Blanche's house of ill repute.

Madam Blanche took the call and clucked her tongue in sympathy when Jack told her the news. "I'll get Mr. Loring dressed and to the hospital pronto." She went upstairs to the Madame Pompadour suite where Willis Loring was doing the unspeakable to the unlovable, who sighed with relief when Willis excused himself hastily and went to the bathroom to tidy himself up before dressing.

Annamary had begun to pull herself together and prodded Jack into phoning their lawyer, Marcus Tender. Awakened from a deep sleep, the dull man groaned and grunted and coughed while his wife pulled the comforter around her ears and hoped she could resume doing with former heavyweight champion Jack Dempsey what they had been so deliciously doing in her dream before the phone rang.

In the waiting room, Jack kept asking Annamary, "Do you think Mama's really dead?"

"If she was, they would have told us."

"She looked dead. She . . . she didn't look like herself."

"Don't go on about it."

"What'll we do if she dies?"

"Bury her."

"How can you be so cold-blooded?"

"If she's dead, she's dead." And she didn't add what she was tempted to add. If she's dead, I'm free. No more nagging, no more browbeating, no more screams and shouts and obscene language. No more Mama and her schemes and her deals and her shenanigans and dear God in heaven! I can be rid of Willis! I'll go live in Europe and he can go to hell! But what about you, Jack. What becomes of you? You're useless on your own. You're over thirty, but you've got the mind of a twelve-year-old. Mama's got your money tied up in knots and Christ knows how long it'll take to untangle it. You weren't as smart as me. I made sure Marcus Tender set up my annuities, my beautiful, gorgeous, million dollars' worth of annuities. And set up so Mama couldn't lay her fingers on them. I paid Marcus plenty to go behind her back and do this for me and bless Alex Roland for having helped me.

Alex. Someone must tell Alex. "Jack, do you know Alex's private number at home?" He didn't. "Wait. I think I have it in my address book." She rummaged in her handbag, found her address book, and there was Roland's private number at home. She crossed to a nurse at the desk and asked to use the phone.

"Why, of course," said the nurse dolefully, a middle-aged spinster who had entered the profession as a teenager because she adored watching people suffer. Poor thing, she thought as Annamary dialed the number, I read she's been so devoted to her mother all these years, they were like sisters together. She turned and stared at Jack, who was sniveling into his handkerchief. There's a weak link if ever I saw one. I can't believe these two are really brother and sister. He's weak, she's strong. Look at how her chin juts out while his recedes. It takes all sorts to make a world, it really does.

Alex Roland held the phone and gasped, "Oh my God, no!"

Alarmed, Helen cried, "Who's dead?"

"Marie's dead!" Helen's chin dropped. "Wait! She's not dead! She's had a terrible stroke!" He was listening to Annamary at the other end and relaying the news to his wife like a sportscaster on the radio by remote control from a football game. "Now calm yourself, Annamary. Of course you mustn't work tomorrow. Yes, yes, I understand. We'll postpone. No, no, my dear, I wouldn't dream of replacing you."

"But you must," insisted Annamary. "I know the trouble you're in and if Mama needs me, it may be weeks before I can return to work. Please, Alex, I insist."

"But who can I get?" mourned Roland. "There's nobody." Helen was refreshing their brandies. Annamary made a suggestion and his face was a study. "Annamary, let me handle this. Have someone call me if there's any change. And Annamary"— his voice softened—"my thoughts are with you."

"Thank you, Alex," said Annamary. "I'd knew you'd understand." She hung up and the nurse was offended by the aura of happiness that suddenly enshrouded the great star.

I'm free and I'm happy and I don't have to make any effing talker and I shall soon lose myself in the paradise of obscurity. She looked at her brother and said sharply, "Pull yourself together, Jack."

"You sound just like Mama."

Annamary sat next to him on the couch. "Stop sniveling. It sounds ugly."

"Why'd you say Mama was dead?"

"It was a slip. My nerves."

"You don't care if she dies, do you?"

"I don't want to talk about it."

"You know what happens to me if she dies? Alex Roland won't

go ahead with my talker. He'll cancel it. He was only doing it to get you for Alicia's picture."

"Well . . . maybe. There's always Sam Goldwyn."

"No. I'm finished." He sank back and his eyes met those of the nurse. She awarded him her standard smile of sympathy and he resisted the urge to stick out his tongue.

"Oh no, Alex. Not me!" Helen waved away Roland's request that she take over for Annamary Darling in *The Bride Wore Sneakers*. "I'm too old for the part, to begin with. And I can't stand the thought of acting with Arnold Holt. He's so boring."

"He has a good, deep baritone."

"He has a good, deep, boring baritone. What is it, Reynolds? I thought you'd be in bed by now."

"I'm sorry, Mrs. Roland, but this envelope came for Mr. Roland while you were out and I dozed off and forgot to give it to him." The butler handed Alex the envelope. He asked Helen, "Can I get you anything?"

"No, nothing. Go to bed." The butler thanked her and departed while Alex slit open the envelope with a desk knife.

The strange expression on Roland's face as he read the letter alarmed Helen. She went to him and put her hand on his arm. Their eyes linked and he said, "Remember at dinner I said sometimes the past catches up and—"

"What's wrong? Who's the letter from?"

"It's from Marie Darling. She must have written it some hours ago. It's on studio stationery. It's about Jack."

"Insisting he direct his first talker?"

"No, demanding I help him out of a jam he's in. And it's going to be very nasty. Sit down, Helen." She sat in a Morris chair. "Sweetheart, I should have told you long ago. Jack Darling is my son."

SIXTEEN

Word of Marie Darling's stroke was not yet public. It had therefore not reached soundstage 5 at the Diamond Studios where Villon, with Mallory and Hazel Dickson in attendance, was talking to the sound technician who had been engaged in discussion with Jack Darling earlier that day. The man's name was Ken Butts and he had been sent from the East several months earlier to supervise wiring the stages for sound.

"As a matter of fact," Butts told Villon, "I'm working late because of a smart theory of Jack Darling's."

"What's that?" Villon couldn't believe Jack could possess any technical knowledge this engineer might find useful.

"How to make the microphones movable. I've tested it and it works. I'm installing an apparatus, like a fishing pole, which can move the mikes with the actors. It's damn good, let me tell you." His enthusiasm made him look boyish.

"Ken, was Jack with you up until the time the body fell from the flies?"

"All the time? No, not all the time. He excused himself and said something about having to find his mother. I didn't see him again until I noticed him talking to Rita Gerber."

"Any idea about how long after he left you that was?"

"Let me think. I can't say for sure. But I had a long session with my assistants about Jack's suggestions and that was at least half an hour."

"At least half an hour," repeated Villon. "Thanks a lot, Ken."

"I'll be here most of the night if you need me again."

"I don't think I will." He said to Mallory, "Let's find Jack Darling." Mallory and Hazel followed him out the studio's side door. There they encountered Ethel Swift, arms laden with costumes. She told them the Darlings had left and were probably at home in their mansion by now. Villon phoned the mansion and it was Dakota McLeod who took the call on the kitchen extension. Hettie was at the table with a sober expression. Annamary had telephoned from the hospital and told them of Marie's grave condition.

Villon listened to Dakota's litany of the tragedy that had struck down and incapacitated that mountain of strength, Marie Darling. Dakota told him the name of the hospital then said, "You're welcome," and hung up.

"Dakota," said Hettie with her Wurlitzer organ of a voice, "it's the end of an era. The old lady ain't going to survive this one no how, and if she does, they'll condemn her for life to a nursing home. We better start making plans."

"You're right, but let's wait until the family comes home."

"Honey, Annamary's been aching for ages to make tracks out of here, and once she does, I'm not staying on with that fruitcake son. No way, not me, not Hettie McLeod. Dakota, what do you think of rehearsing that old act of ours?"

"Maybe yes, maybe no. It's been a long time ago, Hettie. Times has changed and so has tastes. I don't think audiences today would go for that old coon act of ours. And anyway, we should move forward, not backward. I want some respect before I die."

"I'll get the coffee going. It's going to be a long night."

Helen was staggered by what her husband was telling her. It was incomprehensible to her that he had been Marie Darling's lover thirty years ago. Helen couldn't imagine that awful woman as ever having been attractive. And his eloquence astonished her. He was talking as though what he had shared with Marie had happened just a few days ago. When Roland courted her, was it because she reminded him of the Marie of his youth? Would she one day become a dragon breathing fire and dominating her children with an iron fist?

Children. Will I ever have children?

"We were so young," Roland was saying. "I was the juvenile in the company and Marie was the soubrette. Her husband was up the river in Sing Sing on a robbery and attempted murder charge. Annamary was living with Marie's mother. She was maybe five, six years old at the time. So precocious even then, always dancing around the living room like an enchanted fairy. Even then, Marie had ambitious plans for Annamary."

"What about Jack? How did she explain Jack to her husband?"

"She didn't have to. He committed suicide before the boy was born. He hung himself." He sipped brandy and then rubbed his temples. "I often thought Marie must have written and told him she was pregnant with another man's child."

"Why didn't she try to abort?"

"She wanted the baby. She wanted my baby."

So do I, Helen wanted to cry, so do I. But now, will I ever? Is it too ? You're twenty years older than I am, are you too old to be a father?

"Why didn't you marry her?"

"I did." He had the decency to look shamefaced. "It seemed the honorable thing to do."

"Were you in love with her?"

"No. And she wasn't in love with me."

"But she called him Jack Darling, not Jack Roland. Why? If you married her, why didn't you insist he have your name?"

"You know Marie! You know what a scheming harridan she is! Why didn't I recognize the truth then, that's what you should be asking me. Early in Marie's pregnancy, Annamary got her first job onstage. It was a comedy. She had a small but important role. She was a huge success. Marie had plans for her, big money plans. There was a very important producer after Marie and Marie intended for him to catch her and make a star of Annamary, so Marie dumped me."

"Does Annamary know Jack is your son?"

"Yes."

"Does Jack?"

"If he does, he's never confronted me."

"Perhaps he's been obeying Marie. Perhaps she told him to

keep the subject in the family. After all, you made him a star of the silents. I suppose Marie dumped her Broadway producer when she realized how important you had become in the industry."

"Not right away. She was smart enough to wait until Annamary was well into her teens. She groomed Annamary to rival Mary Pickford and Mary Miles Minter and Maude Adams, all of them spectacular hits in the same kind of roles. But Annamary had something different. She was more womanly than they. Her children were child-women. While playing the innocent naïf, Annamary subtly projected an erotic femininity that eluded her rivals. That's why I think now she could be an even greater star in the talkers. But I don't think she wants that."

"Do you think what Marie writes in the letter is true? Do you think he's insane? Do you believe he murdered four people, his own wife whom he professed to love so passionately? Do you believe Marie? Did you ever really believe Marie? Have you never thought someone else might be Jack's father? You said Marie was promiscuous. It's possible, isn't it?"

"Do you know how often I've tortured myself wondering if I'd been a patsy? But then I'd study the portraits of Jack that were made when I signed him to a contract. He's me three decades ago. He's my son. Helen, I want to go to the hospital."

"I'm going with you." She left her chair and headed for the hall.

"Are you sure? You don't have to. It will be unpleasant."

"I belong with you. Let's not bother the chauffeur. Let's take the sports car. I'll drive, and with the top down. I need to clear my head."

Bertha Graze was laughing hysterically as she danced around the table holding the crystal ball with the gracefulness of a mastodon in heat. "Marie is dying! Marie is dying!" Her spy at the hospital, the nurse in the waiting room, had phoned her the minute the Darlings' chauffeur had entered the emergency room. She whirled and twirled until her lungs begged for mercy and she sank onto the couch fighting for breath. "Marie is dying, Marie is dying." She stretched out a hand until it connected with a plate of marzipan on an end table, and then crammed a chunk of the sweet into her mouth, chewing away with the intensity of a cement mixer.

Willis Loring arrived at the hospital at the same time as Dr. Sibelius. Willis asked Annamary, "How's Marie?" but Annamary ignored him and instead accepted the doctor's familiar warm embrace.

"I'll do my best for her," said the doctor.

Annamary wanted to say, "Don't. Let her go. Don't let her linger. Give her a quick send-off!" Instead she said, "I know you will." The doctor was led to his patient by a young intern whose personal opinion was that Marie would soon be off and running on one of the two tracks that led out of this life. Everyone in Hollywood knew Marie's reputation.

The nurse assigned to Marie had removed her jewelry and handed it to another nurse for safekeeping. "She won't need these where she's going," she said coldly.

"Why? Afraid they'll melt?"

Willis was annoyed by Annamary's brush-off. "How did this happen? What brought on the stroke?"

"What does it matter?" Annamary was staring at her brother. Jack was talking to himself. His lips were moving and she wondered if he was sneaking drugs again. What indeed had brought on the stroke? she now wondered. What had Jack told Marie when he got her alone in the wardrobe room? And what were the two detectives and that reporter doing here?

Herbert Villon entered with Jim Mallory and Hazel Dickson dutifully in attendance. Hazel was all atingle; her intuition told her she was on the verge of a great news break. This might be the story that could elevate her from her stagnant plateau as a sob sister. She had phoned in her story of Marie's tragedy as soon as Herbert Villon had heard it from Dakota McLeod. Her editor had caressed her ear with, "Great work, Hazel! You're a terrific reporter! Stay on the story, get the rest of it." Oh, happy day. Now if Marie Darling would be a true darling and kick the bucket within the next ten minutes, she could provide her editor with a double explosion of scorching news to send across the world with his wire service.

She heard Jack Darling saying to Herb Villon in a tiny voice, "I killed them. I'm sorry. I didn't mean to. I took the musketeer outfit and, you know, after seven years it's still a perfect fit? I haven't gained an ounce. Mama would be so proud of me. And aren't you smart! That's exactly what I did with that smelly slob's body up in the flies. Aren't you smart! Annamary, isn't he smart?"

Alexander Roland and Helen came hurrying in.

Annamary agreed Villon was smart.

Jack continued. "I knew Alex was in trouble. He was giving Mama a hard time and so I decided he must be punished. I knew if I killed the women it would bring the productions to a halt and cost him a lot of money. I didn't figure on his replacing Alicia, poor sweet Alicia, with Annamary. But by that time I had planned on how I would kill the smelly singer, and it seemed a darned shame to cancel my plan, it was so clever." He shrugged like a little boy. "So I killed her."

"What about your wife and Ezekiel Lovelace? Who killed them?"

"Well, I hate to do this to Mama. But I think Mama killed them. Mama's very neurotic. She used to see an alienist for a while. She used to get hallucinations like I sometimes get."

Alexander Roland asked Villon if he could talk to him in private. "It's very important. I have something I want you to read." As he led Villon away from the others, Hazel put a consoling arm around Annamary's shoulder. Annamary smiled while Willis Loring wondered if Alex Roland would honor his deal or would he be forced to go back to Joseph Schenck with his cap in hand. At least, he thought gratefully, now I can divorce myself from this accursed family.

Herbert Villon read Marie Darling's letter, every so often looking up into Roland's tired and troubled eyes. "She writes he killed all of the victims."

"Marie had a magnificent gift for stretching the truth. Still, so does Jack. I was glad to see you here. I'd like to see this wrapped up as soon as possible." They rejoined the others.

Villon gave Marie's letter to Jack. "Read this. Your mother sent it to Mr. Roland shortly before the stroke."

Jack read the letter and exploded. "It's a lie! It's a goddamned rotten lie! I didn't kill Dolly! I didn't kill them! I love my Dolly! How could Mama do this to me?"

Annamary wrested the letter from Jack and read it. Villon in turn claimed it from her. "Evidence, you know." Hazel thought he looked so cute. She had taken command of a phone and was dictating her story to rewrite.

"Wait a minute! Hold it! Jack Darling's going berserk!"

Jack was on his feet and striking out with his fists in all directions. "Why is Mama doing this to me! She promised I'd be on top of the world! Is this what she calls the top of the world? Annamary? It's not fair! It's not fair! Just because I got drunk and told Dolly everything about me and my real poppa and she told that louse Ezekiel and he told Bertha and the hell with all of you! The hell with all of you! Dolly! Dolly! I need you sweetheart! Come to me Dolly!"

He struck Mallory in the face. He pushed Willis Loring to the floor with a maniacal show of strength. He tore past an intern, who tried to restrain him, and soon was outside and punching the Darling chauffeur, knocking him to the ground. He gunned the motor of the limousine and headed it toward the hills of Hollywood.

"Good heavens!" exclaimed Marie's private nurse. "Look how sweet she looks."

Dr. Sibelius had to agree. In death, Marie suddenly looked thirty years younger. Even her death rattle he found rather melodious. He began figuring in his mind the enormous bill he would present to Annamary. He said to the nurse, "I'll inform the family. I'm not sure if Miss Darling will permit an autopsy, so wait until I give you further instructions as to the disposal of the body."

*   *   *

Villon and Mallory were chasing Jack. Hazel remained behind to stay with her story, hoping Mallory would remember to inform her of Jack Darling's fate as soon as he could get to a telephone. Jack had a clear road to his destination, whatever it was. Villon at the wheel marveled at how Jack took the twisting turns in the road without going over the edge. The roads in the Hollywood Hills were narrow and dangerous, with sheer drops on either side into ravines below.

Mallory said, "I think the nut's heading for the sign."

The sign lay ahead of them. It was treacherously high and loomed over the area ablaze with its electric bulbs. It proclaimed itself proudly, if gaudily, HOLLYWOODLAND. It was the city's most famous whore and pandered to everyone's dreams and ambitions without fulfilling any promises.

They heard a screech of tires as Jack bore down on the brakes. "Will you look at the damn fool! He's climbing up the H! He'll electrocute himself!" shouted Mallory.

"Fine," said Villon, "that'll save the state money."

Jack's climb was slow and laborious. He kicked some bulbs on his way up, which exploded with pops that echoed and re-echoed throughout the hills. Villon and Mallory watched him, in silence.

Soon Jack reached the top of the H. "Hey!" he shouted. "How about me? I'm back on top! Mama! I'm on top! And I did it by myself! I didn't need you to get me here! Do you hear me, you fucking traitor? I didn't kill Dolly! I didn't kill Dolly!" His sobs even touched the steel hearts of the lawmen below. "Top of the world, Ma! Top of the world!"

Jack Darling sailed gracefully into space and into film history. He joined the other dinosaurs of the silent film in extinction. In years to come, there would be occasional retrospectives of his work given by colleges, universities, film societies, and film museums across the world. He was idolized in communist Russia as a victim of capitalism, and there's a bust of Jack on display in the town square of the village of Baronovich, where it is respected by everyone but the pigeons.

192

SEVENTEEN

♦

Hazel Dickson scooped the world and made immediate plans to write her autobiography. Herbert Villon was proud of her and made immediate plans not to propose marriage. Jim Mallory decided to have an affair with Marie's private nurse, who seemed very agreeable. Willis Loring continued to live under the same roof with Annamary, though they never exchanged a civil word. Alex Roland honored the deal Marie had made for Willis who became one of the great legends of the talking screen, to his own great shock.

But Herbert Villon was unhappy. In his office with Mallory, he read and reread Marie's letter to Alexander Roland. "There's something wrong with this."

"You've been saying that for two days. Are we going to the funerals?" Annamary had decided to make it a doubleheader, a real treat for the vandals she expected to invade the chapel at Forest Lawn.

"I'll pass. I'm sure it'll be much like Dolly Lovelace's."

"Worse," said Mallory. "This one's a double feature. Do you suppose Annamary's planning to give away dishes?"

"There's something wrong in this letter."

"You keep saying that," responded Mallory with impatience, anxious to get away to a rendezvous with his new inamorata.

"Would Marie really finger her beloved Jack as a four-time killer to protect herself? I don't think so. I really don't think so. And I'm positive he didn't kill the Lovelaces. Why are you so fidgety?"

"Look, Herb, I've got this date. I mean, you really don't need me any longer, do you?"

"Go on, scram. But I want you here bright and early tomorrow morning."

"Um, actually, I was thinking of going to the funerals. I've never been to a Hollywood party; I'd kind of like to see one. You know, to tell my kids about it someday."

Villon waved him away and continued staring at Marie's letter. He wondered if he was supposed to have dinner with Hazel. He'd have to dump her soon. That ego was getting both boring and dangerous now that she'd been made an editor. Still, she was pulling down a hefty salary now, and if he married her, they could maybe get in on some property in Bel Air. He'd been tipped by a real estate broker it was the next up-and-coming area.

At the Diamond Studios, the sadness of the murders was now overshadowed by the injection of fresh blood into the two jinxed productions. Helen Roland's rushes were glorious and her husband was predicting great things ahead for her in the talkers. It wasn't easy to ignore that she was increasingly unhappy, but it did not reflect in her performance. She was a real trouper. She had arranged with her business manager to acquire a property for her in Juan-les-Pins, France. Alex could join her there or not, it no longer mattered.

Even the news that Roland was Jack Darling's natural father was taken in stride by the industry. Louella Parsons, the empress of gossip, was livid with anger that she'd been scooped by the upstart Hazel Dickson. She was positive the betrayal had come from the spiteful Hedda Hopper, while Hedda Hopper had excoriated Erskine Simpson-Thwaite for not gleaning that tidbit when he was in the Darlings' employ. Ernest pooh-poohed Hopper, happy in his new position as keeper of the towels at Madam Blanche's.

The funerals were much as Villon had predicted. Except this time, the police were prepared and were able to keep the blood-thirsty mob from invading and disrupting the services. In a front pew, Sam Goldwyn whispered to Frances, "I'll tell you one thing. This funeral is no laughing matter. So why is Annamary laughing?"

Annamary sat between Willis Loring and Alexander Roland. They couldn't quiet her. They had mistaken what they thought were her grief-stricken sobs. Roland was the first to recognize that the sobs were actually ugly guffaws. "Hush dear, hush dear," he said nervously while patting her hand.

"Ha ha ha ha ha ha ha!"

It made headlines.

The next afternoon, a subdued Annamary, suitably dressed in black, paid a visit to Bertha Graze. She carried in her hand a peace offering. Bertha had been astonished and then pleased when Annamary phoned her the previous evening requesting a cessation in their hostilities and a reading in the crystal ball. Annamary drove herself to the rendezvous. In response to her knock on the door, she heard Bertha shout, "Come on in! It's open!"

The living room was as Annamary remembered it, shabby and worn, the paisley shawl she'd given her years ago still draped across the piano. And Bertha herself. Impossible to believe this once slim, petite, and lovely ingenue had inflated into this surreal monstrosity.

"You look real good in black. Real good. Well, so now you're an orphan. When you getting rid of Willis? I don't need the crystal ball to predict that. But let me tell you, I've been looking into it and I'm sorry to say, there's a dark spot. A real big one. A real beauty of a stinker. Is that for me?" She grabbed the package greedily from Annamary. Her pudgy fingers were abnormally nimble as they tore off the string and wrapping paper. She uncovered the box and emitted a yip of delight. "Oh, what gorgeous cookies!"

Annamary finally spoke. "Try the chocolate ones. I baked them myself."

Bertha stuffed a chocolate cookie in her mouth and munched contentedly. Then she munched a second and then a third as Annamary opened her handbag and brought out a tiny medicine bottle filled with a colorless liquid. Bertha was staring into the crystal ball as she plunged a fourth chocolate cookie into her dangerous chasm of a mouth. "Damn it! Now there's two dark spots, criss-crossing the way they did with Thelma Todd!"

Those were her last words.

She clutched her stomach, emitted an agonized belch, and then her head fell back. As though performing before a camera, Annamary uncapped the medicine bottle, went to the dead woman, and poured the liquid into her mouth. The acid worked immediately.

Annamary walked to the telephone and gave the operator the number for Villon's headquarters. When she heard the switchboard operator at headquarters speak, she asked for the chief inspector.

"Mr. Villon? This is Annamary Darling." Her voice was sweet and beckoning, like a harp glissando. "I missed you at the funeral yesterday. I thought you'd be there. I'm sure you've read how I misbehaved badly." She laughed. It felt good to laugh. "Mr. Villon, I'm calling from Bertha Graze's home. I'm afraid I've been a very naughty girl again. I just brought her some poisoned cookies. She ate four of them. Two would have been enough, but of course, with her size and her constitution . . ."

Mallory wondered at the strange look on Villon's face. It was a mixture of pleasure and sadness. He wondered who was on the other end of the phone.

Villon heard Annamary saying, "It was simpler with Dolly and Lovelace. You understand, of course, it was me Mama was trying to protect in her letter to Alex. Poor Jack. Poor unstable Jack. All those drugs and all that alcohol. He didn't know he was dying. He had almost no liver. I guess Mama thought she was doing him a favor in betraying him. Poor baby. Maybe if Alex had—oh well . . . maybe maybe maybe. Mr. Villon, I'm waiting for you."

"I'm on my way."

Dolly's picture was on the grand piano along with that of several other Bertha Graze clients. Annamary wandered into the bedroom, made a nose at the unmade bed, studied the stuffed parrot, the only fatality from her previous attempt on Bertha's life, and then wandered back into the living room.

She gazed into the crystal ball and saw nothing but her own reflection. She looked into the box of cookies. They looked temptingly appetizing. She picked up the box, took it with her to the sofa, sat down, and then selected a chocolate cookie. She popped it into her mouth and looked content, alone with her thoughts, alone with her memories, yet feeling not at all lonely.